This one's for Val - thanks for everything

Sunset Val's
Final Boarding
or,
The Sinking of Atlan

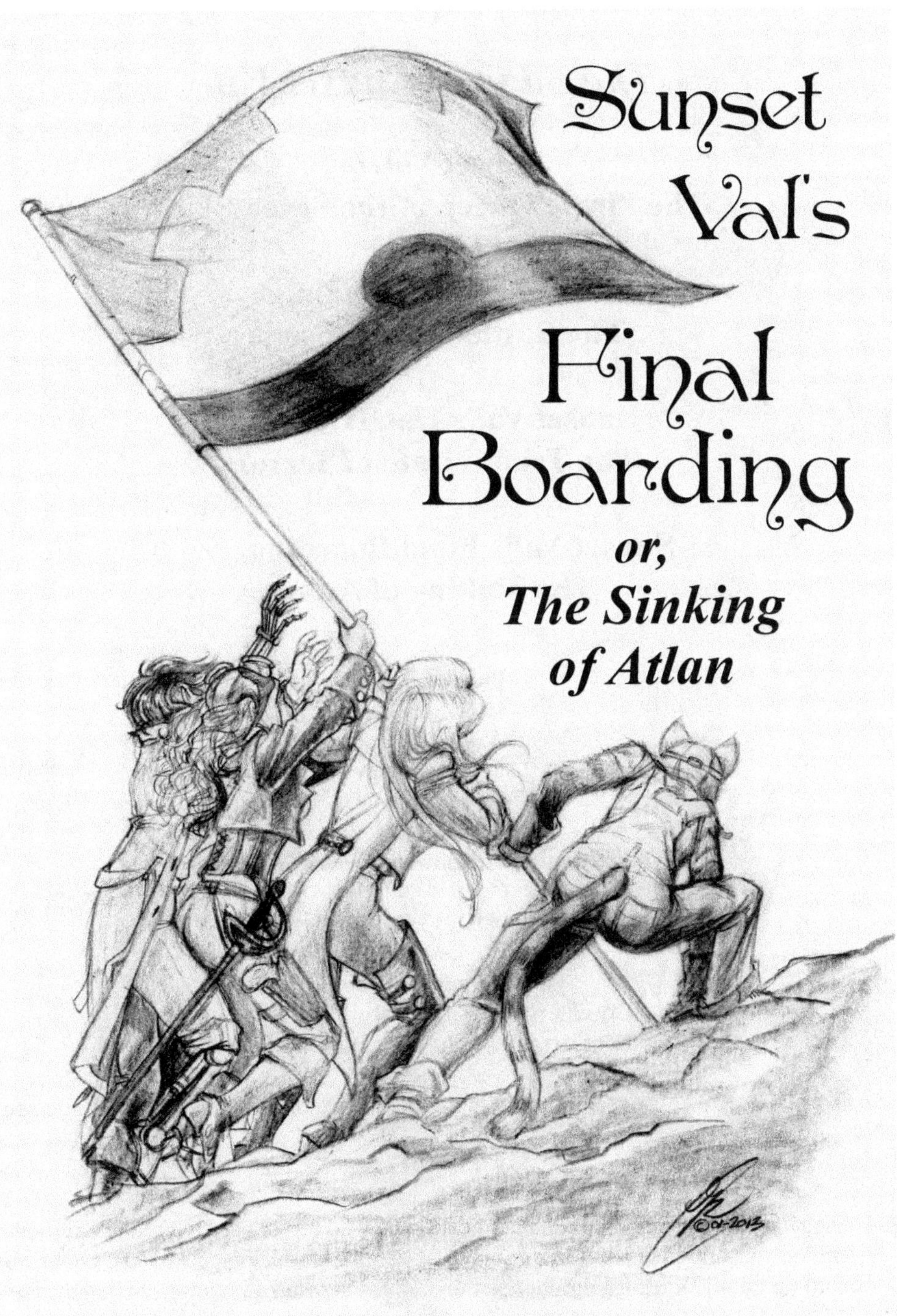

A true accounting, in her own words, as told to

R. M. St.Martin, esq.

The Saga of Sunset Val

**Sunset Val, *or*,
The Pirate Queen of the Seven Skies**

**Sunset Val Flies Again, *or*,
The Battle Over Libertia**

**Sunset Val's Hat Trick, *or*,
The Triumvirate of Terror**

**Sunset Val's Final Boarding, *or*
The Sinking of Atlan**

Published by:

Weird & Wondrous Books
33A Broadview
Pointe Claire, QC
H9R 3Z1
http://www.weirdandwondrousbooks.com

ISBN 978-0-9917472-1-4

A Pretty Impressive Political Prologue

Neptopolis.

So named for the ancient explorer, Nepton, who first landed there, the glorious capital of the Atlan Empire sits upon an island in a river estuary. Eight bridges link the island to the mainland, each a marvel of Atlan ingenuity. In the harbour, on an otherwise unremarkable small island, another marvel stands, a glittering beacon to all the world: the statue of Atlan Triumphant, a five hundred foot statue of gleaming brass. Personified as a beautiful woman, Atlan Triumphant raises aloft her Sword of Victory, while the other hand holds forth a brilliant ever-burning lantern, the Light of Civilization.

Two million people dwell in the capital. Politicians and lawmakers. Captains of Industry. Generals and Admirals. The Atlan Senate lives there, meets there, rules there. The Chancellor of the Senate, a Senator elected by his fellows (and all Senators are men), sets the Senatorial Agenda, presides over Senatorial Hearings, chooses which Senators will serve on which committees. Committees that rule Atlan and the world beyond. Committees that allocate funds to certain projects, certain people. Committees that serve as judiciary boards over trials of great import. Committees that appoint Governors to their provinces, promote officers within the military, grant rights and privileges to various companies.

The Chancellorship begins with an election within the Senate and ends five years later with retirement from the Senate. Each Chancellor only serves one term. It is considered by many to be an honourable end to a distinguished career in politics, though more than one Chancellor has been elected to the post in order to be rid of him.

Senators, unlike Chancellors, hold their positions for life. Once raised to the Senate from the ranks of appointed Governors and promoted Generals and Admirals, the only way a man might leave behind his

Senatorial responsibilities is by election to the post of Chancellor, or death. There are always one hundred and ninety nine Senators, though not all may be present in the Senate Hall at any given time. One hundred and ninety nine men rule Atlan. One hundred and ninety nine men decide the fate of fifty million citizens... and five hundred million slaves, patchworks, animen and automatons.

Half of the population of Ayrth lives and dies under Atlan rule. Of those fifty million lucky enough to be born or descended directly from at least one parent born on the island continent of Atlan, twenty six million are women, who of course cannot vote. Of the remaining twenty four million, almost half are under twenty-one years of age, the age of majority. From twenty-one to twenty-five years old, every Atlan male must serve a term in the military, be it Aerial, Terrestrial or Nautical, placing seven million men in uniform. Survivors of military service are granted full citizenship, including the right to vote in General Referendums and the right to hold public office.

Even with advanced medical techniques and life-preserving technology, average life expectancy of an Atlan male citizen is not even sixty. Seven million men have completed their military service.

Of these seven million, perhaps as much as forty percent are unable to attend General Referendums, which determine those issues deemed too important, or too politically volatile, for the Senate to decide. The last General Referendum, fifteen years ago, allowed animen the right to education. The narrow victory of the Pro-Education camp is still a hotly contested argument in the drinking establishments of Neptopolis. There are even those who still mutter darkly about giving women the right to an education, thirty years ago.

But General Referendums are few and far between. The day-to-day operations of the Empire rest firmly in the hands of the Senate, their puppet Governors and the City Councils the Governors control. The Councillors oversee those tasks too unimportant for the Governors and far too trivial for the Senators. The Councils oversee building projects, traffic, crime prevention, trash and sewage. They ensure the cities of the Atlan Empire are the cleanest, safest, most beautiful in the world. Councillors on Atlan itself take special pride in their cities, and to be elected to the City Council of Neptopolis is considered a great honour.

For Neptopolis is a clean, safe, and above all, beautiful city.

Gleaming marble buildings rise high into the sky, none greater than the most recent project, the Grand Atlan Tower. At a projected one hundred storeys high, when it is completed it will be the tallest building in the world, with an airship docking station at its very peak. Many buildings in Neptopolis have ornithopter landing pads, but until the Grand Atlan Tower is finished, airships must dock across the river.

Majestic parks grace the urban landscape. The Great Park at the centre of Neptopolis boasts a zoo and a man-made lake, for the enjoyment of all citizens. Most neighbourhoods have implemented tree-planting along their cobbled streets, and the unpleasantness in Afric has led many families to plant vegetable gardens in their yards. But only 'for the duration', as they say.

Beneath the towers and parks, a network of tunnels allows electric locomotives to transport the teeming masses here, there and everywhere. The Tunnels have alleviated the growing traffic challenges of the successful modern city. Steam-powered horseless carriages still clamour for dominance of the cobbles, frightening actual horses and auto-horses alike, but the Tunnels have provided some refuge for the masses.

Unfortunately, it is also a haven for the unsavoury unmentionables of society, the criminal sort. They have made the Tunnels their highways, flitting unseen beneath honest citizens.

For even safe, beautiful Neptopolis is not free from the scourge of civilization. Crime will ever thrive in a society where there are those who have without want, and those who want but do not have. And so even safe, beautiful Neptopolis must have its police force, its courts of justice and its prisons.

Beneath the Great Hall of Law lies one such prison. It is but a temporary place of incarceration, meant for those criminals awaiting trial and sentencing. Most criminals will be sentenced to slavery. Some, whose crimes are more unspeakable, will be sent to a patchwork manufactory, in the hopes that some good might be salvaged from their existence. And a very, very few will be sent to Blackiron Prison, to live out the rest of their lives in penal servitude, mining coal and other ores from the mineral rich mountains that run along Atlan's western coast. Everyone knows that being sent to the Pit is a death sentence, for the life expectancy of the criminal population is less than three years after arrival. One man lived five years in the Pit, surviving through ruthless cannibalism, until he was killed by his fellow inmates... and eaten.

Most criminals brought before the Committee of Justice, a tribunal of five Senators, plead for leniency. Those bound for the Pit beg to be patchworked. Better a quick death than a long slow descent into madness, cannibalism, and finally, death. The criminals sentenced to patchworking plead for leniency and a lifetime of slavery. And the majority who are bound for slavery, well, they insist on their innocence.

But one criminal stands differently from the others. Petite would be a charitable description of her stature, though long hours of physical labour have granted her a lean musculature. Her skin is tanned and freckled, due to an unladylike amount of time spent outdoors, and tiny creases mar the skin at her eyes and forehead, aged before her tender years by the winds of airship travel.

Her hair is her most notable feature. A deep russet hue, the tangled curls she had when finally captured have been shorn, as is typical of all prisoners of Atlan justice. The stubble dyes her scalp in bloody tones.

Shackled at wrist and ankle, she stands in the Prisoner's Ring, a circle of marble set in the centre of the Trial Hall. Facing her accusers wearing nothing more than a simple grey dress that covers her from shoulder to knee, she seems little more than a child, contritely bowing her head.

She has not been beaten. She has not been starved. She has been allowed adequate rest. Dark circles of guilt do not underscore her haunted eyes. Gaunt cheeks do not pale with terror at her fate.

Her bare arms tell a tale of violence. Numerous scars etch a lacework of swordfights and knifefights, at times punctuated by a puckered bullet wound. Above them all, most notably, a crudely-formed slave tattoo.

The Chief Justice, a Senator of some twenty years of honourable service, reads the charges. His voice is deep, resonating in the Hall.

"That the criminal before this Tribunal of Law did knowingly commit the following crimes: Fugitivism. Piracy. Murder. Robbery. Pillage. Destruction of Private Property. Destruction of Government Property. Plotting to Overthrow the Government. Sedition. Suffragism. And... Treason."

The audience that has gathered to witness the trial roar their outrage. The Tribunal allows them several minutes of this before issuing a call for order.

The Chief Justice continues. "Prisoner, if you are found guilty, the heinous nature of your crimes demands a sentence of imprisonment in Blackiron Prison. How do you plead?"

She raises her head, smiles contemptuously, and utters a single word:

"Guilty."

No, no, wait, I should totally back up a bit.

Chapter One

I Back Up A Bit

"Brace for impact!"

My voice was rough from roaring out commands for three days of battle. The radio unit smoked and sparked, but I hoped it still had enough power to relay my commands. Argenta lay in pieces, her directivation tapes unspooling out onto the floor in a gruesome parody of the blood spilling from Domina next to her.

The Atlan Hammerhead slammed into us, a thundering crash mingled with the shriek of tearing metal and screams of my girls. The ship was bigger than the Furies. They had more men.

"Prepare to be boarded! All hands on deck!" I yelled, hoping someone was relaying my orders belowdecks.

Angel stepped over Argenta's body to help Domina. Restless, Molly and I left the bridge and headed topside. Swords out. Pistols cocked. From two decks below I heard Inga bellow, "FIRE!"

To ram us, the Hammerhead had to let us cross her T. Fifteen cannons and twice that many volley guns tore into them. Of course, their bow had thick armour plating, but not thick enough. The prow exploded in a shower of splintered wood and shrapnelled metal. I felt something hot and wet spill down my cheek before Restless tackled me to the deck.

Then they boarded us. Atlan Aerial Marines, shooting, slashing, hacking, killing. We met them with steel and screams, the bloodthirsty howl of The Furies. More than one Marine stepped back from the hate, the bloodlust, the hunger for vengeance in our screeching shriek.

Our batgirls descended on them, grabbing the men and dropping them over the side to plummet to their deaths far below. Some of our batgirls died the same way.

I emptied my guns into the crowd of Marines, pulled my epee and main gauche free from their scabbards and dealt them swift steel death. Gone were the days of elegant ripostes and measured attempts at a prise de fer; this fight was butchery, pure and simple. Kill or be killed.

Blood slicked the deck in seconds. Our blood, their blood; all running red, the ruin of lives lost.

We repelled the boarders. I ordered the batgirls and the sailmakers into the rigging to untangle our lines from theirs.

"Incoming, Cap," Restless said, pointing into the sunset. Silhouetted shapes soared toward us.

"Let 'em," I said, teeth clenched with ferocious fury. "What do you see, Restless?"

"Two Great Whites, a half dozen Hammerheads, couple dozen Barracudas... oh shit. Captain, they've got one o' them Leviathans we been hearin' about!"

A Leviathan. The biggest, most massive vehicle in the seven skies. A floating city. A weapons platform that could crush cities to rubble in minutes, and had. South of here, they'd been used against us. I hadn't seen one in action.

Yet.

"Unleash the hounds," I ordered. Restless ran to the bridge to try and relay my words to the rest of the fleet.

Apparently our radio worked well enough to get through to the Mistress O' Merit, because not even a minute later the skies were filled with the buzz of aircycles. Then the Vulka-rey passed us, howling. It sent chills up my spine. The crew cheered. My smile, if anything, got more fierce.

I suppose, by then, I was more than a little crazy. I mean, we'd been fighting pretty much non-stop since we'd gotten Lemuris the allies they needed to take the war up a notch. Three months of hard fighting would end, today, one way or the other. Merraq was Atlan's last stronghold on the continent. Once we took Merraq, Afric would be ours.

We'd run north first, capturing Aegyptia and Saud, then swept south. The Z'lauwe had welcomed us with open arms as liberators, adding troops to our ranks. Then west, a long slow grind through jungles and across grasslands. Mountains and lakes. Dusty badlands of bare dirt and trickling streams. Insects and illness dogged our every step.

But finally, finally we'd pushed Atlan forces back, back, back until their backs were to the Atlan Sea. Here, they would make their final stand. Here, we would crush them.

We hadn't waited. No long siege while they waited for rescue. We'd attacked, and three days and two nights of fighting had brought us to this final battle for the fate of Afric.

Off in the west, bright explosions shattered the growing darkness as the sun slipped beneath the waves of the Atlan Sea.

With the sunset, Serena's slumber subsided. Her hunger hit me hard. A shiver shook me as she woke.

And the two dozen other vampyri in our Booty Bay woke up too.

Seconds later I felt them race past us, their shapes a blur as they leapt across to the Hammerhead. A flash of concern for my injuries from Serena, and then the almost physical pleasure of her joy of combat, of unleashing her killer instincts, of slaughter and blood.

I wanted to scream. I wanted to laugh. I wanted to throw up.

I didn't do any of those. I ordered my girls back to their stations, confident that twenty five vampyri could slaughter the nearly two hundred Atlans aboard the Hammerhead. Eight to one odds? No problem for them.

Our lines freed, we left the Hammerhead to the vampyri and got ready to face the last of the Atlan Afric Fleet.

If you've never seen one, a Leviathan was a long narrow rectangle of a ship, its gas bags scattered throughout its interior. Bristling with cannons and volley guns, it looked a little like a sperm whale mated with a puffer fish. Dozens of launch bays cratered its hull, able to let loose dozens of ornithopters and hundreds of aircycles in minutes. Three huge smokestacks belched black clouds into the sky. Not pretty, but deadly as the Blight.

We formed up alongside the Tallyho Sisters and the Mistress O' Merit. Flagships to the fore, that was Remy's style. Behind us, fifty pirate ships, a hundred or so Lemurisian air drakes, and maybe forty Zhou junks. We had them outnumbered, but they had us outgunned.

I went down to the command bridge. Restless was at the wheel. Gigi and one of her girls, Sonia I think, were repairing the wireless radiophonic communicatron. Gigi shook her head and swore in Gallian. No sign of Domina, other than the puddle of blood staining the floor. Most of Argenta had been cleaned up, too.

I climbed up beside Gigi. "Anything?"

"Maybe," she answered. "Give me a... there!"

Static crackled from the radio's speaker.

"Furies to Mistress," I said into the microphone.

Remy's radio operator, a guy I'd never met but had spoken to often, answered. "Mistress, go ahead."

"This isn't going to be pretty."

"No kidding."

"Orders?"

I waited as the guy, whose name I never learned, talked to his captain.

"The Admiral says, take 'em out."

Captain Remarkable Jones, Admiral of the Fleet and King of the Pirates, master strategist, and that's all he came up with? I bit down my frustration.

"Yes, okay, but how?"

"We take the high road, the Zhou take the low road, Lemuris keeps the babies off our tails."

I rolled my eyes. The high road meant doing things the hard way. "Understood."

See, we'd learned from those Leviathans we'd fought down south. And by we, I mean our side, not necessarily me and my crew. Anyhow, what we'd learned was the Leviathans had a weak spot.

That's to say, they weren't especially well designed. Before the war had started, Atlan had a grand total of one Leviathan in service. It had been built mainly to make jobs for certain Senators' friends, and they'd been skimming off the top from the start. So it had lumbered into a battle in Mpongwa with only half a crew complement. The cannons had rusty parts and substandard housings, which basically meant half of them didn't fire at all and maybe half of the ones that did fire blew up. Armour plating had fallen off during the fight. Rumour had it one entire floor had collapsed on the one below it. Our spies reported that the official inquest had revealed that almost two hundred men had died in a fire, because their compartments all led to one bottlenecking escape hatch. Apparently several Senators had chosen to take their own lives over being thrown in the Pit.

Unfortunately for us, that had sent the Leviathan back to the drawing board, and they'd employed an army of Eire shipbuilders to get the Mark IIs into service. Construction had been overseen by armed guards, and weekly audits of the books ensured every sovereign spent had gone into the ships. The Mark II Leviathans were a lot better designed and built that the first one, but they'd been in such a rush to build them they'd forgotten a few key points.

Like the Mark I, the Mark II had been designed to be used against a land-based populace, not a fleet of fast-moving airships. So more than half of the guns aimed in a generally downward direction. Only a quarter of the cannons even swivelled. And the ship moved so slowly, and turned so widely (I mean, seriously, it could take them miles off course to turn around), that its basic method of attack was to either fly straight through the thick of a battle, come out the other side and pound our land forces, or else aim for the biggest concentration of our ships, plant itself in the middle of us and slug it out.

Now, we were pretty foolhardy, but we weren't stupid. We weren't about to try to slug it out with something the size of a small city. We'd draw it in, wait for it to slow to a stop, then scatter to the four winds. And exploit the last and biggest problem of the Leviathans.

See, they were armoured like nothing you'd ever seen. Six inch thick steel plates in some places. It was mad of them to even try to get something that heavy in the air, much less bring it into battle. But they brought it to battle, so we brought the battle to them.

Our fleet split into three. Lemurisian airships raced ahead of us, drawing as many of the escort ships into a firefight as they could. The Zhou junks and our pirate airships headed for the Leviathan.

Remy had given us the tougher job, but the Zhou would have a tougher time, under the Leviathan's guns while we tried to blow her from the skies.

How, you ask? I'll tell you if you give me a chance.

Even though we'd used this tactic successfully twice before, the Atlans fell for it again. I continued to be grateful that promotions could be bought for enough money in the Atlan military, because it meant rich Senators could buy captaincies for their idiot, unqualified sons. Most of what remained of their fleet swerved off to engage the Lemurisians.

Unfortunately, our victories meant that we'd killed off a lot of Atlan idiots, leaving smart, qualified commanders in their wake, or survivors of battles at least. So not all the Atlan airships followed our bait. Some were left behind, setting themselves up to cross our Ts. And we flew straight at them.

Inga fired up Old Sparky and gave them a hell of a time. Nothing like ten bajillion volts of lightning to knock some of the arrogance out of an Atlan airship crew. And The Furies wasn't the only ship with prow-mounted cannons. Maybe a quarter of the pirate armada took it on the chin in that one assault, maybe a third of the Zhou. But we blew past their blockade and let them have it with both banks of guns on our way past. We shredded them to pieces.

Then we were through. Restless spun the elevator wheel so fast it blurred. The Furies gained altitude as the Leviathan came closer, closer.

The air filled with the buzz of Atlan aircycles and the thick black smoke of the Deathwing Guard's batwing backpacks.

"All hands on deck!" I ordered, and ran up the staircase to join the battle.

"Running low on ammo, Cap'n," Molly said, taking her time to aim at an incoming Deathwing.

"We survive this I'll get you all the ammo you want," I said, reloading my guns.

"I dunno," she said, then fired her rifle right into the Deathwing's face. His batwings spiralled him right into our hull with a crunch. "I want a lot of ammo."

My furies fought fiercely, ferociously, famously. Deathwings died in the dozens. My girls got gunned down too, giving Doc Regan, Eve, Mary and Angel more work than they wanted. I felt something punch my shoulder. I ducked down, checked the wound. It was nothing that couldn't wait.

Deathwings landed on the deck. Ironically I knew we were safer then, since the aircycles wouldn't risk firing on their own troops. Of course, that meant the Deathwings had less support. And, y'know, were in sword reach.

Bloody doesn't begin to describe it.

When it was over I ordered my girls to confiscate the batwing backpacks and carry the bodies to the Booty Bay. I got back to the bridge just in time.

The Leviathan was huge, enormous. It filled the shattered windows of the command bridge. The far off ocean disappeared behind grey steel plates and cannons. Lots and lots of cannons.

It seemed to me they all opened fire at once. The air itself seemed to disintegrate. I saw the Mistress O' Merit take a direct hit. Her spine shattered, she cracked in half. I saw pirates tumble out. Some were on fire.

Flames licked up her lines.

"Restless!"

"I see her, Cap," Restless answered. Her voice was so calm. So calm.

Restless turned the wheel hard to starboard, just in time. We veered away as the Mistress O' Merit's balloons exploded. The entire ship went down, straight onto the deck of the Leviathan.

Remarkable Jones was dead.

No time for grief. No time for rage. No time for oaths of vengeance. No time to mourn.

"Get us back on course," I said.

"Aye Cap."

"Argenta!" I said, turning to face the radiophonic communicatron.

It wasn't Argenta. I didn't care, or even notice until later.

"Open the bay doors. Drop our cargo."

"Aye Captain," Svetlana answered for the missing Argenta.

First the bodies of the Deathwings. Maybe the troops inside the Leviathan would freak out a little, seeing their supposedly toughest, most vicious troops gutted like fish and dropped from the sky.

Then the ornies, the batwings, everyone we had left. Everyone carrying firebombs, a special little cocktail Inga whipped up. Something that would burn hot, really hot, hot enough to melt metal. And sticky. And couldn't be put out with water or smothering. Something nasty the girls called Doomfire.

Even high above the flames we could feel the heat. I wouldn't want to have been an Atlan soldier inside a metal gun turret hit by a Doomfire bomb.

And finally, our big payload. Bombs. Big, big bombs. Dropping so fast I could hear those descending whistles over the roar of battle, the rush of wind, the thunder of the engines, the screams of the wounded and dying. Sometimes, when I'm just falling asleep late at night, I hear those whistles and it jolts me awake. I don't try to go back to sleep then. I know too well the nightmares will come those nights.

The bombs blew craters in the armour plating of the Leviathan, not enough to kill it but enough to keep it busy. See, the bombing run along the Leviathan wasn't the way to kill it.

Actually, the ornies were.

Every ornithopter in the air carried one special bomb. Small, but very powerful. Designed by top Lemurisian scientists to react with the exhaust scrubbers deep inside the ship. One bomb dropped into the scrubber would cause a chain reaction that would destroy the whole ship.

The only problem was getting it there. The only way to get the bomb into the scrubber was to drop it straight down one of the smokestacks along its back. The only vessel agile enough to fly close enough to the smokestacks and not get hit by their cannons was an ornithopter.

We had done a practice run, about three weeks ago, when we'd heard Atlan Aerial were moving their last Leviathans. One was recalled to Neptopolis to protect the capital. And the other, well, we were flying right over it.

The practice run had gone pretty well. Of my six ornies, two had hit the target, a flaming pool of pitch in the middle of a long canyon. We figured weaving through the canyon would simulate dodging the cannons, and the black smoke of the pitch burning was pretty similar to the junk being spewed out the smokestack. Two orny crews out of six were pretty good results.

Problem was, three days of fighting had halved my ornies. We'd stacked the deck a little by letting our ornies fly inside a formation of pirate airships, making targets of ourselves to give the ornies a chance at hitting the target, but still.

The Tallyho Sisters took a hit to their stern and black smoke started pouring out their hull. Exploding rounds shook us, shattering what was left of the windows.

"Gun Deck!" I yelled at Svetlana.

"Gun Deck, aye," she answered after relay.

"Fire at will!"

Svetlana turned to the wireless, spoke, then listened. She turned to me. "Inga's due respect, Captain, but she asks, what exactly do you think they're doing?"

"My ass she said that," I muttered. Whatever Inga had said, it hadn't been with due respect. She was right, because I mean seriously, it was a stupid order. But I had to do something besides sit there, watching Restless steer us through a nightmare.

The Tallyhos veered off course. I ran up the staircase to the wireless and snatched the headset away from Svetlana.

"Furies to Tallyhos, Furies to Tallyhos, come in!"

The longest seconds of my life passed while exploding cannon shells shook the ship and I waited to hear from my friends.

"Dreadfully sorry about this, but we're going down," Gwen finally said. "All hands abandoning ship, wot?"

"Gwen! Guinny?"

"We're just fine ducks. Or should I say, Admiral?"

"What?"

"Remy's gone and we'll raise a glass later, but right now, that leaves you in charge, your Admiralship, mum."

I hadn't thought of that. I didn't want to think of that.

"Orders, Admiral?"

Something wet trickled down my cheek. I thought the cut there had reopened and reached up to wipe the blood away, but my hand came back covered in clear liquid. Tears. "Just one. Survive."

"Aye aye, Admiral. Tallyhos, over and out."

The line went dead and all I wanted to do was curl up into a ball, scream, hit something, anything. Instead I hit the talk switch.

"This is Captain Val of The Furies. With the Mistress O' Merit destroyed I'm taking command of the armada. All ships report in."

"Scirocco, reporting in."

"Hammer, reporting in."

"Bloodfang, reporting."

"Predator, here."

"Skysword, reporting."

"Steam Queen."

"Revenge, reporting in."

"Seashell Ghost, reporting."

"Blindsider."

"Lightning Strike, reporting in."

"This is The Fist. Our captain's dead! What do we do?"

"Hang on there, Fist," I said. "Is that everyone?"

"Lion's Share reporting! We're going down! Somebody help!"

A painful shriek of electrical feedback screeched over the wireless. That was the last anyone heard from the Lion's Share. One hundred seventeen pirates. The pilot managed to take her down into one of the bigger gun turrets, though, so there was that, at least.

No, I know it couldn't possibly be enough.

We were down to twelve ships, half the number we'd started out with four days previous. The rest of the pirate armada were patrolling the Afric coastlines, making sure there were no Atlan attacks.

Just then we passed over the Leviathan's stern. Her rear gunners kicked the shit out of us. We lost the Bloodfang and the Steam Queen in that. But then the last of us were out of the range of their guns.

"All ships, did anyone hit the target?"

"She's still there, ain't she?"

"What do we do? What do we do?"

"Blast the bloody blighters!"

"Everybody calm down!" I yelled. "Listen. We have a job to do and we've got to finish it. If none of our ornies hit the mark, we've got to try again."

"Are you mad?!"

"Try it again?"

"What are you talking about? We can't survive another pass!"

"Listen to me! LISTEN!" I took a deep breath. "If we don't take out these bastards, they're going to pound the troops on the ground, wipe them out. The war will be lost if we let that happen! I don't know about you, but I won't be able to live with myself knowing that I personally lost the war. So we're going to turn around and try again. Once we're past the rear gunners most of their guns aim forward. They won't be able to fire on us until we're past them! Then we drop whatever we have left. Everything we have left! Understood?"

"Furies, this is Seashell Ghost. Sorry, Captain Val, we're out of this fight. Our guns are empty and our engineer says the engines are going to give any minute."

"Get out and stay alive, Seashell Ghost," I said. "The rest of you, all I ask is that you stay with us until the first smokestack. Get me there and I'll take care of the rest."

Molly limped onto the bridge. Ever since she'd lost her mechanical foot and we'd replaced it with a brass peg, she'd been limping. Gigi was working on replacing the brass peg in her copious spare time.

"None of our ornies made it," Molly reported.

"None?"

She just shook her head.

I closed my eyes for a second, exhaling the anguish. Three ornies gone. Nine more of my crew, dead. Good girls, gone.

I took a deep breath, then said into the microphone, "All ships form up on The Furies. We're coming about. Stay with us until that first smokestack, then scatter to the four winds. It's go time, get me?"

"Aye."

"Aye aye, admiral."

"We get you."

"Do what you like, you suicidal bitch, but we ain't coming along this death ride."

"Who's that?" I shouted. "Identify yourselves."

"This is Captain Ardent of the Blindsider. If you think getting us all killed will win the war, you need to think again. We can't beat this blighted bastard. Cut an' run is what we should do!"

"Leviathans have been beaten before, by less ships than we have here, Captain Ardent," I answered him. I'd met him a couple of times. Lean and vicious like an alley cat. Never liked him. "You want to turn tail and run, go ahead. Then we won't have to share our glory with the likes of you. That goes for anyone else who wants out, too. Go now, or go time. Your choice."

I cut the line and ordered Restless to bring us about.

"We're still going in?" Molly asked as I climbed down from the wireless.

"Go time, Molly. We have a job to do and I aim to get it done."

"You think we can get close enough to those smokestacks?"

"I think Restless can," I answered. Restless straightened at the compliment, squaring her shoulders at the responsibility. If I had an entire crew of Restlesses, I could have won the war with just one ship.

"And throw what at them, harsh words?"

"Tell Inga to get down to the Booty Bay and drop our last three scrubber bombs. She's got three chances to get it right. Get as many spotters as she needs down there, too. Order the crew to mask up, that smoke is a killer and will blind us."

Molly just stared at me, her face stunned, her one human eye filled with something strange. Fear? Admiration? I couldn't tell.

"Molly?"

Her mouth opened and she said, almost despite herself, "Aye aye, Captain." Then she left.

"Course, Cap?"

"As close to those smokestacks as you can, Restless. Keep us steady, no matter what."

"Aye aye, Cap. No matter what."

I climbed back up to the wireless, took the microphone from Svetlana and said, "Pirate fleet, this is Cap... Admiral Val, of The Furies. Stay on our stern, and drop everything you have on them. Bombs, bullets, cannonballs. Rocks and heavy objects, if you have them. I want to rain doom and destruction on their heads so that if there are any survivors, I want them to remember this day with terror in their hearts. I want them to piss the bed dreaming about it in their old age! Let them know they messed with the wrong people. Let them know that whatever they do to us, it will come back to them a hundred times worse! With any luck, we'll see you all back at the airfield soon. The first round is on me! And every other round is on the crew who comes back with the most ammo, so make sure you use yours all up!"

I switched off the microphone and sat down on the staircase. Someone brought me a leather gasmask, making me look like a hideous bug-eyed monster. But hey, they kept us from choking to death, so we didn't mind too much.

The Leviathan's stern guns opened fire as soon as we were in range. Volley guns followed their cannons moments later, shattering whatever glass was left in our bridge windows. I ducked behind the stairwell, for whatever good that would do.

Inga let loose with Sparky, keeping their gun crews busy staying alive instead of firing at us. An explosive near-miss rocked our ship. Another explosion pounded our hull. I heard screams from my girls.

Then we were past them. I didn't bother asking the other pirates to report in. We'd find out soon enough who had died in the assault. Or else we'd die trying and it wouldn't matter.

Our guns opened up. The thunder of gunfire filled the world, louder than the explosive replies of the Leviathan's guns, louder than the steady beat of our engines, louder than the pounding of my heart in my chest, louder than my own thoughts. All was gunfire, everything, everywhere.

Smoke from their stacks seeped into the command bridge, thick, sooty and black. Their scrubbers didn't work as efficiently as ours, probably due to their being rushed into service. All I knew is, if we could get our bombs down one of those smokestacks, it would be bye bye Leviathan.

Pretty soon the gunfire stopped, both ours and theirs. They couldn't see us in all the smoke. We were out of cannonballs and bullets.

I turned to Svetlana to give the order to drop the bombs and that's when I noticed she'd been hit. I rushed to her side. She slumped over the wireless control panel, shielding it with her body, and when I pulled her away I saw her gasp an anguished breath, coughing blood. There was blood everywhere. The bullet must have gone through her back and out her chest.

"Help! Someone!" I yelled, but my mask muffled my voice. Luckily Molly came in just then, and she rushed up the stairs to help me carry Svetlana away.

"Get her to the Doc!"

Molly didn't say anything, just hauled Svetlana over her mechanical shoulder and left.

I raced back to the wireless, but between the blood and the bullet holes, I couldn't be sure it was working properly. I flipped the switch for the Booty Bay.

"Inga! Drop the bombs!"

I saw through the video console that the bomb doors were open. Through the smoke I could see someone using the loading crane to lower themselves out the bomb doors.

"What the?! INGA! DROP THE BOMBS!"

"Coming up on the first stack, Cap!"

"I know, Restless!" I jumped down the staircase. "Steady as she goes, no matter what! I've got to get down to the bay, they can't hear me!"

"Aye Cap!"

I ran. Hard. Maybe harder than I ever have in my eighteen years of life. Ordering girls out of my way, let me through. Slipped on a puddle of what I hoped was grease but was more probably blood. Slid down stairwells and ladders, never touching a rung. Got to the Booty Bay.

"DROP THE BOMBS! DROP THEM! NOW!"

Through the smoke I could see three girls standing near the last three bombs. We must have passed the first smokestack by then, because through the open bomb doors I could see a huge vague cylindrical shadow pass. The second smokestack.

Inga dangled by one hand out the bomb doors, the other hand raised. "Hold!"

I ran to the bomb doors. "Inga, what are you doing?!"

She ignored me completely. "Hold!"

"INGA!"

"HOLD!"

I turned to face the three girls. "Blight take you, DROP THOSE BOMBS!"

"HOLD!" Inga yelled over me.

Below us, the edge of the third smokestack came into view.

"INGA!"

"NOW! BOMBS AWAY!"

The girls shoved, and the bombs dropped over the edge of the open bomb doors, whistling through the air, dead centre on the mark, into the smokestack and disappearing from view.

I ran to the intercom, flipped the switch for the bridge, and hoped the speaker was still working. "Restless, this is Captain Val! Get us out of here, as high as you can go!"

I turned back to Inga and her bombadiers. "What were you thinking?"

Inga looked confused. "Following the Captain's orders?"

"What orders?"

The deck tilted and the air began to clear as we gained elevation, so I pulled off my mask. Restless must have heard me.

"Oh, it's you! I didn't recognize you in that mask. You could have been anyone."

"What orders, Inga?"

"Three chances, you said."

"Yeah, three smokestacks."

Still dangling from the crane chain, Inga laughed. "I thought you meant three bombs! Three in one smokestack!"

The entire ship shuddered then and a huge *WHOMP* noise filled my entire world. I must have lost my balance, because the next thing I knew, I fell out the open bomb doors.

Inga's huge hand closed around my wrist, though, so basically I had a gorgeous view of the Leviathan's death.

The scrubber bombs were basically a big chemistry set, designed to react with the chemicals in the Leviathan's exhaust scrubbers, making all those chemicals into a highly volatile, super-heated liquid. Like nitroglycerin, I guess.

Anyway, flames shot out of the smokestack, the path of least resistance. Then the entire Leviathan sort of bulged in the middle. Smaller explosions began to burst out of weaker points in their armour, sending shrapnel into the air to rain down on the troops below. I really hoped our troops were smart enough to get out of the way. Of course, hanging there, dangling from Inga dangling from a chain, I wasn't in much of a position to complain about the intelligence of others.

After the smaller explosions began, another, even bigger *WHOMP* shook the Leviathan, and the smokestacks toppled. Then greenish flames shot out of pretty much every orifice on the ship, which I suppose was the gases in their internal balloons exploding. Gotta hand it to those Atlans, though, because the main frame of the ship held together.

Right until it smashed into the ground.

I guess that speech about the survivors living the rest of their lives in terror of our attack was pretty much pointless, since there weren't any survivors.

The Battle for Afric was over. We'd won.

The rest of the war was just beginning.

Chapter Two

Admiralizing Ain't Amusing

Svetlana didn't make it.

She wasn't the only one we lost, either. All of my orny crews, dead. Nine women. Fourteen injured, six dead from the gun crew. Twenty eight injured, twelve dead from the boarding crew. Six injured in the engine room. Three Vulka-rey killed. Domina lost an arm, too much damage to repair. Mrs. Shorty almost died from a heart attack. At least she didn't wind up like poor Jenny Squall, who just sort of... shut off, one day about three weeks before that last battle. She didn't talk, didn't move unless told to, had to be fed, had to be bathed. She just stared at the ceiling above her bed. I made a point of visiting her until one day she moved on her own... to roll away from me and stare at the wall until I left.

Argenta was in so many pieces, Gigi didn't know if she'd be able to fix her. The Union of Automated Gentlemen offered to help, and sent a couple of other former automaidons to put Argenta back together. Even so, it might be weeks before she was fully functional again.

And Restless got hit. She kept us in the air, piloting the ship wounded, the stupid, crazy, awesome kid. I wanted to yell at her when I found out. I wanted to hug her when I found out. If the pirates gave medals, I would have given her one. I would have given every one of my girls a medal.

The Furies had been beaten, battered and broken. We took so much damage it was a miracle we were still able to fly. One of the outrigger engines had been blown off completely, which made Restless' flying all the more impressive. Even our balloon had taken damage, a sure sign that the Leviathan's gun crews had been desperate. Would you shoot at a giant ball of potentially flammable gas directly over your head?

Gwen and Guinny had followed my orders for once and survived. The Tallyho Sisters had crashed and burned, though. I immediately offered them a place on The Furies, which they gladly accepted.

Of the seven ships who followed our second charge, two were blown out of the skies, three more were put out of service. Scirocco survived, barely. Only The Fist, without a captain, who stuck to us like glue, came through it relatively whole.

Which was more than could be said for Mistress O' Merit. She went down with all hands.

Leaving me in charge of a fleet that was scattered to the seven skies. Those that weren't were left without ships, without crew, without a captain. I called a conclave.

But, of course, it wasn't as easy as that. First of all, Afric is a huge continent. And without long-range radio, word didn't spread that fast. And anyway, they were all doing something important for the war effort, and needed to be replaced. Which meant I needed to discuss their replacements with the other leaders of the war.

Two nights after we won the Battle for Afric, I got an invitation from General Komodo to meet with him and the other leaders. It was the first acknowledgement of my admiralty outside the pirate fleet. But I should have know he'd make me work for it.

"Ah, Captain Val, join uss," he said as I stepped into his tent, his Lemurisian accent almost completely gone. It was sort of ironic that constant use of Atlan as a common language helped us fight against our common enemy.

Now, when I say tent, I mean, this thing had canvas walls and was supported by wooden poles, but don't think it was tiny or cramped. There were multiple chambers. The main one, where I met the other leaders, was bigger than Gigi's workshop on The Furies. Carpets covered the dirt floor, and lanterns hung from every available space, making it seem unnaturally bright inside.

I walked across the carpeted floor, trying to stay calm, despite my pounding heart. "Admiral Val," I corrected him.

"Pardon?"

"Remarkable Jones named me his successor, as both Pirate Queen and Admiral of the Pirate Fleet. You called me Captain Val."

He smiled a tight little smile, lantern light glinting from his facial studs. "Of course. My apologiess."

"General Komodo was just arguing the merits of pressing our advantage," the Fist of the Zhou Way of Three said. I nodded to him; he nodded back with a slight, very slight, almost unnoticeable smile. My heart pounded just a tiny bit less hard. Not relaxed, no, but nice to know I had a friend on this war council.

"And Mr. Mahogany here is asking uss to consolidate our holdingss here in Afric, before continuing onward," General Komodo continued.

I turned to look at Mr. Mahogany, an Afric rebel leader. He was tall, and as dark skinned as the wood he was named for. Despite his age, and he had to be nearly fifty, he had a full head of short dark hair. His wrinkled face was clean-shaven, his eyes bright and perceptive. He wore a simple, pale three-piece suit, crisp white shirt unbuttoned at the throat and no tie.

"Admiral, we have not yet met," his Atlan flawless, unaccented.

I shook his hand. "Mr. Mahogany, your reputation precedes you."

He'd led a rebel uprising the day the news had reached his small town that the Lemurisians were on the march. He'd turned a group of desperate peasants into warriors and gained the trust of nearby bands of brigands to augment his growing movement. Town after town joined him and his cause, a Free Afric. When Lemurisian land troops had reached his pocket of resistance, he'd convinced them to let his people join the fight. Under his nearly flawless understanding of local Afric politics and history, he'd managed to keep the various groups from infighting. There were a lot of people who wanted to make him King of All Afric, but he kept refusing the title.

"As does yours, Admiral," he answered. "Please, join our discussion. Which do you think is wisest, consolidating our holdings, or pressing our advantage?"

I looked at the table, covered with a map of all Ayrth. Afric was covered in small markers, indicating our strongholds, our troop placements, our airfields and their complements. Similar markers covered Zhou and the Zybarich, the Russankyan lands north of Zhou. They spread through Hindyastan, Anatol, reaching almost to the Saud desert. Other markers noted Daxian movements in Russankya, where vampyri troops were wreaking havoc. In the Sea of Lemuris, between their islands and Afric were more markers showing ships, both airships and ocean vessels.

And the newest markers, showing uprisings in Anglica, Eire, Hibernia. Etrusca was almost completely covered, as was Gallia. Hispania had a few, but as a major source of Atlan industry, and with their proximity to Atlan, any rebellions there tended to be crushed pretty thoroughly.

Bavardy had a few more than Hispania, and Norsica a few more than that. Honestly, it was nice to see so many people on our side.

The only places that didn't have any of our markers were the Thousand Tribes and Amazonia, of course, since they'd officially declared themselves neutral in this conflict. You'd think they'd want in on the defeat of their ancient enemy, but apparently not. The Thousand Tribes stayed out of everything, so I was told, and Amazonia was having problems of their own, something no one was talking about, deep in the jungles of their interior.

Then there were the Atlan markers, which covered Atlan on the map like a swarm of Blighted on an elephant's corpse, and dotted Ys only slightly less. Commodore Crow had turned his island into a refilling station and shore leave/medical leave/rest and relaxation destination for Atlan troops, much to his credit and Ys' profit. I'm told it was once a haven for pirates and other unsavoury types, but Atlan's military apparently had more money to spend. The bars and pleasure houses were raking in cash, hand over fist.

Viewed as a whole, the map looked like our blue markers were winning. Afric, Lemuris, Zhou, all blue. Europa, sort of a purplish. Atlan and Ys, bright red. We covered more ground, but were less organized.

"Neither," I said, finally.

Mr. Mahogany looked surprised. "Admiral?"

"Explain," Komodo said.

I looked at each of the other leaders. General Komodo in his green and gold uniform, his beard trimmed short, his dyed hair in long dreads, his face studded along cheekbones and brow ridge, his teeth filed in the way of the Lemurisian Imperial family. The Fist of the Way of Three, sallow skinned, dark haired, impeccably dressed in traditional Zhou robes in shades of grey. Mr. Mahogany, the leader of Afric. And the other two.

Collective Number Six was, or were, as I understood from what Remy had told me, six individual automatons merged into one being. It? They? Let's say they. They worked together to control the ungainly collection of sensor equipment, spindly arms, pincer hands and tractor-treads that branched out from the central housing of various cylinders that made up its torso. Remy said Collective Number Six never said anything, never offered any advice or contributed to tactics or strategy.

They just observed and reported back to the Union of Automated Gentlemen.

The last person in the room was also the only other woman present. The name I knew her by was Willow Phoenix, though it was a well-known fact that it wasn't her real name. She had one of those ageless faces, so much so that in the right clothes and wig and makeup, she could have passed for anywhere from a worldly twenty to a well-preserved forty. Right then and there, she had sandy blonde hair cut boyishly short, piercing pale blue eyes, a bit of a prominent nose and thin lips. Experience would later show me that she never went anywhere with the same face twice. She was our spymistress.

Of course we had spies! Dozens of them, all over the world. We couldn't have won the war without them getting us crucial information. Men and women, animan and automaton, patchwork and vampyri and faekind.

Oh. Yeah. Spoilers, I guess, we won the war. But you want to know *how* we won the war, don't you? So keep reading. It's gonna get good.

Where was I? Oh yeah. I looked at the General and said, "I wouldn't do either. Sitting still isn't going to win this war and attacking that big cluster of red is a great way to get a lot of people killed. What we need to do is shake them up, get the message out. Disrupt them where they live. I mean, look, when I was in Anglica a few months ago? The people there acted like there wasn't even a war going on at all. Not until I blew up that power plant and shut down the patchwork manufactories. Then the Redcaps took up the cause, shutting down more manufactories, disrupting rail service, that sort of thing. And what they did to the Eire shipping industry was nothing short of brilliant. That got people talking about the war, let me tell you!"

"It's true," Miss Phoenix said. "The Atlan public are being kept ignorant by the government. In some cases wilfully so, but for the majority, they simply have no idea what's happening to the world outside their continent."

Mr. Mahogany frowned. "Surely the disruptions of trade, of food and slaves, has awoken them to the greater conflict?"

"As I said, sir, many are wilfully ignorant," Miss Phoenix answered. "In many cases, they simply blame the so-called Triumvirate of Terror, specifically, the pirates."

What little media attention the war had been getting had been called 'the actions of a Triumvirate of Terror: Zhou criminals, savage Lemurisians and bloodthirsty pirates'. Not half wrong, really.

Everybody turned to look at me.

"Yeah, well." I looked back at the map. "Maybe we can use that to our advantage."

"How so?" the Fist asked.

"Get pirates attacking Ys," I said, pointing at the map.

"It'ss a military stronghold!" General Komodo said.

"It's a military asset for rest and relaxation," Miss Phoenix corrected. "Disrupt their rest, don't give them a chance to relax. It's an elegant method of reducing their capabilities."

"We don't have to actually win a battle," I said. "Just hit and run. Just enough to keep them from relaxing. And if we take their supply vessels, that makes it less fun all around for them."

"What is the strength of your fleet, Admiral?"

I looked at the General. "I'm not a hundred percent sure, actually. We came out of that last battle pretty beat up, the ones who were here for it. The others, the ones patrolling Afric's shores, they're coming in for a conclave. I've already discussed it with the Fist, his air junks are replacing my pirate ships."

"How nice of you to tell uss," the General said drily.

I raised an eyebrow and jerked a thumb at Miss Phoenix. "Oh please, she didn't tell you an hour after we'd talked?"

The General looked surprised but Miss Phoenix didn't show any reaction at all. Remind me never to play six-card with her.

"General? Miss Phoenix? Do you mean to say the responsibilities of a spymistress extend to spying on our own people, as well?"

"Mr. Mahogany, it's not a big deal," I said, keeping my eyes on Miss Phoenix. "We have to guard against treachery and betrayal, after all." I switched my gaze to the General. "I mean, just a few months ago, I had a saboteur aboard my ship. We caught her and her sponsor in the end, but who's to say if they were the only traitors in our midst."

The General had the common decency to look embarrassed, at least. If it weren't for me he'd have been hanged as a traitor months ago, and the true traitor, Admiral Salamander, would have sold us all to the Atlans.

"But I'm not here to make us mistrust each other," I continued. "I just want an end to this war, same as everyone. We've got to work together, or else we'll fail apart."

Mr. Mahogany looked impressed. "Well said, Admiral."

"Indeed," Miss Phoenix agreed. Nothing showed on her face, though. "But to the matter at hand, attacking Ys cannot do more than annoy. After a few attacks, they will simply relocate their troops to another location for rest and relaxation."

"Yeah, I figured that too," I said. "That's why we've got to do something bigger, there on Atlan itself."

The Fist leaned forward on the map table, staring at the markers, looking for something he might have missed. "Did you have something in mind?"

"Actually I do," I answered. "Miss Phoenix, do any of your spies have any information on the Pit?"

That actually got a reaction out of her – mild surprise. "Blackiron Prison? Not as such, no. We've mainly been concentrating our efforts on determining military movements."

"What is this about, Admiral?" Mr. Mahogany asked.

"Seems to me we need to do two things right there, on Atlan. On Atlan? In Atlan? Whatever. First, get the word out about the war. Not sure how we can do that. Drop pamphlets on them, maybe? I dunno. Anyhow, the second thing, and I've been thinking about this for a while, is we need to disrupt the shit out of them."

They chuckled at my choice of words, and I felt my cheeks redden.

"Uh, sorry. But yeah. We need to stir things up, you know? Really get them where they live. Bring the war home. But to do it on a big enough scale to get noticed, we'd need hundreds of agents."

Miss Phoenix raised an eyebrow at me. "We haven't got hundreds of agents."

"No, I didn't think we did. And anyway, they're doing more important stuff than what I had in mind. Imagine a crime spree in the heart of Neptopolis. Already scarce resources being stolen. Or government officials being murdered in their sleep. And I'm not talking senators, here, I mean getting the accountants working in the tax office or whatever. The real people, not the grand high jackasses who claim to be running the show. Imagine if a bomb went off at the public works office. How much road repairing would happen then? Which would affect everyone in the city. One little bomb could throw the entire city into utter chaos. Just by killing off the right people."

"Innocentss, you mean?" Komodo looked disgusted.

"I could make an argument about no one supporting the current regime being innocent, but that's just justification for our actions. No, this is simple math, actually, General. We kill a dozen people working in the tax office and suddenly the military can't buy cannonballs. That saves lives for us. We kill a dozen people in the public works office and suddenly the entire city wants to know what's being done about this war. Maybe calling for a ceasefire. Who knows?"

"Yes, well, as I said, we haven't enough agents to enact your plan."

"But there's hundreds of people who hate Atlan, right there, in the heart of the empire."

"Blackiron Prison," the Fist said, and nodded.

Chapter Three

A Little R&R&R - Rest, Relaxation and Repairs

"So then what did they say?"

Restless sat next to me, just about quivering with curiosity.

"Miss Phoenix said she'd look into getting some intelligence on the Pit, but she didn't have any agents in place for that kind of thing, so it might take a while." I sighed, then shrugged. "So we wait."

"Aww," Restless complained.

I changed the subject. "So let's see it."

Restless reached up and gingerly raised the sleeve of the loose blouse she wore, revealing the puckered gunshot scar she'd earned during the Battle for Afric. The scar had a twin on the other side of her bicep. She'd been reaching for the elevator crank when the bullet had gone straight through.

But Doc Regan's bio-regenerative goop had fixed it right up in a matter of minutes, instead of weeks. That stuff had saved more lives and gotten more people back into the fight than I could count. And after she'd shared the secret with the other doctors in the fleet, well, things turned right around for us. Instead of needing to guard huge hospitals filled with walking wounded, only the very worst cases had to stay more than overnight.

Of course, not everyone had been so lucky. Restless shared her quarters with Domina, and Domina's bunk was empty. Doc Regan was keeping her in the hospital, for observation. Between Doc Regan, Gigi, and Eve, they'd fitted Domina with a new mechanical arm, a real beauty of brass, almost human-looking, the best money could buy. I'd paid for it myself, so I should know. But they wanted to make sure Domina's body didn't react negatively to the new limb. It had been known to happen, which was why Inga still only had one eye, the other a simple copalum sphere.

Which was more than Eve could say. She had to make do with an eyepatch over the eye she lost at Aldgate Amalgamated. I'd offered to get her to a patchworking facility, but she wasn't interested. "Not yet," was all she'd say, whenever I brought the subject up.

"Nice," I said, and Restless grinned, touching her scar carefully, as if afraid it might hurt. "That'll get you some drinks, next time you have shore leave."

"You think?" she asked, and grinned even wider. She flexed her arm, wincing only slightly. "Anyways, when can I come back on duty?"

"You know that's up to Doc Regan. But probably a couple of days. Besides, it's not like we're going anywhere."

The Furies was laid up in drydock, undergoing repairs. And she needed more than I had first thought. Gigi's post-battle inspection had discovered cracks in the keel, which meant weeks of repairs. We decided to take the opportunity to upgrade her, too. When Gigi was done with her, she said, we wouldn't recognize her.

So we moved out, setting up in Remy's old quarters in Maraqaz. He'd commandeered a villa for himself, as Admiral of the Pirate Armada, and I kind of inherited it. Now, when I say villa, I know what you're thinking: a nice little place, white plastered walls, open balconies, maybe a central courtyard. Yeah, Remy was never one for doing anything small. The Admiral's Villa was huge, a real mansion. Practically a palace... or a fortress, depending on your point of view. There were several courtyards, dozens of balconies and hundreds of rooms. More than enough room to accommodate my entire crew, in style, and not cramped six to a room like aboard The Furies.

We made it our oasis, giving us a place to relax and rest up. No one knew when the next battle would be, so everyone took the chance to catch up on our sleep. And baths! There were dozens of private baths, as well as the biggest outdoor swimming pool I'd ever seen. That was better than the wine cellar Remy had set up, let me tell you.

Doc Regan had set up shop not far away in the camp hospital, mixing up batches of her bio-regenerative goop and healing the wounded in a fraction of the time it would have taken them to naturally heal. Broken bones got the ossificator treatment. Anything too damaged or infected to be healed properly got removed, and fitted for mechanical replacement. The only people excused from service were those with some kind of mental trauma, preventing them from functioning. Amazingly, no one I talked to had ever heard of a psychiatrist, or a psychologist. A couple of the doctors I met through Doc Regan seemed interested in the idea, but most of them seemed sceptical. They seemed to think that the only place for the mentally wounded was an asylum. Until the wounded could be shipped back to Kha'ir, where the nearest asylum was, they were kept in a separate ward from the other patients, sedated. The official reason was to keep them safe from hurting themselves or others, but amongst the command, we knew that we had to keep the mentally wounded away from the others to keep up morale.

I spent the next few days in meetings. Organizing the defense of Afric, shoring up supply lines between us and Zhou, establishing support networks for the various revolts in Europa. Food got scarce, because we'd gathered all the farmers up in our push across Afric. Farms and ranches and plantations across the continent lay empty, rapidly returning to the wilds from which they'd been hacked. We had to implement rationing, to keep enough food for everyone. As much as we'd conquered Afric, I began to wonder if we hadn't been trapped here, too.

We still heard stories of uprisings of the Blighted. Once in a while a family would disappear, then days later the entire village would shamble off into the jungle, infected.

Plus, the vampyri in Russankya were bogged down. And the Russ had also launched a counter-offensive against the Zhou. Fighting a two-front war didn't seem like a great idea to me, but I wasn't a military genius or anything.

But it didn't take a genius to see that it was starting to look like we were stalling out.

Finally, the last of the pirate armada straggled into camp. Go time for the conclave.

Chapter Four

The Second Great Pirate Conclave

I had it at the Villa, the only place big enough for all the captains to get together comfortably. There were a few familiar faces from that first conclave, in Libertia, folks like Jackal and Lawless, friends like the Tallyhos and Python. Notable exceptions, like Remarkable Jones. And new faces, too, captains who hadn't made it to the first conclave, all those months ago. Some of the people at the second conclave had voted against joining the war during the first conclave, only to have changed their minds later. Remy had welcomed them with open arms and given them shitty jobs until they proved they weren't spies or traitors. Once they'd convinced him, they'd been given better missions.

Of course, when you're talking about pirates, 'better' always means 'more profitable'. To show off how well we were doing, I put on a banquet in one of our bigger courtyards. To get enough food to make it worthwhile, I bought off all my crew's rations for the day. Then I got Brunhilde and Hilda to cook up a buffet for us. I personally hadn't eaten that well in weeks.

Once everyone had a chance to grab a plate of food and fill a cup with their beverage of choice, I called for their attention and proposed a toast. "To fallen friends."

They echoed my words and drank from their cups. Some of them drained their cups and called for more.

Farthing Lawless stood up, crazy tall and ginger-haired. He'd shaved his ginger goatee, making him look younger. "So tell us, Sunset, what's the purpose of this conclave?"

I set aside my cup of watered wine. "Seems to me we need to decide what's next for this armada."

Gwen stood up. "Tallyho, of the Tallyho Sisters. I say, not everyone here knows everyone here. Let's do this right and proper, shall we?"

Lawless shrugged. "Fair enough. Farthing Lawless is my name. Highwayman II is my ship. What is it you think we need to decide?"

"Captain Val, acting Admiral, of The Furies," I introduced myself, even though I knew everyone present knew who I was. Conclave protocol demanded it.

I looked around at the assembled captains. Just to give you an idea of how things stood, of the nearly forty captains at the conclave, only ten were women. I was one of them. Only two were nonhuman – Josiah Axe, Captain of the Bloodbucket, a patchwork; and Arthur Rage, a bear animan, of the all-animen Menagerie. At eighteen, I was the youngest captain present, though it was a near thing with Captain Richard Robin of the Red Crest being only twenty. The next youngest woman present was Gwen Tallyho, five years older than me and only minutes younger than her twin, Guinevere. Who was also in attendance, since the two had shared captain's duties, taking turns as the commander.

"I think we need to decide what this armada wants to do next."

"First things first," Captain Axe said, standing. He was huge, taller even than Farthing Lawless. Lean. A hard look to his scarred, pale face. "Axe, Bloodbucket. We need to vote us up an admiral."

"Remarkable Jones named Sunset Val his successor," Gwen said simply. "Most here know that. Some here even witnessed it."

"Some of us even remember it!" Guinny laughed.

Yeah, that had been some kind of party, let me tell you. After we'd brought the Zhou and the Daxians and upset patchworking in Anglica and nabbed us the Redcaps to boot, all into the war, Remy had thrown a festival to officially declare me his successor as Admiral of the Pirate Armada and Pirate Queen-in-waiting. My own hangover had lasted two days, even with Doc Regan's Impossible Hangover Cure, and I hadn't nearly partied as hard as some. The Vulka-rey had kept things going for almost as long as my hangover had lasted.

"Remarkable Jones ain't here," Axe said. "And I ain't sure I'm willing to let her take the helm."

"Did you have someone else in mind?" Lawless asked.

"Sure," Axe grinned. He was missing some teeth, I saw.

Lawless grinned back. "Let me guess. You?"

"And why not?"

"Anybody here trust Axe to lead the armada?" Lawless asked the gathered captains. No one answered.

Axe shrugged. "Alright then, you do it."

Lawless laughed. "Me? No thanks."

A tall, gorgeous woman with fiery red hair stood. "Bridget Flame, of the Blaze. Call the vote, Captain Val, and let's get on with this."

I stood up and waited for Lawless, Flame and Axe to sit. "A vote's before this conclave. All in favour of naming me Admiral of the Fleet and Pirate Queen?"

The Tallyhos shot to their feet. Newly named to the captaincy himself, Captain Cooper of the Fist stood quickly after the twins. Then Python, wrapped in her skins. Lawless and Flame. Richard Robin. Then the rest of the women captains: Storm, Cyclone, old Nan Pistol, Shrike, Darling, Orchid, Cerise.

One by one, the men stood for me, too. I won't bother with naming them all, but basically, Axe was the last to stand.

"Just didn't want it to be an automatic assumption of power," he said, grinning that horrific grin.

"Thank you all," I said as they sat back down, then took a drink to work the lump in my throat back down. "Right. So. What do we do next? The war's about to take a change of direction, and we need to know which way the wind's going to blow. Command wants us to start in on Ys, disrupt their rest and relaxation. Other options?"

"Arthur Rage, of the Menagerie," the bear animan said, standing. Nearly as tall as Axe, he was also massively built. I was beginning to wonder if I was not just the youngest, but also the shortest and the lightest captain at the conclave.

Rage looked around at the gathered captains. "Why not go straight at 'em? Bring the war to Atlan's shores."

Lawless stood up. "Let me guess. Too much military presence?"

I nodded. "That's it, alright. They've pulled a lot of their forces back home. Russankya and Europa are set to fall, now that Atlan's abandoned them. Good for us, but it makes their island that much more of a problem. With their military all in one place, and so-called loyalist refugees jumping ship from Europa and the men being recalled into active service, they're too much to handle head on."

The refugees were news to the captains, I saw. They exchanged glances and muttered amongst themselves. I'd only found out about it a couple of days previous. Seems some people hated the idea of change, hated the idea that they might be in the wrong, so much, that they left behind everything they knew and emigrated to Atlan. According to our sources, a lot of native Atlans weren't especially thrilled about the new waves of foreigners on their shores.

The men being recalled into active service was especially troubling. It meant Atlan military command had convinced the Senate to change Atlan laws. Supposedly if a man survived his military service, he was released into society as a free citizen. Being called back meant someone somewhere had convinced the Senate that the war was going badly enough they had to enact extreme measures. As if unleashing the Blighted and patchworking their own troops hadn't been extreme enough. I wouldn't say it then, but I'll say it now: some of our own command were worried about how much more extreme Atlan was willing to go. The Fist in particular had this idea that in war, the side that won was the one that was willing to sacrifice more than the other. Atlan military command had already proven they were willing to sacrifice all honour. The Fist hoped we wouldn't have to beat them at that game.

I let the muttering go on for a while, long enough to let them get it out of their systems. "So Atlan herself is too big a nut to crack. Command wants to consolidate its holdings, here in Afric, in Zhou, Hindyastan. Then we take Europa, which won't be easy, not by a long shot. We could get bogged down in Europa the same way we nearly stalled out in Afric, before the Zhou and the vampyri sided with us. Could drag on for another year, or more."

"I am Capitaine Cerise, of ze Stiletto," the pink-haired Gallican pirate said, standing. She was supermodel thin, with golden brown eyes and obviously dyed, braided hair. "Zis plan, eet ees 'ow you say, not such a good idea, no? A long war cannot benefit anyone."

"Don't see how hit and run raids on Ys will do enough harm, neither,"Axe said. "They'll just pull their troops back to Atlan, like everywheres else."

"Alright then, let's talk options," I said. "Anyone?"

After a long uncomfortable pause, Guinny said, "This is where we recognize Remy's brilliance. Never at a loss for words, that man."

Those who'd known Remy chuckled.

"Seems to me," Lawless said, "that when your opponent curls himself into a big protective ball, you either hit him with a big enough stick to break his back, or else you nibble him to death."

"Brightly Burning Orchid, of the Alabaster Moon," said a petite Zhou woman with an eyelens and a mechanical arm. "The Death of Ten Thousand Cuts, this, yes?"

"Hit and run raids everywhere at once," Lawless said. "Supply lines, base camps, cities, even."

Richard Robin stood. "Rick Robin, the Red Crest. You mean to hit innocent civilians?"

"Ain't no one on Atlan innocent, boy!" Axe laughed.

"Women and children? They'll be killed!"

"Women and children are already being killed!" someone yelled. Everyone looked my way, so it must have been me.

"Women and children are already being killed," I repeated, milder, trying to get a hold of the raging fury I felt. "Women and children are taken by slavers. Sold to workhouses and pleasure houses. Families destroyed. Lives ruined. So that the people of Atlan can maintain their precious lifestyles. So that the people of Atlan can live on, blissfully unaware of how they have ruined the rest of this planet. So that they can keep bleeding Ayrth dry.

"Women and children are already being killed. In Zhou. In Libertia. All across Afric, all these months. And Atlan is responsible. So now it's time for Atlan to pay for their greed, their corruption, their crimes against the people of this entire world. It's time for Atlan to suffer, as they've made others suffer. And then maybe, maybe, women and children won't be killed any more."

I sat down. Trembling, I reached for my cup.

Captain Flame stood up, and raised her cup toward me. Captain Cerise did the same. The Tallyhos. Python. Storm. Old Nan Pistol. One by one, all the women captains stood and raised their cups to me.

Captain Lawless stood next, the first of the men. Captain Cooper. Captain Axe, grinning. I suspect he was more in favour of killing Atlans than saving countless generations of women and children from bondage, abuse, and slavery, but hey, whatever. Captain Rage. Captain Anniz. Captain Jackal. Captain Corsair. Captain Muldoon. Captain Barnacle. Captain Talespinner. Captain Orca.

I lost track of who stood when, then, but they were all standing soon enough, even Rick Robin.

I stood and raised my cup to them all, a silent vow to them. To see it through, to the end. To do whatever it took to end Atlan tyranny and well, save the world. Or die trying.

I know, right? No pressure.

Chapter Five

An Admiral's Land Battle

Nothing much else was decided that night, because Atlan forces launched a counter-assault and we all scrambled. Those who still had ships got them into the air. Those of us without found other ways to be useful.

See, the thing of it was, we'd expected them to attack from the west, toward the ocean. Maraqaz had been the capital of the province of Cartha, a nice landlocked town surrounded by plains. Easy to spot any oncoming attackers, which had been one of the reasons we'd made our headquarters there.

But Atlan Aerial hadn't led the attack, for once. Instead, Atlan Terrestrial and Atlan Naval had coordinated to launch a massive assault across the Straits of Nepton, where Hispania nearly touched Afric. The port city there, Abyla, had mostly been pounded into rubble the first time we'd taken it from the Atlans. The refugees from the city had pretty much all settled in Anfa, a much smaller port city to the southwest of Abyla. We'd left a couple thousand troops to defend the ruins of Abyla, which looking back I suppose had been a mistake.

Atlan Terrestrial and Atlan Naval had crossed the Straits while a couple dozen Barracudas and Groupers from Atlan Aerial bombarded the ruined city, then they'd killed or captured our remaining troops and charged southward, toward Maraqaz. The attack had been so sudden and successful our troops in Abyla hadn't even had a chance to send word.

We didn't know any of that at the time, though. All we knew was we were being attacked, from the north. Our airships completely outnumbered the Barracudas, who were defending the Groupers as they offloaded the troops they were carrying.

Not just troops, either. Blighted.

Atlan Terrestrial warcrabs and lobster-tanks and octopods kept their troops safe from infection, but we didn't have any of those. And our mega-saurs, the Lemurisian dinosaurs we'd fitted with Gigi's shrinking-growing machine, had all died out from massive heart failure. Turned out Gigi's machine still had a few kinks to work out. Too much strain on a living creature. Yeah, I cried when Fluffy died, let me tell you.

But we had aircycles and batwing backpacks. And a couple of Afric geniuses had fitted together some construction walkers, fitted them with armour and weapons, and sent those giant, steam-driven man-shaped mechanical marvels out into the battlefield. Just the sight of one of those fifty-foot mechmen was enough to set our troops cheering and Atlan warcrabs scurrying for cover. So far we only had about thirty or so, but we had lots more in production.

The Vulka-rey had learned the hard way that they were pretty much immune to the Blight, so they traded spots with other girls in our crew, regulars to the aircycles, werewolves to the fray. From the happy looks on their faces, you'd think the Vulka-rey had been ordered to a week on a sunny beach while good-looking men massaged their feet and brought them cold drinks.

Once the captains had left the Admiral's Villa, and I made sure the villa's defences were properly seen to, I realized I had no idea what I had to do next.

Luckily, Serena and Tring were at my side.

"Admiral, you'll need to coordinate the pirates," Serena said.

"From the safety of the Admiral's mechman," Tring added, taking me by the arm.

"Serena, you've got a portable wireless?" I asked as Tring escorted me away.

Serena grinned. Portable was not the word I wanted to use, but that's what the Union of Automated Gentlemen insisted the thirty-pound steel boxes were. "Yes Wal. Good hunting!"

And with that she was off and running, a silver-blonde blur.

"This way, Admiral," Tring said, pulling me along.

We went out one of the side doors to the Villa, rushing past girls who were arming themselves. Guns were loaded, ammo shoved into rucksacks alongside as many jars of Doomfire as they could safely carry. A lot of the girls had long shirts of ringmail – basically a leather tunic with steel rings sewn onto it. It had saved a few of them from catching the Blight and none of them wanted to take the risk.

In addition to mechmen, which were run by crews of three or more (mine needed five to keep her up and running), there were stiltwalker suits, which were worn by a single operator, and three-man pachyderm platforms, four-legged walkers with a either a single cannon or a pair of volley guns. These had all been put into service because of the Blighted, keeping our troops out of reach.

My mechman stood at the end of the back yard, fifty feet tall and already belching black smoke into the night air. A pair of huge shoulder-mounted spotlights stabbed through the smoke into the sky above, spearing airships as they soared past us.

She looked a little like a garbage can with a glass bowl on top. Stubby legs and long arms gave her an ape-like appearance. One arm ended in a pincer claw, the other had a forearm-mounted repeating harpoon launcher. Someone had painted a red and orange sunset on her torso. I still hadn't named her.

Tring shoved me onto the ladder that rose up into the mech's undercarriage. Spare me the jokes, please? I didn't design the thing. Anyway, the ladder led to a platform, where Gigi was waiting.

"Welcome aboard, Admiral," she grinned, offering me her hand to help me up.

"Thanks. Everyone aboard?"

"Yes."

"Set... well, not sail. Go time, I guess?"

Her green eyes flashed with delight as she and one of her girls hauled the ladder up. "Go time!"

I climbed the inner staircase that led to the command deck, a circular room about fifteen feet wide. Two pilots were needed to work the mechman, and two or three engineers to keep the engines and machinery functional. Usually one of the engineers doubled as a gunner.

I nodded to the pilots, Inez and Antonia, two dark-haired, dark-eyed Hispanians who'd been with us a couple of months. I sat in my chair. A wireless communicatron had been set up next to it. I grabbed my special set of goggles and strapped them on.

"Orders, Admiral?" Inez asked.

"Get us to the fight," I answered.

Antonia turned off the running lights. The pair of them had nightvision goggles to let them pilot the mechman. My goggles were totally tricked out – nightvision, telescopic, flare guard, the works.

The engines rumbled louder and the whole mechman started to shake. Then Inez pushed a lever and we took a step forward. She pushed another lever and we took another step. Lever, step, lever, step. Slow going at first, but we built up momentum soon enough.

I pulled the intercom tube to my mouth and said, "Gigi, as soon as we're good, I need someone on our weapons."

There was a pause, then Gigi answered, "I'm sending Beatrice up."

Beatrice, short and stocky and brunette, climbed through the stairwell door soon enough and went to the weapons station. The harpoon launcher wasn't the only thing we had at our disposal. Inga had really tricked us out with some death dealers. Shin-mounted Doomthrowers to take care of any Blighted or regular troops trying to climb aboard. Two belly turrets, fore and aft, with large calibre volley guns to deal with any warcrabs we might run into. Shoulder minicannons to handle anything bigger, like the lobster-tanks or the octopods.

Our mechman's legs were twenty feet long, but it took a lot to move that much metal. Our fastest speed couldn't keep up with the stiltwalker suits or even the pachyderms. As we made our way to the battle, stiltwalkers zipped past us. I thought I saw Molly with them. Ever since we'd started fighting the Blighted on land, she'd volunteered for every mission.

The stiltwalker suits had once been used by message couriers, navigating the crowded streets of Maraqaz by going over the traffic. Imagine a pair of mechanical hip-wader boots attached to a set of giraffe legs and you get the basic idea. The legs were extendible to an extent, so anyone wearing them could vary from twelve to twenty feet tall. Pretty much perfect for wading into a gang of Blighted and bashing their heads in. There were stories of single stiltwalkers taking on a dozen Blighted or more, solo, and surviving the fight, uninfected.

When Molly had heard about that, she'd found herself a suit and that had been that. She'd grown quite the legend about herself on the battlefield, taking on huge crowds of Blighted, pulling our troops to safety, rescuing civilians. But I know something that the legends never mentioned.

After that first fight, her first time out in combat in the stiltwalker suit, she'd come to find me. We talked. She told me about how the Blight had taken her father, how she'd had to put him down herself. I'm not ashamed to say I cried, and I'm sure she wouldn't mind me telling you that she'd wept, too. Huge, gutwrenching get-it-all-out weeping. Next day, she acted like it never happened. But every time the chance came to get into it with Blighted, Molly was the first on the field and the last one standing.

The pachyderm platforms were walking gun emplacements. Their legs bent like an elephant's legs, and most of them had forward-facing cannons. Between Inga and Gigi they'd managed to figure out how to reproduce lightning cannons on a smaller scale than our own Sparky, and by then about a half dozen pachyderms had been outfitted with a L'il Sparky of their own. They were great at killing warcrabs and lobster-tanks.

The other mechmen had already reached the battlefield, halting the Atlan advance. The thunder of gunfire and cannonfire, the flashes of muzzles and explosions, the fires from our dropped Doomfire grenades... The night had been truly shattered. Above us, Barracudas locked in combat with our pirate ships. I saw right away that the long weeks patrolling Afric's shores had given our ships a thirst for blood or vengeance or violence, because they soared straight at the Atlans and pounded them into paste. I don't think the Atlans knew what hit them.

Down on the ground, Blighted were being herded into kill zones, places where our crossfire could chew them to pieces. Stiltwalkers waded into the thick of it, braining the Blighted with heavy hammers and axes and shovels. Doomfire soon spread everywhere.

Bullets kept pinging off our mechman, sounding like we were under a tin roof in a hailstorm. I was glad Gigi had convinced me to thicken the glass panels and reinforce the ribbing of our dome. It wasn't quite bulletproof, but it came close. After the battle we picked bullets out of the glass for souvenirs.

Just then, though, I had to keep an eye on my ships. We got to a patch of higher ground and I ordered our feet planted. It was a technique that would keep us from being bowled over if we got caught by cannonfire. Basically the feet of the mechman clenched, grabbing onto the ground beneath us. That would give us enough time to get moving again, if we were hit.

Gigi stayed in the engine room to mind her machines, and her engineers made their ways to the gun turrets. Soon our guns added to the roar of battle. Our shin guns began spitting Doomfire out, a sign there were Blighted attacking us. I was glad I couldn't see them. Couldn't watch them burn. I had enough gruesome images in my head to keep my nightmares supplied for the rest of my life, thanks.

I scanned the skies with my supergoggles. We were doing pretty well. The pirates had gotten into the air quicker than anyone else, and they were really letting the Atlans have it. But there weren't any Lemurisians or Zhou in the air.

I toggled the switch on the wireless. "Admiral Val to fleet command. Come in, over."

"Admiral Val, this is fleet command. Go ahead."

"Where is everyone? We're just barely holding the line. Over."

"Admiral Val, the Fist sends his regards, but the attack from the north is just a feint. Zhou, Lemuris and Afric forces have engaged an attack from the south. Over."

"So, no backup? Over."

"Sorry Admiral, but you're on your own."

Chapter Six

Why Do Things Always Go From Bad to Worse?

I put the speaker tube back in its cradle, my mind whirling.

"Admiral!"

I looked up. Inez was pointing at something in the distant sky, silhouetted against the moon. I twisted the lenses on my supergoggles to zoom in.

Three Hammerhead battleships. Fan-frickin-tastic. More Barracudas, too. Oh and a bunch of little darting silvery shapes that were probably Piranha fast attack ships. Not good.

"Orders, Admiral?"

"Gimme a sec," I stalled. What could I do? We were about to be heavily outgunned. But we had to stop them from reaching the city.

So I did what Remy would have done.

"All ships, all ships, this is Admiral Val. Break engagement with current opponents and head due north at all speed and engage those Hammerheads. Over."

The wireless burst into noise, the chaos of dozens of voices all talking at once.

"Say again?"

"You want us to what?"

"We're right in the middle of something here!"

"I repeat, this is Admiral Val, break engagement and take on those Hammerheads!"

"Are you crazy, girl?!"

"Who is that?!"

"Captain Axe, who else?"

"Axe, you'll follow my orders or I'll set your head on a pike! You understand me you Blighted bastard?!"

There was a long pause. Everyone was trying to figure out how serious I was.

I spoke quietly into the tube. "Axe. I have the means to keep you aware while you're on that pike. Severed from the rest of your body. Maybe I'll leave it to rot, somewhere you can watch."

"Alright! Alright. Straight at 'em, Admiral?"

"Straight at 'em."

"Aye aye, Admiral Val."

I might not have made a friend, but he followed my orders.

I switched my wireless to the frequency we were using for our ground troops. "All mechmen, all mechmen, this is Admiral Val. I want you to form up on my position."

Standard operating procedure for the mechmen was to keep them separated, because all together they made a nice big target. So they spread out across the battlefield, surrounded by stiltwalkers and regular troops.

"Admiral Val, this is Mighty Max. Form up on you, ma'am?"

"I repeat, all mechmen units to form up on me."

"This is Big Bertha. You want us to abandon our positions?"

"Yes, yes, abandon your positions! There are Hammerheads coming in and we need to give the airships some backup!"

"By ceding the field, Admiral?"

"If one more person asks me one more question, I'll personally give the order to the firing squad that takes care of them, am I understood?!"

"Aye Admiral."

"Yes ma'am."

"Aye aye."

"This is Tall Tom. No disrespect, Admiral, but we're pinned down here and AHHHH!!!"

I glanced across the battlefield, spotting Tall Tom just in time to watch them crash to the ground and explode.

"All mechmen, report in."

"Big Bertha, reporting."

"Mighty Max here."

"Giant Jack."

I waited a couple of seconds, then realized that was all of them. "Form up on me. Over."

Then I switched to another frequency. "Serena, this is Val."

I repeated it a couple of times, but finally she answered. "Admiral, this is Serena. Go ahead."

I didn't ask if she was okay. I already knew she was fine. Our psychic link would have told me otherwise.

"Serena, I need someone to take command of the ground forces while I help the pirate armada with those Hammerheads. I'm promoting you to General."

That shocked the amusement right out of her. "Can you do that?"

"I'm the Pirate Queen. Who's going to stop me? Take command of the ground troops, form a line at the city walls. Don't let anything past you. Keep your vampyri together and under control. Set them on the lobster-tanks and warcrabs. Regroup the stiltwalkers – find Molly, she'll be in the thickest crowd of Blighted – and don't let them get diverted into chasing down stray Blighted. We'll get them all eventually. Break them into squads of ten, with someone in command and a message runner."

"And the pachyderms?"

"Spreading them all over the battlefield is stupid. Bring them back to the walls, spread evenly in the ground troops. HOLD THAT LINE. Nothing gets past you."

"As you command, Admiral."

"Oh and somebody tell the Vulka-rey to get back, too. Put them to work with the vampyri on the warcrabs and lobster-tanks."

"That might be difficult, Admiral, but I'll send someone. Vhat of the octopods?"

"Leave that to me and the mechmen. Oh and Serena?"

"I know, Wal. You too."

I left the Afric irregulars, spare pirates without a ship, vampyri commandos and a squad of Vulka-rey werewolves under the command of a vampyri swordmistress. It was the first time anyone had given a military position to any vampyri outside of the Daxian military, and the first time a female had been given the rank of General. Ever.

Oh sure, I was an admiral, and not the first female in that position, you know, world-wide, but beyond the Lemurisians, I hadn't ever heard of any military leaders being women. Not the Atlans, that was for sure. Not the Zhou, either.

Anyway, I had complete trust in Serena. How could I not?

But back to the battle. I switched the wireless back to the armada. "Axe, I want you to take the lead."

"Why me?"

"Because you want to prove what a death-dealer you are, right?"

There was a long pause, then I heard a growl of frustration. "Straight down the middle, you said?"

"Straight down the middle, everyone firing on that central Hammerhead."

"Why that one?"

I rolled my eyes but held my tongue. "Because, Axe, standard Atlan formation calls for the command vessel to take the central position. You take them out, it will decapitate them."

"Beggin' yer pardon, Admiral, but they have a chain of command for a reason. So they can't be decapitated."

"Yeah, I know that, Axe, but it will take them some time to recover. Anyway, when you're done that, swing around and take out the Hammerhead on their portside."

"Oh, just swing around, she says."

"You take out those two Hammerheads, Axe, and you can scatter. I'll take out that third one myself."

"How the blight are you going to do that, from down there?!"

"You worry about yourself, Axe, and leave me to me."

There was a long pause this time, and finally he said, "Aye aye, Admiral. Good hunting."

"You too."

I could see the other mechmen making their ways across the battlefield towards us. When they got close enough, I flipped over to their frequency and spoke into the tube. "Alright, all mechmen, follow me. Don't be shy about firing on those Atlan bastards, either."

"Fire while walking? Due respect, Admiral, we won't hit a thing."

"We don't have to," I answered. "We just have to make them think twice about getting anywhere near us."

"Aye aye, Admiral."

I was getting pretty tired of hearing that 'is she crazy?' tone in everyone's voices. Hopefully this battle would teach them to stop questioning everything I said. I mean, it's not like I was some military genius or anything. The only training I had came from movies and television shows and books, and anyway that kind of warfare was very different from anything I'd experienced. But I had a pretty good track record so far, and doing whatever they least expected seemed to be working pretty well. Anyhow, all this to say, that tone was getting on my nerves.

Which probably explains what I did next.

"All mechmen, follow us, full speed. Open fire, all guns."

The four of us charged across the field. Now, when I say charged, don't imagine giant robots actually running. It was more of a quick march. Good thing too, because even a quick march was jarring and jolting enough that I bit my tongue twice, hard enough to draw blood. Even belted into my command chair, I felt like I'd been beaten up.

Once we cleared past the remaining crowds of Blighted and got into the ranks of Atlan Terrestrial units, we had the pleasure of seeing them scatter, screaming. Even though our gunners couldn't get a bead on anything, we put enough flying lead, cannonballs and Doomfire into the air that I'm sure we left a swath of dead and dying Atlans behind us.

"Admiral Val, this is Big Bertha. Where exactly are we headed?"

I scanned the battlefield. There was a bit of a hill up ahead. "Make for that hill." Then I repeated the order to Inez, who just nodded. It made a nice change, giving an order and having it followed without question or argument or discussion.

When we got to the hill, though, we saw something that nearly made me sick. Dozens more warcrabs and lobster-tanks. The attack on the north wasn't the feint; the southside attack was.

"What do we do, Admiral?" Inez asked.

"Plant us, right here," I said. I switched over to the mechmen. "Mechmen, this is Admiral Val. Position yourselves around me, and keep them off me."

"Aye aye, Admiral," they answered.

Over to Serena. "General Heartlace, this is Admiral Val, come in."

"General Heartlace, go ahead Admiral."

"General, this isn't the feint, this is the main assault force. Do you see the mechmen on that hill just past the main advance?"

"Yes, Wal."

"If we go down, everyone retreats. Don't let it become a rout, but get into the city and make them pay for every inch. They've got... fifty warcrabs, thirty five lobster-tanks, two dozen octopods. Hundreds, maybe thousands of ground troops."

Serena swore in vampyri, then asked, "Vhat vill you do, Wal?"

"What I always do. The unexpected."

The other mechmen opened fire on the advancing Atlans as soon as they were in range, and I ordered our gunners to do likewise. No sense saving bullets when an ocean of enemies was crashing towards us.

I searched the skies above us. The pirates had made their first pass on the Hammerheads, by then. Two pirate ships were sinking towards the ground, one of them on fire and the other belching black smoke. I couldn't tell which ships they were, but they were headed toward the Atlan troops, so if they couldn't pull themselves out of their long slow crashes, I hoped they'd take a few more Atlans with them.

But the much better news was, that middle Hammerhead was coming down, too. Flames licked at its sides and I saw a dozen safety ornithopters – sort of the airship equivalent of a lifeboat – take to the skies. And it looked like the Hammerhead would come down on the Atlan troops, too. Which gave me an idea, the idea I'd been waiting for. Because yeah, up until then? I'd had no clue what I was going to do.

We waited until the pirate armada had turned around and begun their second pass, long slow minutes in which the Atlans opened fire on us. Bullets whizzed by, pinged off our glass dome, rattling our armoured chassis. Cannonballs crashed into us, making a sound like a huge bell. I still get jumpy whenever I hear a clocktower bell ring. Some of the cannonballs hit the hill, filling the sky with dirt and dust, making it nearly impossible to see what was happening.

Luckily I was staring up at the Hammerheads and not down at the warcrabs and lobster-tanks that were surrounding us. The huge octopods that were bringing up the rear of their advance were the only things I could see in all that mess.

"Admiral Val to all mechmen, I want you to clamp on to us. Grab us and don't let go!"

There was a long pause, then they all answered their affirmatives. The three mechmen swivelled toward us and grabbed on to whatever was most convenient. Since we were at the top of the hill, and they were slightly lower than us, that pretty much meant our legs. The mechman shook with each clamp.

I ordered Antonia to raise our harpoon arm. I knew we had eight harpoons loaded.

"How fast can this thing fire?" I asked her.

"One harpoon every four seconds, signora. I mean, Admiral."

"Pull the trigger, and it automatically loads the next? Four seconds is how long it takes for the next barrel to rotate into place?"

"Si, Admiral."

"Okay. Antonia, open fire on that Hammerhead."

"What?!"

"What?!" echoed Inez.

"You heard me. Spear us a Hammerhead. Fire every harpoon."

"Si, Admiral."

Antonia leaned down to look into the viewfinder, a small circular green-and-grey television screen being fed an image from a camera mounted at the end of the harpoon gun. One hand wrapped around the firing handle; the other manipulated the harpoon arm. She flipped the safety cover off with her thumb, then pressed down on the red firing button and fired the first harpoon.

Now, when I say harpoon, I don't mean the long spears they used to hunt whales with. I mean twelve feet of steel ending in a barbed hook, attached to the mechman by a spool of thick chain. When that baby flew, no one wanted to be in its path.

The first harpoon glanced off the Hammerhead's copalum armour, falling back into the crowd of advancing Atlans, skewering a warcrab. Oh well, not a complete loss, then.

"Take your time, aim and fire, Antonia," I said, resting a hand on her shoulder. Of course, I wanted to scream, FIRE FIRE FIRE!!! but you know, I had to keep my cool for the girls.

Antonia didn't answer, she just fired again.

The harpoon flew through the air, the chain rattling out behind it, and sunk deep into the Hammerhead's hull. The second and third harpoons hit as well. The second one's chain snapped with a crack like a rifle shot, just as the fourth one hit and the fifth loaded up. Harpoon after harpoon flew through the air to penetrate the Hammerhead's hull.

Inez had a hard time keeping us planted. The strain of the Hammerhead, pulling on all those chains, bent the metal of the mechman's arm with a groan. But the combined weight of four mechmen was too much for the Hammerhead.

I know what you're thinking – a Hammerhead battleship was a huge machine with powerful engines and huge propellers. And that's all true.

But the Hammerheads were never designed to carry a huge load like four heavily-armoured, heavily-armed anchored mechmen.

It had been a gamble, I admit. I mean, I was just hoping we might hit that wide command deck at the front, or maybe get our chains caught in the propellers. What we did, skewering its hull, chaining it to the ground, sent the huge battleship way off course. Ever seen a dog on a leash run around its human? It was sort of like that.

Only a mechman, having been designed for use in construction, could swivel on its waist. So instead of the chains wrapping around us or the arm breaking off, we just spun around.

"Reel it in!" I ordered, and Antonia pulled the lever that threw the harpoon chain coils into reverse.

There was no way the little engine on there was strong enough to pull a Hammerhead down, but if we could get her off course just enough...

The first thing that happened was the warcrab we'd speared rattled toward us, spilling out the remains of its crew. Then the chains on the Hammerhead snapped.

Oh well, good idea, too bad it didn't work, right? Wrong.

The Hammerhead crashed right into the advancing Atlan troops, then exploded into a rain of shrapnel and greenish flames.

We'd brought it down without firing a shot.

Unfortunately, while the flaming wreckage was enough to send the Terrestrial troops running, and diverted the warcrabs and lobster-tanks, the octopods just lifted themselves over the flames.

The octopods moved by, yes you guessed it, tentacles, only tentacles is really way too simple a term for the incredibly sophisticated machinery that was able to lift the vehicle and wrap itself around whatever happened to be in its path. I mean, I suppose it was a little more like a spider than an octopus, because they both had a huge spherical chassis under which were eight long legs, but spider legs are stiffer than the octopod's were. And anyway I didn't name the blighted thing.

They came at us, straight over the flaming wreck of the Hammerhead, completely unconcerned with any survivors. Four octopods; four mechmen. Now, the octopods were made to be land battleships, with dozens of crew inside manning eight powerful engines and dozens of cannons and guns. So it's kind of an understatement to say they were bigger than us. More like twice the size, at least.

"Admiral, we should retreat," the captain of Mighty Max said.

"If we do, hundreds of people will die," I answered. "You want that on your conscience? Because I sure don't. So stay with me, and we'll get through this."

I really desperately hoped that I hadn't lied to him.

"We're running low on ammunition, Admiral!"

"We all are," I answered. "We'll just have to do this the hard way."

I turned to Inez. "All ahead full."

"Aye, Admiral. What about that warcrab?"

I grinned. "Bring it along."

So we charged straight at the octopods. Big Bertha had a wrecking ball for a right hand; Mighty Max's was a giant shovel scoop; Giant Jack had a big old hammer. Why our mechman had needed a harpoon launcher I had no idea. (Gigi later explained it had been for putting up fence posts linked by chain. Bit of a waste, if you asked me. I mean, what was wrong with two guys with shovels? Anyway. Back to the fight.)

Our harpoons had been launched and their chains snapped. All but one, and that had a warcrab dangling from the end of it. Which would likely make a pretty good wrecking ball, I thought.

So we closed with the enemy. I ordered everyone to attack the same octopod, hoping that maybe our proximity to their colleagues would keep the others from attacking us. Then I sent Beatrice back down below to help Gigi with the engines, taking over the clamp arm. We jumped the lead octopod and started hammering at it.

Antonia raised and lowered the launcher arm, and the warcrab swung around on its chain and smashed into the octopod's right eyehole window, destroying it. I hoped that had been some kind of command bridge or something. I worked the other arm, grabbing a tentacle and keeping it from snaking around us. Of course, that left three other tentacles to grab us, with the last four being needed to hold the octopod up.

A tentacle wrapped itself around Mighty Max. They chopped at it with their shovel, smashing it to pieces. Big Bertha flailed at it, her huge wrecking ball doing exactly that, wrecking everything in its path.

"Go for the legs!" I ordered.

Giant Jack ducked, *DUCKED!* under a tentacle and went for the legs, slamming that huge hammer into first one leg then another, shattering them. Between them and Bertha, the octopod soon ran out of tentacles holding it up, and had to retract the ones attacking us to keep itself upright. Without anything to defend itself with, we beat the living shit out of it. Mighty Max went down when a cannon shot it, point blank, in the belly, exploding its engine. I had a second to hope some of the crew got out.

Then the other octopods were on us.

Tentacles everywhere. Grinding machinery scraping our hull. The shriek of metal being torn open, of arms being snapped. We lost the warcrab at one point and were left just slamming the launcher arm against the hull of an octopod. Big Bertha was crushed by three tentacles. Giant Jack was pulled apart by the crews of two octopods. Things were definitely not looking good.

I looked everywhere, desperate for a way out of that mess. Above me, I saw a tentacle raised to smash our glass dome and kill us all. Then another tentacle tripped us and over we went, crashing to the ground. Guess the tentacle crews needed some team-building exercises or something.

Anyway we crashed onto our back, shattering our glass dome into thousands of flying shards of cutting death. Inez and Antonia were lucky, being at the front of the command bridge and, you know, strapped into their chairs and everything. See, they were smart. Me, not so much.

I flew through the air, crashing into my command seat and breaking at least a couple of ribs. But I managed to grab onto a strap and keep from plummeting into a knee-high pile of broken glass, at least.

I hung there, gasping for air against the pain of my snapped ribs, dangling, when I saw the most beautiful thing ever.

General Serena Heartlace, leading a charge of pachyderms and stiltwalkers, of vampyri and werewolves, of pirates and Africs, across the battlefield, heading straight for me. She was standing on a pachyderm platform, and I saw her yell the order to open fire. The cannon erupted, and I swear to you, I watched the cannonball go over us. From the explosion that rocked our crippled mechman, it was a direct hit against the tentacle.

Serena jumped off the pachyderm without waiting for it to slow down. She climbed through the shattered dome without any thought for the killing shards of glass.

"Wal!"

"I'm... good," I lied. Talking hurt more than breathing.

She grabbed my legs and helped me down. If it weren't for the blood staining her chin and shirt, I would have kissed her. As it was, I settled for letting her hold me up. She reached down to carry me.

"Don't!" I hissed. "They need to see me walk out of here."

Serena looked like she wanted to argue, but nodded, reluctantly.

I took as deep a breath as I could and pushed off from her. Apparently I'd twisted my ankle, too, so no one was going to see me walk anywhere. Limping would have to do it.

I let Serena lead me out of the downed mechman. Almost all our crew survived. Beatrice didn't make it. She'd been on our rear gun when we fell. Except for my wounds, everyone else only suffered bruises and minor cuts. I'd call that a win.

Chapter Seven

Planning the Pit

Doc Regan's ossificator wasn't any fun, but it was better than stabbing pain every time I moved or breathed or did anything at all. The sprained ankle, there wasn't anything she could do about.

"What?!" I whined.

"Stay off it an' rest, yer Admiralship," Doc said, closing her little black bag. "Sure an' ye've earned it."

I rolled my eyes. "At least give me something for the pain."

She snorted. "I'm of the opinion that maybe a l'il pain'll do ye some good. Remind ye that y'ain't invulnerable. From what I hear tell, that was a blighted stupid thing ye did."

I flopped back into my pillows, crossing my arms. "Which part? You'll have to be more specific."

She just raised an eyebrow and gave an arrogant little smirk. "G'day to ye, Admiral."

She closed the door behind her, leaving me with my pain. I looked around my gigantic room. I think I could have fit six of my bedrooms back home on Earth into this one single room. My bed could have fit a half dozen people. Okay, they would have had to get cozy, or at least know each other really well. But you get the idea.

The room itself still bore traces of Remy's occupancy. The fully stocked bar in the distant corner. The exotic-looking guns on display over the mantle. The gold-plated chamberpot, which I still couldn't bring myself to use. Who gold-plates a chamberpot?!

But the rest was all me. My desk was covered with papers, ledgers, maps and books. Things I needed to know about, now that I was Admiral. I'd started keeping a journal to keep track of everything that had happened, what came first and who did what. There were a couple of armchairs set before the fireplace, but since summer was just coming to a close I didn't feel the need for a nightly fire. The chairs were covered with discarded clothes.

I'd become something of a clothes collector. The sheer amount of stuff I'd had to ship out of The Furies while she was refit was astonishing. I couldn't remember buying so many clothes, and I wondered where Domina had hidden them all. While she'd been in charge of helping me, my room had been spotless.

She was doing well, since I know you're wondering. Doc Regan said Domina was almost ready to return to her duties.

A warm breeze wafted through the latticework windows and the lace curtains hanging there, billowing them softly. Sunlight streamed in when the curtains moved away. Despite the early hour, I could tell it was going to be another scorching hot day.

I decided I wasn't going to just lie there feeling sorry for myself, so I threw off the thin cotton sheet and lowered my feet gently and gingerly to the floor. I limped across the room to my clothes closet and opened the double doors. I'd always dreamed of having a walk-in closet; this was more like another room, just for my clothes. A full-length mirror at the far end showed me how I looked.

A summer spent fighting across Afric's skies had turned my skin into a freckled disaster. Even my freckles had freckles. Even parts of me that never saw sunlight had freckled. Don't ask me how that worked. My hair, however, had brightened so bright a red that I bet I could be spotted from miles away. I was in the best shape of my life, except for all the scars and the sprained ankle.

And the tattoo.

Captain Crow's brand, my slave marker. A terrible rendering of a crow in flight. My daily reminder of why I had to get up in the morning. Because my few weeks as a slave had been horrific enough, and they had been easy compared to some of the horror stories we heard. Beatings, rapings, deliberate disfigurement. Confinement. Starvation.

So whenever I woke up – because it was nearly never that I got a full eight hours, and absolutely never that I had a set bed time - I would glance at that blasted blobby bird and think about all the slaves still out there, still waiting to be freed. And that would chase away the urge to stay in bed and wait for the war to be over.

Anyway, on to happier topics. I was eighteen, in the best shape of my life. My legs were toned, my abs were sculpted, my arms were totally cut. Let's face it, I was hot, something I'd never thought of myself back on Earth. I was lean without being skinny, muscled without being mannish. Athletic, I guess, but not like I spent six hours a day at the gym. More like, I spent twenty-four hours a day trying to keep myself and my crew alive, and hadn't eaten any junk food since I arrived in Ayrth. Just Brunhilde's and Hilda's awesome home cooking. Who knew nearly constant exercise and nothing but home-cooked fresh food would have such an effect?

So yeah, nearly a year on Ayrth had turned me into kind of a hottie, but it wasn't like I had any time to do anything about it. I kind of envied my girls, whenever they went out on shore leave. Partying like it might be their last day on Ayrth, because hey, it might be. But being a captain meant a thousand decisions to make every day, and being Admiral of the Pirate Armada somehow made that twenty times worse. Every day, it seemed, I went to bed more tired than the day before, woke up still tired. But who else was going to do the job?

And anyway, even if I did have the time to spend with some guy, I didn't want some guy, I wanted my guy. Even if he was thousands of miles away on another continent leading a rebellion.

Oh yeah, Bunthorne Bartholomew Tallyho, aka the Hooded Fox, masked avenger of the patchworked, hero of Albion, and I guess you could call him my boyfriend? Sort of a crazy word to use considering we'd only kissed a few times and never been on a date, unless you count that party where I'd nearly been caught by and then nearly killed Commodore Crow, the brother of the guy who'd put the slave tattoo on me in the first place. So anyway, my I guess you'd call him boyfriend, had managed to get himself involved with the Redcap Rebellion, organizing all manner of hijinks, clearing Atlan troops out of Eire and Hibernia and most of Anglica. Oh, and inspiring all kinds of other masked avengers, or so I heard. Between the vigilantes and the faeries, Atlan forces had been forced to withdraw from the other cities in Anglica. Only Albion itself remained an Atlan stronghold, and when that fell, then all the faeries in the world would have a place to call home in Eire, and Hibernia would have its independence, and Anglica would be a bastion of justice for all. At least, that's what he told me in his letters.

The first time I got a letter from him, I had no clue what to do with it. I mean, I read it, of course, but it was filled with all kinds of things. How the rebellion was doing. How Albion society folk were reacting to the changes. Who was siding with whom. And how he felt about me. Those parts made me blush. No, I'm not going to tell you any more than that.

His sisters, the horrid interfering matchmaker busybodies that I loved so dearly, encouraged me to write back. I couldn't imagine writing down some of the things he'd written, so I answered back with you know, regular day-to-day stuff. Funny stories about the girls on my crew. How this battle went, how that city had fallen to our advance. And at the last minute, just as the mail carrier ship was readying to take off, I added a little heart to my signature, sealed the envelope before I could change my mind, and sent it.

And it went like that. He was so much eloquenter than me. Than I. More eloquent. Anyway. He'd poured out his heart and soul into the letters, and I gradually answered back with more of my feelings toward him and less about how Restless spilled Inga's soup. Every word about how I felt about him I wrote made him write ten words about me.

Of course I kept all the letters! In a special, sealed, fireproof box I kept under my bed.

So yeah. Love letters, blah blah blah, missed him like I'd miss an arm, yadda yadda. Okay. Yeah.

Where was I? Oh yeah. Okay. So I got dressed, slowly because of the stupid sprained ankle. Skirt, slippers, blouse, waist cincher. I was in the middle of making a mess of my hair when Restless actually knocked. I mean, she knocked as she opened the door, proving she could be taught, even if she hadn't quite grasped the waiting for me to answer part.

She grinned at me. "Cap'n!"

"Come in," I said as sarcastically as possible. "Oh it's you, Restless. Do come in."

"Huh?"

"Never mind. What is it?"

"Someone at the door for you, Cap'n. An old woman? She says she has a message. Something about ashes?"

'Ashes' was the codeword we'd come up with for a special top secret message from Miss Phoenix.

I nodded. "Alright. Put her in the study, the one with the books? See if she wants anything to drink. And let her know I'll be down as soon as I can."

"Aye aye, Cap'n. I mean, Admiral. Sorry 'bout that."

"It's fine, Restless. Go."

She left without another word, and I started looking for something I could use as a walking stick.

In the end, I settled on using a parasol I'd picked up somewhere. Not very sturdy, but better than nothing. The stairs, I didn't even bother, I just slid down the bannister.

I hobbled into the study. An old Afric woman was sitting in a wicker chair by the window, absorbing the heat of the sunlight beaming in. She didn't move at the sound of my entrance, just calmly sipped from a glass of mint iced tea. Sunlight like diamonds in the condensation on the glass, gleaming from the heavy gold bracelets and hoop earrings she wore. Her clothes were a riot of conflicting colours and patterns.

I cleared my throat as I came near. She turned her head toward me and I saw her eyes were milky white. She was blind.

"Admiral Val?" she asked, her Atlan heavily accented. I'll spare you a phonetic version of her accent, because it often took me two or three times to understand her and honestly, no one wants to read that.

"Yes."

"Are we alone, Admiral?"

"Yes."

"Good. The bird of fire speaks through me."

I sat down across from her. "Go ahead."

"Some events have recently occurred of which you should be aware. First, your actions during the recent battle have some people considering you reckless. Perhaps unfit to bear the title of admiral?"

"Really."

"Second. The majority of the leadership feel that this attack might not have happened if the advance had continued into Hispania."

I shook my head. "So they're going to invade Hispania and get a lot of people killed. Great. Do you have any good news?"

"Alas, the bird of fire sends only words of tribulation."

I sighed. "Fine. Anything else?"

"Yes. Perhaps most disturbing is the news from Atlan. The tides of loyalist refugees have the native-born Atlans calling for restrictions on immigration. Specifically, animen."

"There are that many loyalist animen? They're barely more than slaves themselves, under Atlan law."

"True. But recognizably not Atlan, yes? Their property has been seized 'for protection' and they have been rounded up. For their own safety, them now live in special camps, far from any city."

Camps. The word sent a chill up my spine. I'd seen movies about the camps during World War II, back on Earth. I knew what happened in those places.

"Is there any way to get them out?"

The old woman frowned, confused. "Rescue the animen?"

"They're as much victims of Atlan tyranny as any slave, now."

She nodded. "True."

"So what do we do?"

"The bird of fire, she did not say."

I raised an eyebrow. "You can drop it now, Miss Phoenix."

The old blind Afric woman blinked, confused. "What do you mean?"

"Oh please. I'm supposed to believe you'd send someone barely intelligible to deliver this kind of news?"

There was a long pause, then in perfect Anglic she asked, "Accent a bit much, then?"

"Just a bit. More tea?"

"Thank you."

I poured us both a cup, adding a lump of sugar to mine. "So? What do we do?"

"You're right about the invasion of Hispania. It will get a lot of people killed."

"Tell me about it. So stupid! I mean, the war's got to continue, but there are better ways to win it."

She sipped her mint tea. "Tell me your idea."

"It's not much of an idea. Sneak into the Pit, convince the prisoners to revolt, escape, and spread chaos through the continent, but especially in Neptopolis. Get the citizens of Atlan so riled up, so scared, that they force their leaders to surrender, or at least, open up negotiations."

She thought about it for a few minutes. I sipped my tea.

"You're right, it's not much of an idea," she said, finally. "First, we have no idea where the Pit is. Second, getting you and your famous face into Atlan will be a challenge. Not to mention the fact that as Admiral and Pirate Queen, you're too important to risk on this potentially suicidal mission. Then there are the prisoners, vile, cutthroat, dishonest, dishonourable – and that's the best of them. The bad ones are much, much worse. Convincing them to honour their promise upon their release, which I'll get to in a moment, will be next to impossible. And the prison break, well, if it were possible, it would have been done long ago. And then, assuming you escape your responsibilities here, and successfully invade Atlan, and find the secret, hidden prison, and get in, and convince the most dangerous criminals in the world to work with you, and plan and execute a prison break the likes of which Atlan has never imagined, then we'd have to extricate you from the most heavily defended continent on the planet. Is that it?"

"Pretty much, yeah."

She stared at me a long time, then laughed. "Very well. Let's begin."

"What, now?"

"We haven't any time to lose. The invasion of Hispania will happen as soon as the other leaders feel we're ready. General Komodo seems to think it will take at least two months to get everything organized. The Fist thinks a month is more than is necessary. Mr. Mahogany feels six weeks will be needed, but that it should not be rushed and is willing to side with the General."

I sipped my tea and thought about it. "The General is used to everything being shipshape and squared away. The Fist has a looser attitude. Mr. Mahogany's a little of both."

"Indeed."

"We need all the time we can get."

"I agree."

"I'll see what I can do. Meanwhile, what about the Pit?"

"Getting you into the Pit will be as much of a challenge as getting you back out."

"I could give myself up," I laughed.

She didn't laugh. She stared at me with those blind eyes a good long while.

Then she shook her head. "There's no guarantee they'll let you live long enough to stand trial."

Oh yeah, that. "If I surrendered in a really public way, so that everyone knew I'd been taken?"

She shook her head again. "No. There would be an 'accident'. You would be 'resisting authority' or 'shot while attempting escape'. Or simply, you would 'commit suicide' in your cell. There are too many ways for you to be killed before you reached the Pit. And besides, you're the Admiral of the Pirate Armada. You're needed here."

That, too. "What if I wasn't Admiral?"

"The other pirates voted for you, unanimously. Did anyone even speak against it?"

"Captain Axe," I muttered, thinking. How could I get myself demoted?

We talked about sending other people in my place, but couldn't think of anyone infamous enough to be sentenced to the Pit or convincing enough to get the prisoners to get on board with the plan. Not to brag or anything, but I did convince a group of scared women to rebel against the slavers who'd ruined their lives; convinced a bunch of notoriously individualistic pirate captains to form an armada and stand against an Atlan invasion fleet; convinced a gang of Zhou criminals to make a stand against their Atlan overlords; convinced the vampyri to risk genocide to gain their freedom; convinced the faefolk of Albion that the time for revolution had come. I was pretty sure I could convince a gang of people who had to hate Atlan with an epic hate to, you know, go out make as much trouble for Atlan as possible, including killing as many Atlan leaders as they could.

No, it had to be me.

But how?

Chapter Eight

Can't be Inhuman Without Humans

We kicked around a few ideas for a few hours but nothing solid sorted itself. The biggest problem, aside from the fact that I was an admiral, was getting into the Pit. No one knew where it was, how it was guarded, or even how many prisoners were still inside. There wasn't much point of even planning this mission if there were only four guys and a couple of shovels down there. Everyone knew being sent to the Pit was pretty much a death sentence. A few weeks, a few months, maybe a few years, but eventually everyone sent there was worked to death.

Seemed like a stupid way to get coal out of the ground. I mean, there *had* to be a better way. The more I thought about it, the less the whole 'coal mine prison' made any sense. We needed more information, and we didn't know how to get it.

See, the problem was, there had to be someone who knew where the Pit was. More likely, a whole bunch of someones. The prisoners unlucky or infamous enough to get sent there didn't just disappear. They had to be transported there, somehow. Which meant guards. Which meant drivers. Which meant more than one person knew.

Unless, of course, they were a lot smarter than we thought, breaking the trip from the jails of Neptopolis to the gates of the Pit into pieces, with no guards, no drivers, knowing the entire way. Maybe even doubling back and looping around to lose any pursuers. That's what I'd do.

But even if they were as smart and suspicious as me, it still meant there were a lot of people who knew the way to the Pit. So maybe if we could find one of those people, we could somehow get them to work with us. Bribes seemed to be the least violent option, though the likelihood of the Tribunal of Justice giving the transport of an infamous prisoner to a guard whose loyalty might be purchased seemed pretty slim.

"So I'm asking for ideas," I said to my crew chiefs, once we'd finished the main course. I'd asked them to meet me in the Admiral's Villa for a late dinner.

"Admiral?" Tring asked, standing up.

I nodded. "Yeah, now please."

Molly looked like she had something to say, but I held up a finger for her to wait.

Tring whistled and her Open Hands appeared at the opened doors of the balcony. They closed the doors and turned their back to the doors, staying outside, on guard.

Tring went to the huge double doors of the dining hall, looked out into the hall, then closed them and stood with her back to the doors. The only other door was the servant's entrance at the other end of the dining hall, and Tring could keep an eye on it from where she stood. She looked at me and nodded. I motioned for Molly to speak.

"Seems to me, Admiral, we need to focus on one problem at a time. First of all, you're the Admiral of the Armada. You can't just turn your back on that."

"Who says?" Inga asked, pouring beer from a pitcher into her pewter mug. "She's the Pirate Queen!"

"That is a problem, though, isn't it?" Mrs. Shorty said. "You're an inspiration to the fleet, Admiral. People follow you, not some noble cause of freedom and justice. They follow *you*. And if you disappear for a month, this time it won't be like our whirlwind tour of Zhou and Daxia and Anglica. People will want to know where you've gone. People will want to follow."

"I doubt they'll want to follow if they know where I'm going."

"Getting you into the Pit isn't the problem at hand, Sunset," Gigi said. "Getting you out of the Admiralty is."

"I could retire. Say the pressure of command was too much for me. I mean, half the other leaders believe what I did during that last battle was reckless, stupid, pointless, whatever. Not that they'd believe that I knew what I was doing at the time."

"Did you?" Miss Merryweather asked quietly.

I shrugged. "Did I know we'd be able to take down that Hammerhead? Or that Serena would save us from the octopods? Of course not. But did I think that sitting back in the city and waiting for the attack from defensive positions was the smarter thing to do? No, I didn't. Sitting and waiting doesn't suit me very well."

They chuckled at that.

"So if you're asking, did I know charging into a battle, outnumbered, outgunned, overmatched, would succeed? Yeah, I did. Because it wasn't what they expected. And we've seen that by doing what they don't expect, we win. Just about every time. Playing their game by their rules, they're experts. But by playing by our rules, they can't adapt fast enough to deal with us, and we win."

Miss Merryweather nodded. "Admiral, I believe I may have the solution you're looking for. If Miss Phoenix can get me into Neptopolis, I may be able to get us the information we require."

I stared at her. "What?"

"Mattis?" Mrs. Shorty asked.

"You all know that before being taken as a slave, I was a governess. I don't believe I've ever told you for whom."

I raised an eyebrow. "Nooo...?"

"My employer was Senator Mason Maplethorn."

"You vorked for a Senator?" Serena asked. "I can understand vhy you vould not vish that fact to be common knowledge."

"Well, I can't," I said. "Why not tell us before?"

"When Crow took us slaves, it seemed prudent not to mention that I had intimate knowledge of a Senator whose stance on piracy had always been shall we say, harsh. Since the death of his sons, I have heard he has made it something of a personal vendetta to eradicate piracy."

"Pirates didn't kill his kids," I argued. "Slavers killed his kids. Their whole corrupt system that allows and encourages slavery killed his kids. Not pirates."

"I shall be sure to mention that to him," Miss Merryweather said.

"Mattis, are you sure of this?" Mrs. Shorty asked.

"Elegiac, I can be sure of nothing," she said, taking her friend's hand and squeezing it.

Miss Merryweather turned to me. "But I believe I can get the information we need."

Out of the corner of my eye, I saw Tring open the door, say something quietly to someone outside, and close it again. She caught my eye and nodded.

"Alright, then," I said. "Make a list of the things you need. The rest of you, come up with ways to get her into Neptopolis. Gigi, can I see you for a minute?"

"Sure," she said, and we both rose from the table.

I led her out the room and down the hall.

"What's this about, Sunset?"

"Better I tell you all at the same time," I answered, opening a door and letting her go in before me.

Inside the room – one of the hundreds of little sitting rooms in the Admiral's Villa – were the four other animen on my crew. Audrey, a tall, lean ostrich; Moira, a curvy rabbit, who despite having white fur also had long strawberry blonde hair; Belle, a chestnut horse; and Vivienne, a fox with a gorgeous head of red curls and one of the best swordfighters on the crew. I'd asked Gigi once why some animen had human hair and animal fur, why some had animal legs and others had human. She said it had something to do with how solidly the animanization process took hold on the unborn child. See, animen aren't born naturally, they have to be made. When a female animan found out she was pregnant, the parents would decide which animal to attribute to their unborn child, and the process would infuse the fetus with that animal's … well, the word Gigi used was 'essence'. Apparently how well the essence grafted into the fetus determined how animalistic the child would be. And it was different for every animan child. I'd asked her if any animen were born fully animalized, or if they ever had a human head on an animal's body, but she'd shrugged and said she didn't know anything about that, having never been pregnant and never knowing any animen who'd been through the process. She'd told me what her parents had told her, when she'd been old enough to get curious about it.

"It seemed like a messy, inaccurate process," she'd said at the time. "Give me a reliable, predictable machine any day."

Now, though, she wasn't saying anything. She just went to stand with her fellow animen.

"Sit down, please," I said, taking an armchair for myself.

They sat, and I leaned forward to rest my elbows on my knees, lacing my fingers.

"Admiral?" Vivienne asked. "What is it? What's wrong?"

I took a deep breath. "There's no easy way to tell you this, so here goes. The authorities in Atlan have rounded up every animan on their island and put them into camps."

"What?" Audrey asked. "Why?"

"The recent influx of loyalist refugees is creating a shortage of resources and space, making the native Atlans really cranky," I said, sitting back. "So the authorities decided that seizing the assets of a visible minority and redistributing them would calm people down for a while. They're saying it's for the animen's protection, to keep them safe from 'delinquent and seditious elements' who might have 'infiltrated' their shores, 'under the guise of loyalty'."

"They've given the people someone to hate, someone to blame, and someone to fear, all at once," Vivienne said. "Rather ingenious, really."

"What does this have to do with us, Captain? I mean, Admiral?" Belle asked.

"I just wanted you to hear it from..." and I almost said 'the horse's mouth' but considering who I was talking to, I changed it to "... someone with actual facts, not the rumour mill."

"Is anything being done about it?" Gigi asked quietly.

I looked at her. "Done? By us, you mean?"

She narrowed her eyes and her ears started to go flat. That and her twitching tail gave me a rough idea of how pissed off she was. "Yes. Are the Triumvirate of Terror doing anything about it?"

I sat back in my chair. "Like what?"

"Like mounting a rescue mission? Like trying to get people out of those camps? LIKE ANYTHING AT ALL?!"

I looked up at her, keeping eye contact instead of being distracted by the glint of firelight on her extended claws. "Gigi, sit down, please," I said, as calmly as I could.

"You know as well as I do that those so-called camps are just another word for killing pens," she hissed, but she sat down again.

"I do know that," I answered. "And the Triumvirate will get to that, I promise."

"When? After we've rescued the pixies and the vampires and all the other, more human-looking, people?"

"Okay, I know you're upset, but that's not fair."

"You're blighted right I'm upset! And blight take your 'fair'! It's not your people being herded into the slaughterhouse!"

"Gigi, are you listening to yourself? When have I ever said anything that would make you believe I'm going to put the lives of one species of people ahead of another?"

She scraped her aviator cap off her head, then ran her fingers through her matted head fur. "Ah zut. I'm sorry, Sunset. But animen are going to be killed, for no better reason than because they're animen!

"My father... He was a true genius with machines. He could have been one of the greatest engineers this world has ever seen. I mean, I'm good, but he was something incredible. A true gift. And without any education! Not one day of school. But people in our town would bring him things to fix. Not one day of school, and everyone in town knew that Jean Fantastico Lyon could fix anything. Not just our town, either! And when he'd fixed it, whatever it was, and people would ask, how did you know, Jean? How did you know how to fix it? He'd just shrug and say, well, it just made sense, didn't it?"

She stared into the fire, her green eyes glimmering. "And not one day of school to explain it. Because he was an animan. Not fit for education. A beast. But he could make an engine purr! And the day they changed the law against us being educated, that day he started saving up. Because he wanted his child to have the best education he could afford. He didn't care that I was born a girl. He didn't care what I wanted to study. 'Anything you want, Melly, I promise!' he'd tell me. He was the only person who called me Melly, you know. Meliora, my real name," she explained to the others. I have to admit, I'd forgotten it myself.

"Anything I wanted, and all I wanted was to make motors purr like he could. So, engineering. He was so proud when I was accepted at the University of Lutis! So proud. Out of a thousand students, only five of us were animen. Only five, at first.

"Papa would write me. Not often, he had no gift for writing. But once in a while. Asking me about university. Asking me about what I was learning. Mechanical stuff, you know. And sometimes he would ask how the others were treating me. How could I tell him the truth? That we animen were belittled, degraded, humiliated? Laughed at behind our backs and to our faces, teased, taunted, reviled? In four years I don't think a week went by that I didn't find a saucer of milk outside my dormitory door. At least once a semester there would be a dead mouse or bird in my bed. I learned to hide my tail under my skirts, rather than work it through the hole my mother had so painstakingly tailored for me. Because after the third time I had to untie a can from my tail, I decided that it wasn't worth the effort.

"I never complained. I never said anything. None of us did. Phillippe Fidele, a dog animan, had the word 'cur' carved into his door, and he never said anything, even when the administration accused him of defacing his own door.

"At first, I tried to make friends. I played nice. I smiled. I made polite conversation. Eventually I stopped. I decided that if they wouldn't like me, they would at least respect me. I made it my mission to be the best in my class. My first exam, I received a failing grade. When I questioned the professor, he accused me of cheating. It was impossible that I should receive a perfect test score. I challenged his assumption. It went to the Dean. They made me write the exam over again while they watched. Standing there. Two hours. And when the grade was once again perfect, the Dean consoled the professor by saying, 'Well, even a horse can learn a few tricks.' No offence, Belle."

She blew through her lips. "None taken. What a jackass."

"How could you stand it?" Audrey asked. "How horrible. I'm glad I never went to school, if that's how they treated our kind."

"I had it easy compared to some. Poor Marie Cloche killed herself in the second year. Too much pressure. No one to turn to but the other animen, and we all had our own problems. We found out, later, that she'd fallen in love with a human boy, and, impossibly, he loved her. But when he told his parents, they forced him to break it off, and transferred him to another university.

"So then there were only four of us in the second year, and only two new animen students in the first year. It was hardest for us four, and Luc Chevron dropped out in third year. Just Philippe, Auguste Rennet, and myself. And me the only female.

"They made our lives horrible for four years. The students. The professors. The administration. They treated us worse than they would treat their family pets. Humiliation, embarrassment, and yes, even fear, became our daily companions. Auguste was a bear animan. The bigger human boys were constantly calling him a coward, trying to get him to fight them. And when he fought, they would beat him down. One would challenge, then six more would join in once Auguste had agreed. I can't tell you how many times he wound up in the infirmary, where more often than not he would be refused treatment. 'This isn't a veterinarian's clinic!' they'd say."

"Charming," Vivienne said, disgusted.

"And all because we were animen. Just like those animen in Atlan. They've done nothing wrong. Committed no crime. And for their loyalty to the empire, they are rewarded with humiliation, degradation, and fear. Robbed of their possessions, denied their livelihoods, herded like beasts into camps. We can't let that continue, Sunset."

"You're right. We can't," I said. "To that end, I'm prepared to release you all from the crew of The Furies, if you want to join Captain Rage's Menagerie. He'll be told next, and I imagine he'll have some ideas about this whole situation."

"You told us before you told him?" Moira asked.

"You're my crew."

"Thank you, Admiral," Belle said, standing. I stood up, too. "I've enjoyed my time with The Furies, but I want to be a part of some action that will fight this. I understand that the flagship of the armada will be needed elsewhere."

"Yeah," I said, offering her my hand. We shook, and she left.

Audrey stood next, and Moira. We shook hands. I never saw them again, after that. Captain Rage accepted them with open arms.

"I... I need to think about this," Vivienne said, then nodded to me politely and left.

A long pause.

"Gigi?"

She was staring into the fire. "My mind says that I could make a difference on the Menagerie. That together with an all-animen crew, we could help those people. Save them from the camps. We might be the only people who could do it, now. Those animen, how can they ever trust anyone but another animan again?"

"I don't know, Gigi." I couldn't say more around the lump in my throat, faced with the very real possibility that I might lose one of my best and only friends.

"But my heart..." she said, looking up at me. Tears gleamed in her huge cat eyes. "My heart says I belong here. With you. With The Furies."

"You're sure?"

Gigi stood up and hugged me. "How could I leave you? You need me too much."

I hugged her back, laughing, and it was half sob of relief. "Yeah."

"Stop it, you'll mess my fur," she laughed, pulling away. "But there has to be a way we can help."

"We'll figure something out," I said.

Captain Rage took it about as well as you might expect, immediately vowing to find the camps and liberate the animen. I wished him well, and promised him any resources he might need.

In the end, Vivienne chose to stay with The Furies, too. "This mission, to end slavery, and overthrow the Atlan government, is bigger than saving a few lives," she explained. "I want to be a part of that."

"Glad you're with us," I said. She was very nearly as good a swordmistress as Serena, and we'd need all the swordfighters we could find in the battles to come.

Chapter Nine

On The Pirate Queen's Secret Service

Miss Merryweather met with Miss Phoenix and discussed a plan. Well, when I say plan, I'm not sure it went much past "Get me to Atlan and I'll take care of the rest." Miss Merryweather was being especially cryptic about what she had in mind. She wouldn't even tell me. "The less people who know, the less chance of it being discovered. Besides, I'm not sure you'd approve."

"You don't need my approval," I answered.

That's when she did something completely unexpected. She reached out and touched my cheek, softly. "Dear child, you don't realize the power you have. It's not just about your approval. You do more than just lead, Sunset. You believe in people. No, more than that. You help people to believe in themselves."

I hugged her, hard, and yeah, I cried.

"Now, now," she said, stroking my hair. "None of that."

I eventually sniffled my way clear, knuckling away any more tears and wiping my messy face with the back of my hand.

"I should be back in a week," Miss Merryweather said. "If you've heard nothing from me in two weeks, you must assume I've been compromised and proceed with another plan."

"Well, we don't have another plan, so don't get compromised," I laughed.

"I shall do my level best, Admiral."

And off she went. She and Miss Phoenix had arranged to have her smuggled into Atlan, somehow. It bothered me a little that we didn't have any more details than that, but Miss Phoenix insisted that we didn't need the details, and it might risk the success of the mission to tell us. General Komodo wasn't thrilled about that, let me tell you. The Fist seemed to understand, and Mr. Mahogany just shrugged it off. And the Collective, well, they just sort of sat there like they always did.

Miss Merryweather was gone for just over a week. Just long enough for me to get worried enough to start planning a rescue mission. When she got back, she wouldn't tell us anything about what happened. She'd just say, "We got the information we require. That's what's important." I never did find out what happened on that mission, but I have my suspicions...

The submersible rises slow and silent out of the inky black ocean, the waves lapping its metal sides hidden in the crash of waves against the rocky coast. A hatch opens, a figure appears. Clad in black, she lowers herself carefully into the shoulder-deep waters, then makes her way cautiously to shore. Behind her, the hatch closes, the submersible disappears. When she reaches the shore, her hip throbbing with unaccustomed effort, she slips out of the waterproof black jumpsuit, hiding it away beneath the roots of a gnarled tree. Beneath the jumpsuit she wears the clothes of a slave – a simple sleeveless tunic, long skirt and low soft shoes. She pauses, briefly, catch her breath. This sort of thing had once been so much easier, in her youth.

Rested enough to catch her breath and for her aching hip to quiet down, she sets off inland. From the maps she's memorized, she knows how far it is to the nearest road. From the clock she glanced at aboard the submersible, she knows she hasn't much time until dawn.

The rocky coast gives way to scrubland and eventually, forest. Forest eventually opens to a dirt road, and it is here that she turns right, heading north. Neptopolis awaits.

Dirt road becomes gravel highway. On the gravel highway, she is able to beg a lift from a passing truck. The corn farmer doesn't want to sully his cab with a slave's presence, but takes pity on the old woman limping along the highway and allows her to ride in the corn crib.

The rumble of the truck's engine, the sway of the corn crib, and the fatigue of her efforts lull her to sleep. When she awakes, the farmer is yelling at her to get out, get down. Not uncharitably, but because he suspects she might be hard of hearing.

"Thank you, master," she says. Her Atlan is flawless, twinged slightly with the nasal accent of someone born and raised in Neptopolis.

"Ain't no master o' yourn," he answers. "Off wi' ya now."

"Yes master."

She steps down from the corn crib to touch foot to the cobbled streets of Neptopolis. All around her the city bustles. Shopkeeps opening their shops, early customers seeking early purchases. Which is to say, shopkeeps ordering their slaves to open the shops. Customers trailing slaves along behind them to carry the early morning purchases. Once in a while, a trusted slave is allowed to travel alone, to enact purchases in the name of their owner. Her presence as a single slave without a nearby master is unremarkable.

She sets off, heading uptown. Everywhere she walks, she sees slaves. How odd that before, as a citizen, she had hardly ever remarked on them. They had faded into the background, like furniture or plants. Now that she is masquerading as one, she sees.

Slaves doing work their overseers could easily have done for themselves. Carrying packages. Cleaning up. Minding children. Tending animals. Conducting vehicles.

And these are city slaves. Out in the countryside, slaves would be working the fields of corn and cotton and hemp, tending herds of cattle and sheep. Working as long as there was daylight. On clear nights with a full moon, all night as well. Worked until their hands bled, their backs ached. Worked even to death, though that was rare enough that it generally made the news and was frowned upon by polite society. But the disapproval of their peers would be the only sanction the offending slaveowner would suffer. No legal ramifications would follow. No justice for the dead slave.

A disproportionate number of them are women. Not surprising, since by tradition slavers only enslave women, captured from airships high above in the seven skies, where jurisdictions are difficult to enforce. Male slaves, such as there are any, are generally the bastard children of a female slave and her master. Those born to slavery have even less legal standing than those who are enslaved, if possible.

Miss Merryweather knows that male slaves are needed in the fields and factories. So much the better for her, weaving through the crowded sidewalks of Neptopolis. All around her are the sounds and smells of a city that knows little deprivation, even now, with the war raging on two continents. Even with the food from the farms of Afric denied them, there are no lines of starving citizens. Fruits and vegetables fill the shopkeepers' stalls. Freshly slaughtered pigs and geese. Fish by the barrel-full.

She has only the barest idea of a plan, and no clear idea of her destination. A bit of sleight of hand snags her something to eat, an apple stolen from a stall. The shopkeeper will not notice its absence. A walking stick will be harder to come by, and her hip is aching. If she cannot find some place to rest soon, she'll be in real trouble.

She ducks down an alley, eating her apple as quickly as possible. She finds a pile of wooden boxes to sit on, and rests for a half hour, thinking. Above her, lines of drying wash drip slowly through a shaft of gritty sunlight.

A plan has almost formed.

Three days. It takes three days to find her quarry and locate her destination. Three days of sleeping in alleys, under stoops. Three days of stolen meals. Those three days wear her down, grind her into exhaustion and hunger, steal the wilful gleam from her eyes, the careful coiffure of her tightly bunned hair. Three days to complete her disguise. From her misshapen tattoo to her filthy clothes, no one would ever suspect she is anything but a slave.

The great house stands, a marvel of granite architecture. It has been over a decade since she's seen it. Though she hasn't heard otherwise, this solid, squat building is the home of someone whose aid she has no right to ask.

From a distant corner, she watches the morning unfold in the relatively posh neighbourhood. Nothing too fancy, nothing that might announce a claim to climb higher or better than their neighbours, who guard their positions in the social strata with an almost fanatical attention.

Delivery men chastise slaves to make the deliveries faster. Milk in bottles. Bread by the loaf and bun. Fresh cut flowers for the mistresses of these domiciles. Fresh cut meat for the masters.

Finally the carriages arrive, two-wheelers pulled in most cases by actual horses, though here and there an autohorse can be seen. One by one the masters leave their homes, climb aboard carriages, heading downtown toward the business district, or uptown to the various ministries. Leaving their homes and all its residential domesticity behind them. Leaving their wives to conduct their slaves in cleaning and cooking and childcare.

Miss Merryweather makes her way around the block to the alley that runs behind all the homes, a gravel road, deeply rutted from carriage wheels and delivery wagons. Weeds line the alleyway to either side, wildflowers left rampant, a sure sign that all is not well within the stately homes. If all were well, the slaves would be instructed to pull the weeds and tear up the wildflowers. Instead, they are being kept busy keeping the mistress satisfied and the master oblivious.

A piece of stolen paper, carefully folded to take the semblance of a letter, is all it takes to get past the slaves in the garden. "A message for your mistress," is all it takes for Miss Merryweather to be directed to the back door and summarily ignored.

An hour passes before a house slave deigns to speak to the bedraggled old woman at the door.

"Give it to me then," the slave says.

"Direct to your mistress, I was told," Miss Merryweather answers. "Else it's a beating for me."

"Your mistress beats you?" the house slave asks. Her eyebrow rises sceptically.

"How d'you think I got this limp, then? Fighting pirates?"

"No, what I meant was, your mistress can afford to beat you, but can't afford to keep you clean?"

Miss Merryweather's ignorance of slave life has led her into a verbal corner, but some quick thinking uncorners her. "Making me stay dirty is another way she punishes."

"Real piece o' work, your mistress," the house slave mutters seditiously.

"Tell me about it," Miss Merryweather agrees in the same hushed tones.

"Follow me, then. Mind you don't track on the rug."

"Right. Thanks."

That simple word of gratitude earns her another odd look.

She's brought to a sitting room where she's told to stand by the fireplace and wait. A half hour passes to the slow tick-tocking of the tall clock standing in the corner. Fatigue nearly gets the best of her, but her screaming hip keeps her alert.

"What's this about, slave?" a woman asks imperiously.

She's just a bit shorter than Miss Merryweather and matronly stout. Once golden hair gone grey, the beauty of her youth not stolen, merely matured. Hard lines at her brow and jowls indicate years of frowning.

Miss Merryweather looks at her cousin and wants to weep. For years lost, for youth perished.

"A message from my mistress," Miss Merryweather says, eyes flicking to the house slave standing ready to serve the house mistress.

"Well? Give it here, slave."

"Beg pardon, mistress, but this paper is not the message. My mistress had me commit it to memory, under orders to only speak them to you. Privately."

The ruse is calculated to appeal to her cousin's sense of intrigue and adventure. As children, they'd gotten into several adventures together. Marriage and children have robbed her cousin of the opportunities for adventure, or so she had said the last time they'd spoken in person, almost a decade ago.

But perhaps the years have taken away all desire for adventure. Perhaps years of comfort have softened her adventurous cousin.

Or perhaps not. "How very... mysterious of your mistress." Without turning her head, she orders, "Leave us," and the house slave leaves with a quick bob of a curtsy.

"Now, what is this message?"

"Olivia, look at me."

Immediate outrage. "You would presume to use my given name?! No wonder your mistress punishes you!"

"Livvy! *Look* at me."

Clearly her carefully constructed world view does not include slaves speaking with such reckless authority, for Olivia sputters in confusion for several seconds before her eyes narrow and, finally, she sees what she is meant to see.

"Mattis...?"

"Yes."

"Mattis!"

"Quiet, Livvy." Miss Merryweather steps closer to her cousin, lowering her voice. "I haven't much time."

"Mattis, we were told you were dead!" Urgent words, but cautiously quiet.

"Evidently I'm not, am I?"

"The... the boys?"

"Killed."

"Oh Mattis, I'm so sorry."

"Thank you." Unexpected sympathy brings unwanted, distracting emotion, pushed aside with abrupt, brutal haste. "Olivia, I need your help."

"But Mattis, what happened to you?"

Resisting the urge to simultaneously sigh and throttle her cousin, Miss Merryweather capitulates. "I was taken as a slave. Not for long. We were led in rebellion." A fond chuckle. "By a girl who reminds me not a little of us, in our youth."

"What? Who? How?"

"Dear Livvy, I promise all the explanations I can give you, I promise to answer any question you might ask, but after."

"After what? After when?"

"Afterwards, my dear. I promise."

"Well, you were never one to break a promise."

"Quite. Now. I need you to bring me into the Great Hall of Law."

"Whatever for?"

"I can't tell you that."

"Wait." Olivia rises from the chair she doesn't remember sinking into and goes to the sideboard, reaching for the sherry. She pauses before pouring, changes her mind, and reaches for the whiskey, pours herself a stiff drink, and downs it in one swallow. Then she pours another for herself, and one for her cousin. "You can't tell me why I'm to assist in this... I must assume it is some form of treason?"

Miss Merryweather takes a sip of whiskey. It's very good whiskey, oak-aged, two decades in the cask at least, and she's sorely tempted to slug it back, but resists. "I can't say it's legal, but I wouldn't call it treason."

"So what is it, then?"

"Change, dear. It's change, if we succeed."

Despite herself, Olivia looks around her comfortable home. She smiles nervously. "I can't say change holds the same appeal as it once did, Mattis."

"We live in a society that condones the murder of children and the enslavement of its citizens, Olivia."

"Just women." The words are out of her mouth before she realizes the depths of their horrid nature. Her eyes dart to the misshapen tattoo of a crow her cousin now wears. She claps a hand over her lips, sits, places the crystal glass on a nearby decorative side table.

"I'm sorry," she says eventually.

"No, it's not your fault. We've been raised on lies, Olivia. Women are not capable of responsible citizenship. Voting is only for men. Leadership comes naturally to men. Women who aspire to more are unbalanced. The nature of a true woman is subservient. Docile. Willing to please. Eager for domesticity."

Tears spill down her cousin's cheeks. "No more, Mattis, please."

"Livvy, something has to change. This society is corrupt to its core. Change must happen. You have children. Three sons and a daughter." She searches her prodigious memory and retrieves the name of her cousin's child. "How would you react if you found out Catherine had been taken as a slave and sold as a house servant? Or worse, to a pleasure house?"

Rage and indignation colour Olivia's cheeks. "Never. It would never happen, Mattis."

"But what if it had? What then? There is no legal recourse, Olivia. 'Those taken as slaves are forfeit of all civil legality.' How is that law just? How can any thinking society consider it reasonable?"

Olivia buries her face in her hands. "No. Stop. Please, I beg you."

"Then help me, Livvy. Get me inside the Great Hall. That's all I ask. I'll do the rest."

"You?" A curious, sceptical look. "What can a governess do inside the Great Hall, alone? A former governess, that is?"

A long pause. Then, "I think you know I was more than a mere governess."

Olivia wipes her face, downs her whiskey. "No, I don't know that. I suspected, of course. The whole family did. Those long, unexpected trips. And that fever you came home with, the one that left you..."

"Barren, yes."

"I'm sorry, Mattis."

"No matter. What's passed is past, Livvy."

A wry chuckle. "No one calls me that any more, did you know?"

"Not even Hector?"

She rolls her eyes. "'Dear', mostly. 'Darling' when he's feeling amorous, which is nearly never these days. This whole unpleasantness in Afric and Europa has him so dreadfully worried, Mattis."

"It won't end there, Livvy. That 'unpleasantness' will reach these shores soon enough."

A nervous laugh. "Surely not."

A quiet, resolute smile. "You don't know her, Livvy. The young woman I follow, she'll see it through. Change is coming, for the better."

"Better for who?"

"Better for everyone. Now, can you help me? Else I must be gone."

A long pause, then a frustrated sigh. "Fine. You always did get me into all kinds of trouble."

"I'd also get you out of all kinds of trouble, didn't I?"

A shared grin.

The next day, Mrs. Olivia Woodworth pays an unexpected call upon her husband, a mid-level secretary to one of the law ministers. Trailing behind her is an old slave, mercifully cleaned up and wearing new-to-her clothes, who somehow manages to disappear somewhere between the front doors and Mr. Woodworth's office. No words of goodbye, no farewell embraces. The slave simply vanishes into the maze of corridors and offices of the Great Hall of Law.

Other slaves in the building take no notice of the old woman with a limp. There are always slaves coming and going in the Great Hall, carrying messages, fetching food and drink, ensuring their masters' carriages are ready and waiting, cleaning. Miss Merryweather procures a mop and bucket from a supply closet, becoming even more invisible to her fellow slaves.

The free citizens who tread the corridors notice her even less. If she were a piece of furniture, they might remark upon her more than they do a slave with a mop.

She spends two days in the Great Hall. Luckily for her, the war has people working around the clock. A slave with a mop in the middle of the night is no more noticeable than in the middle of the afternoon.

Finding the right office proves challenging, at first. Despite its identity as the seat of Atlan Law, the Great Hall is anything but logically organized. Current case files are crammed into legislators' offices, and when those run out of room, whatever nearby space is available is commandeered. Past case files are shoved into boxes, and the boxes stacked into piles near the stairwells, with the understanding that any passing slave is to grab as many as they can carry and bring them down the nearest flight of stairs, unless direct orders prevent them from doing so. It is, she is informed, an efficiency measure designed to keep the boxes flowing downstairs without an interruption of daily tasks.

The slaves, of course, have managed to find ways around the standing order, keeping certain stairwells completely clear so that they don't have to carry any boxes. This has two results – while those stairwells serve as proof of the success of the program, other stairwells have become crammed with boxes.

"What a terrible fire hazard," Miss Merryweather mutters to herself, ideas percolating in her mind. But her mission must come first, and she puts aside her ideas.

What the boxes do offer is a long trail to the archives, a trail she follows to the basement. She knows that beneath the basement lies the central prison of the Great Hall. Beneath her feet are criminals deemed too dangerous to risk martyrdom. Most will wind up patchworked. But some will be sent to The Pit.

Getting into the central prison presents too much risk to her mission, and she decides against the attempt. The files will offer her everything she needs to know, if she can find the right office.

Another day spent in the basement, mopping the floor, watching the comings and goings of slaves and ministers alike. Even here, most doors are unlocked. All save one. That one, she watches intently.

Evening comes, and the minister in the locked office steps out, locks the door, and walks off toward the stairwell. She waits a half-hundred heartbeats, then approaches the door. Skills mastered long ago make short work of the lock, her picks once again hidden in her hair bun. In she slips, silent as a shadow.

Filing cabinets. A large desk. A lamp, a chair. She splashes some water on the floor as pretense, then sets to work. The cabinets are just as locked as the office door and present even less of a challenge. She scans the files quickly, quietly. Convicted criminals all, every file she opens is a testament of atrocities that would have turned her stomach a year ago. Every last one of them, found guilty and sentenced to the various options the Great Hall prefers: death, patchworking, or the Pit.

Every last file is stamped with a single word: Ferronegri. Her education in classical languages, nearly forgotten in the many decades since, nevertheless serves as translator. Ferronegri. Black Iron.

Despite their official sentence, every criminal who is tried in the Great Hall has been sentenced to the Pit. The realization stuns her into pausing to contemplate the ramifications. But there will be time enough for thought later, and she hurries to complete her task.

A search of the desk reveals a ledger, filled with columns of numbers. Delivery schedules. Daily mine yields. But the numbers cannot possible speak of coal, since coal would be measured in tons. Instead, the daily yields speak of ounces and, rarely, pounds.

A note left in the ledger speaks of an upcoming trial and the convicted criminal's delivery to the Pit. An unexpected flood and a washed out bridge will require use of the Atlanopolitan Way. The minister is to anticipate any problems and brief the security detail accordingly.

A date and a place. All they will need to intercept the detail and hopefully follow them to the Pit.

She quickly memorizes the information and puts everything back where she found it. She is just reaching for her mop and pail when the door opens.

The minister from before stares at her, shock clear on his face. "What are you doing in here?"

"Just moppin' up, marster," she replies, waving at the water on the floor as though the answer were self-evident. This time, her Atlan is heavily accented with Anglic.

"The door was locked."

"Beggin' yer pardon, marster, but it were open when I come in."

"Impossible. Come with me."

"Yes, marster."

She briefly contemplates silencing this pompous self-important fool with a swift blow of her mop, but it might prove too much trouble, should he be discovered. Instead, she follows along, meekly carrying her mop and bucket.

Straight to the offices of the director of security. There, three Great Hall guards are enjoying a quiet cup of coffee and a light snack, but straighten at the presence of the minister.

"Minister," says a guard, obviously their superior.

"This slave was found in my office," the minister says. "Find out how and why."

"Right you are, sir," the lead guard answers.

"Come with us, slave," says another guard.

Better she had taken out the minister in his office, quickly, quietly. With a mental sigh, she makes a decision.

A faceful of dirty, soapy water momentarily incapacitates the lead guard. Swing around with the bucket to slam the minister into unconsciousness. Mop handle smacks against one guard's face breaking his nose. Wet mop head splashes into the other guard's eyes, blinding him. Spin. Crack the blind guard across the head to stop him from screaming. Spin back, take out the broken nosed guard the same way.

The lead guard has his firearm out, but the spinning mop handle sends it flying without a shot being fired. Before he can cry out, the handle reverses direction and cracks across his head, sending him to the floor with a crash as he knocks over the tea cart.

All four are unconscious. Her breathing is not as laboured as she might have expected, and her heart is hardly racing at all. She remembers this, this calm, her mind racing as her body reacts seemingly without effort. Her screaming hip is the only reminder of the decades behind her.

She leaves the broken mop and empty bucket behind her, abandoning crucial elements of her disguise in favour of crucial moments to escape. Up one flight of stairs, and another, to the main level. Through the warren of corridors. The nearest exit lies a hundred paces away, seventy, fifty, twenty.

And then Livvy's husband steps out of an office, into her way, colliding with her.

"Beg pardon, marster," she says, stepping around him.

"I say, slave, watch where you're..."

He looks at her.

And inconceivably, recognizes her. "Mattis?"

"Not me, marster, beg pardon."

He grasps her arms. "Mattis! But, we heard you were dead!"

"Hector, let me go."

Distantly, a shout. Someone raising a cry of alarm. Hurried footsteps on the stairwell.

A trick she learned from Tring's Open Hands has Hector face-first against the wall, his arms pinned behind him.

"Listen to me, Hector. I don't have time to explain. You have to take Olivia and the family out of Neptopolis. Do you understand? Neptopolis will not be a pleasant place to be in the next few months. Leave, now."

"Leave? Nonsense. Mattis, unhand me."

A shove of his arms, a bend of the elbows just a fraction past comfort. Hector was a big man, the strength of his youth not lost but buried beneath years of rich foods and padded armchairs and long evenings of too much drink. Leverage, however, can work wonders in the right hands.

He grunts in pain.

"Are you listening, Hector? Get out of Neptopolis. At least send Olivia and the family to the Orchard. You still own it, correct?"

"Of course. Mattis, unhand me, I mean it."

"Goodbye, Hector."

She's gone and out the door before he can turn and face her.

Down the side street, hurrying but not rushing. Calm. Or at least, the outward expression of calm. The confrontation with Hector set her heart racing in a way the altercation with the guards had not. Putting a personal impulse ahead of the safety of the mission. An astonishing lapse of judgement. She must be getting old and sentimental.

Yells and shouts, whistles and finally the klaxons of the constabulary. Briefly she wishes she had purloined the lead guard's firearm, but a slave with a firearm would have drawn attention from every person on the street. An old slave hurrying away from the alarm being raised behind her was hardly of note.

The alarms don't die down as she makes her way through back alleys and side streets. Constabulary men rush to and fro, on foot, on horseback, in steam-driven carriages. The evening comes alive as people crowd into the streets, trying to follow the commotion. She avoids all but the largest crowds, gleaning from hurried gossip the news: the Great Hall of Law has been attacked. Dead guards and ministers. A traitor walks among them. The rumour mill goes wild.

Women and children are hurried back into their homes. Neighbourhood men organize themselves into makeshift militia. She slips into the shadows, avoiding all human contact. A stolen autocycle will get her out of the city. She pushes it a block before mounting it, slipping the goggles on, firing up the boiler. The sound of the steam engine shatters the night's silence.

Off into the night. The city's streets are alive, even at this late hour, and the inconspicuous old slave woman is suddenly, decidedly conspicuous on the autocycle. Shouts follow her. Soon, alarms are ringing behind her. She dares a glance back to see two steam-carriages distantly pursuing her. Will she make it out? Can she escape the gathering noose that surely must be tightening even now?

Out, out, out into the countryside, past the city's limits but not beyond the law. Two steam-carriages have become five, the beams of their electric lamps stabbing the night ahead of her. The owner of the autocycle has generously provided her with the best nightsight goggles sovereigns could buy, and she pours on the speed.

The gravel road is both smoother than the cobbled streets and more uneven. She quickly learns to avoid the wheel ruts, for they have the greatest dangers, lying beneath still puddles of muddy water.

Gunshots ring out over the steady rumble of her autocycle. Freed of the confines of civilian onlookers and the potential of injuring some hapless bystander, the constables are indulging in their need for vengeance, ignoring the evidence of the impossibility of their actions.

Not so impossible, she thinks to herself. Her shoulder suddenly burns with a glancing gunshot. The pain fades into the background of aches and fatigue threatening to overtake her. Her mind burns with only one goal. Escape.

Two of the constabulary steam carriages fall back, unexpectedly, and a third takes a sudden dive into an unseen ditch. The two remaining steam carriages don't seem nearly so ready to give up the chase, however.

For three hours, they chase. It becomes clear that they no longer seek to kill her. Instead, it's obvious they intend to dog her heels until her engine runs out of coal or she reaches her destination, whichever comes first. A glance at the gauge tells her the coal will betray her first.

She decides to deny her pursuers the opportunity. A jerk of the handles and the autocycle careens into a cornfield. She rolls with the crash but three hours hunched over the autocycle have left her stiff. Her arm is numb with the blood loss of the gunshot wound, but it erupts in agony with the impact. No time to wait, no time to rest.

"Up," she says, her voice a harsh rasp. Despite it all, she rises. Despite agony and exhaustion, she disappears into the corn.

Shouts from behind her. The steam carriages drive into the stalks, eager to run her down.

Idiots, she thinks. *The ground's too wet.*

And it is, for something of the steam carriage's weight. Her pursuers are soon trapped in mud, their wheels of their steam carriages spinning with futile finality.

Several miles away, she emerges back onto the road, hobbling along, her hip a perfect symphony of agony, her shoulder throbbing with the tempo of her pounding heart, her breathing harsh gasps of exhaustion.

Midnight, her rendezvous. Midnight, not long now. A thousand paces to the beach, maybe two. Fatigue and blood loss are making her doubt herself, clouding her judgement. The dark of night has obscured the landmarks she memorized, the nightsight goggles broken in the crash, discarded long miles ago. Or were they? Where was the crash? How long ago?

She stumbles. On hands and knees, she finds her way to the beach. Tries to remember where she left the wetsuit. Decides she doesn't care. So tired. So very tired. Her eyelids are the heaviest thing she's ever had to lift. Heavier even than the dead bodies of her boys, lost now, her boys, her sweet boys, dead too young, dead on the end of a pirate's blade. Dead for trying to defend her.

The memories drift into dream, into nightmares that snap her to sudden wakefulness, as they have so often since that terrible day.

A sound. A splash. Not the splash of the waves against the rocky shore. Something else. Something out there, in the water.

And suddenly, the blinding stab of headlights, slowly panning across the beach.

She's in the water, unaware of how she got there, or what she's done with her heavy slave skirt. Without the protection of the wetsuit, the ocean is frigid, numbing.

Behind her, a shout.

Before her, the submersible.

Slowly drifting away from her.

A shot rings out, the bullet slicing into the water nearby.

She swims. Never her best skill. She swims, not for her life, but for two dead boys who should never have died.

The submersible is drawing away, sinking beneath the waves.

Another gunshot, and another.

She reaches the submersible. Bangs against the hatch, the agreed-upon two times, pause, three times, pause, once.

Another gunshot clangs against the submersible, ricocheting into the night.

The hatch opens. Relief floods into her as water floods into the submersible.

She'd done it.

Chapter Ten

A Parting of Ways

I know, right?!

Okay, so all that wasn't a complete fabrication. I mean, I put it together over the weeks that followed. She did come back from the mission with a bandage around her arm and her limp was a lot worse after that. She spent days in a sick bed, too exhausted to do much more than sleep and eat soup. And there were little things she said, too, like knowing how a slave feels, being invisible in plain sight, that sort of thing. Slowly bits and pieces formed in my mind. Maybe I'm bang on with that story. Maybe I couldn't be further from the truth. But she got the information we needed. We just needed to put it to good use.

While Miss Merryweather had been off on her mission, we hadn't been exactly idle. During a staff meeting Molly had been complaining about our losses to the Blighted. Seeme the stiltwalkers had a tendency to get surrounded and needed some better guns. Something that wouldn't jam or run out of bullets. Or at least, if it ran out of bullets, would still be useful. Inga suggested making hand-held Doomthrower pistols. Then at least the stiltwalkers would be surrounded by a ring of fire, keeping the Blighted at bay.

"I like that idea," Molly said. "But eventually one of the bastards will get through. And if the stiltwalker's out of ammunition, it won't be pretty."

"Vhy don't they carry swords?" Serena asked.

"Not good in tight quarters," Molly answered. "Those bastards are clawing up your legs, you need something short and quick."

"Like a hatchet?" asked Mrs. Shorty.

Molly nodded. "Yes, that could work. It would be yet another thing to carry, though."

Inga laughed. "We could weld them onto their pistols!"

Everyone laughed along, except Molly, who seriously considered it. "We'd have to reinforce the pistol housing. And it would be heavy."

"The reinforced housing would mean you could increase the powder charge," Inga added. "And the weight of the hatchet would help control the recoil."

They decided to work together to come up with new weapons for the stiltwalkers. I agreed to it, even though I mostly didn't understand it. They seemed excited, though.

Oh, and Gigi told me she'd figured out how the aetheric portal worked. The only problem would be powering it, and tuning it to the right Earth. I mean, Dr. Sweetwater had described the aether as milk in a glass filled with pearls, each pearl another universe, another Earth. Finding the right Earth might take a while. Powering it, though...

"We'd never be able to power it with just the engines," Gigi explained. "You told me that when you arrived, Sweetwater's airship was flying through a lightning storm, right?"

"Yeah, exactly."

Eve cleared her throat. "We were collecting lightning to power the portal."

"You can collect lightning?"

"Not for long, but it is possible."

"Okay, so we fly through the next big storm and collect as much as we can."

Gigi looked at me, one eyebrow raised, a very clear 'you don't realize how stupid and/or impossible what you just said is' look on her cat face. "Um, that would be almost suicidally dangerous."

"We've flown through storms before."

"This would be different. This would mean deliberately finding the worst storm imaginable, and flying around trying to be hit by as much lightning as we could find."

"Can we find another way to get that much power? On land?"

"No, the portal could open up inside a mountain, or underwater. An airship avoids the possibility of you materializing inside something."

That made a lot of sense. I mean, there was no way to tell where on Earth I might show up. The chain that hauled me to Ayrth was only about twenty feet long, but the airship had been hundreds of feet over the Atlan Ocean.

"So we need some way to get all kinds of power into an airship. How?"

Gigi shook her head. "No idea. Maybe if we covered the airship in photonic converters, like the Forgotten Frigate? But otherwise, I mean, the whole ship could be filled with steam engines and not generate the kind of electricity we need."

"Too bad we didn't capture the Frigate when we had a chance." I checked my pocket watch, a gorgeous wood-and-gold piece that had been a gift from some of the townsfolk. The Admiral's Villa had dozens of visitors arriving daily, leaving gifts or asking for favours. I'd had to put Domina to work, organizing them all. Most of the gifts we regifted to people we wanted favours from, except the gifts from kids, the artwork, and the food. The food we gave to the shelters that had been set up for people whose homes had been destroyed in the battles.

"I have a meeting," I said, snapping the watch shut.

"Another one?" Gigi snickered.

"Don't laugh or I'll make you come with me on this one."

"Good luck, Admiral."

I left the ship, the noise of hammers hammering and drills drilling and welders welding, the smell of sweaty women working hard to make our ship the best ship in the sky. I wanted nothing more than to join them, pitch in and lose myself to honest work. Instead I had to go and face the other leaders of what we'd finally begun to call The Revolution.

Not the Citizen's Revolt or the People's Push for Power or anything all the history books started calling it after the war. We just called it The Revolution. We'd even decided on a flag to rally the troops – a gold half-gear on a blue and red background. Why a half-gear? Because The Revolution was a work in progress, and if we had our way, always would be. That had been Mr. Mahogany's idea.

Yeah, it took a long time for me to realize it kind of looked like a sunset. I wasn't the one who designed it, so don't blame me!

Anyway, off I went, leaving the repairs of The Furies behind me, aching to get back into the sky. Miss Phoenix was hosting, this time, and her quarters were on the top floor of a converted hotel filled with refugees. Yeah, right. If every single person in the hotel wasn't directly reporting to Miss Phoenix, I'd be amazed.

But her quarters on the top floor were empty. Not completely empty, mind you, I mean, we were sitting in chairs around a table, but as far as I could tell that was the only furniture on the entire floor. And yes, I looked, by which I mean I asked to be excused at one point to go to the washroom and snooped around a bit. No doors were locked, but there wasn't anything in any of the rooms. Just weird.

Anyhow, by the time I got back from 'refreshing myself', they'd progressed from the invasion plans to how things were going in the rest of the world. Zhou troops in the Zybarich had seized all the oil fields and coal mines, and Russankyan troops had pulled back all the way to Muskov, the last hold out. The Zhou were consolidating their hold in the East, unwilling to send their troops to the distant West. The Fist had flown to Zhou to see to their efforts personally, but the capture of Muskov had fallen into the laps of the Daxians, who were insisting they needed support.

"They don't need support, they need effective leadership," Mr. Mahogany observed quietly. "They spend so much time infighting and undermining each other, I sometimes wonder if they remember who the enemy really is."

Then I had an idea.

"I could go," I heard myself say. Seriously, my big mouth...

"What?" General Komodo asked.

My mind was racing. "No, listen. I'm not much use in tactics, right? Straight at 'em, that's pretty much my motto, but it isn't going to work every time and anyway, the invasion, I mean, it's pretty much planned, right? So I'll go to Russankya and whip the Daxians and vampyri into shape, finish the job there, turn us around and then Europa will be fighting on two fronts. We'll crush them between us and then we'll be set to take on the big prize, Atlan itself."

But I was thinking, *This is the perfect chance for me to get out of being Admiral. I'll send Serena in my place, she can take over the Daxian Army. She understands their politics much more than I ever will. Then I'll be able to slip into Atlan, use Miss Merryweather's information to get into The Pit, I mean, more prisoners has to be better for my plan anyway. And then we break out, stir up trouble, and end the war before millions of people die.*

"What about your prison break?" Miss Phoenix asked. "You've been pushing for that for weeks. Did your bosun risk her life for nothing?"

"No, we'll still work on that. One way or another, I still believe it will work. I just won't be involved with the exact details, that's all."

It was the first time I'd lied to them. I looked at them all, but the one I was most worried about was Miss Phoenix. She stared me in the eye for a long, uncomfortable moment. I was about to say something and probably blow the whole thing when Mr. Mahogany saved me.

"I like it," Mr. Mahogany said. "It shows that we are willing to send our very best to help our brothers and sisters in need."

I grinned. "Oh, well, I don't know about the best, but thanks."

"Who will lead the piratess in your absence?" Komodo asked.

"I have to pick a second-in-command anyway, right? In case something happens. I have a short list of options."

"How soon can you leave?" Miss Phoenix asked.

"Give me a couple of days to get everything organized," I said, standing. "I'll let you know as soon as I'm ready to go."

I called a meeting of my staff as soon as I got back to the Villa. It took a little while to get everyone, since Gigi was down by the dockyard and some of the girls had gone off into town to shop.

"You vant to vhat?!" Serena asked, nearly spilling her drink when I told them.

"Deliberately deceive the leaders of The Revolution, send my second-in-command to deceive the Daxians, name a second-in-command to lead the pirate fleet here, and sneak into Atlan myself to organize the biggest prison break in history."

"You know, if anyone else had said that, I'd have thought they were mad," Gigi said.

Molly hooked a thumb at me. "Doesn't mean she isn't."

"Yes, thanks," I said. "Okay, so. We send The Furies to Russankya, Serena at the helm, with orders to let her take over their efforts."

"I do not like that idea at all," Serena said, shaking her head. "Vhat vill happen if ve are found out?"

"What's to find? The orders will be perfectly legitimate. The leaders will sign orders placing me in charge, and I'll sign orders putting you in charge."

"And vhat vill the leaders say vhen you do not report back?"

"Oh, I'm sure you'll be too busy for regular reports, and they'll be too busy to wonder why they aren't receiving them."

Serena thought about it. I could feel waves of something I couldn't remember ever feeling from her before, nervousness.

"You'll do great, Serena," I said. "Look what you did during the battle. You're a natural general."

She raised an eyebrow at me. "Ordering a group of nearly panicking citizens, regrouping soldiers and leftover pirates into an effective fighting unit is fine vhen they fear you. My countrymen vill not fear me, and some of them have had centuries to master the intricacies of betrayal. Make no mistake, Wal, this is not a simple thing you ask of me."

I reached across the table and took her hand. The contact let her hear my thoughts. *There's no one I trust more to do this, Serena. I believe in you.*

Ah, but do I believe in myself?

I let go of her hand and smiled. *You'll be fine.*

"So you're sending The Furies to Russankya?" Molly asked.

"At first, yes. But I have a personal request for the rest of you."

"Oh?" Mrs. Shorty asked.

I took a deep breath and plunged in. "You all know the aetheric portal that brought me here, from my world, right? Well, Gigi tells me that there's no way to power it, unless we do something stupidly suicidal. Or something that might seem like a fool's errand."

"And that is?" Miss Merryweather asked, the first words she'd said during the whole meeting.

"I need The Furies to find the Forgotten Frigate. If we can capture that ship and take her photonic conversion cell things, we can power the aetheric portal without having to fly through a lightning storm. And we can use them to keep Sparky charged without leaving us a floating target."

"You're splitting us up?!" Molly asked.

"Well, I mean, I thought that was pretty obvious, with me going into the Pit and Serena going to fight the Russ."

"An' th' Daxians," Moonchance laughed.

"Yeah, and her own people. I'm sorry, Molly, I didn't think you'd get so upset by the idea."

"No, it's not that, it's just..." She sighed. "Look, I know people think I'm kind of a bitch. Hard, you know? I wasn't always. My dad was all the family I had, and the Blight took him from me. That makes you hard. Or you go mad. Then I was taken by Crow's crew. And that bitch Enerva did *this* to me." She curled her mechanical hand, flexing the fingers, then raised that hand to touch her eyelens. "And I know, I went mad a little, then. There was no way I could get hard enough to handle that. But I came back from that madness. You brought me back, Sunset. You and this crew. The only family I have left."

I didn't know what to say. It was the longest speech I'd ever heard her make. Normally getting her to open up was like pulling teeth.

"And now you want to split the crew up. Send us off on all kinds of missions. Well, that's your prerogative, Admiral. But I'd be lying if I said I was happy about it. If I had my druthers, we'd stay right here."

"The war isn't going to stay here, Molly," Miss Merryweather said. "We must go where the effort needs us most."

"Chasing after a ghost ship is where the effort needs us most? Look, I get it, Admiral, you want to go home. We all do. But sometimes you can't go home. Sometimes that home is gone forever. And who's to say what the war effort will need most, anyway? Seems to me there are plenty of folks in Afric who'd be happier if the war effort stayed here and made sure there weren't any more Blighted roaming the jungles."

"The Blighted are not the problem, Molly," Serena said. "They are a symptom of a larger illness: Atlan. Atlan must be stopped."

Molly snorted. "And then what? Has anyone even thought that far ahead? So we give the vote to women and animen and patchworks. Automatons too, why not? Then what? Who do they vote for? Another Senate? Just as corrupt and treacherous as the old one? Why bother?"

"Because a new Senate will be formed from the will of all the people," Violette answered. "Not just a select few."

"And that's somehow supposed to make me feel better?"

"Yes, actually," I said. "Molly, if you had all these issues with our mission, why didn't you bring it up sooner?"

She stared at me for a long time.

"I suppose I thought that if you were with us, we actually had a chance of making the world a better place," she said, finally. A tear traced its way down her cheek. "But you want to deliberately imprison yourself in the worst prison in the Atlan Empire, and if you somehow survive that, you're going to return back to your world."

"Molly, it's not like that," I said. "I just..."

"No, it's fine. I get it."

"Molly..."

Molly stood up, her chair scraping along the floor. "Admiral, I hereby tender you my resignation from The Furies. Good luck with your mission. You're going to need it."

"Molly!"

And with that, she left.

We were speechless.

All except Moonchance.

"Well, seein's as she's done brung it up," Moonchance said, and she, Wren and Apple stood up on the table.

"See, fing is, we's lookin' t' git back 'ome, like," Moonchance said.

"They needs us, they do," Wren added.

"The Redcaps, you mean?" I said. My voice sounded like it was coming from a long ways away.

"Too roight, we do."

Moonchance took her mouseskin leather cap off. "Now, don' take it personal, like. 'S bin a roight pleasure, Cap'n Val."

Wren elbowed her in the side. "Adm'ral!"

"Roight, Adm'ral. But see, 's like this, innit. There's them what's fambly by blood, and them's what's fambly by choice, and sometimes the first ones gotta come first, get me?"

"Sure."

"We ain't leavin' you in no lurch, like. 'em gulls you gimme, well, they ain't no seamstresses no more, see? We trained 'em up roight and propah. Real airship sailmakers, they are."

"Too roight," Wren said, and then she sniffled.

"Oh don't you start!" Apple said, and bawled into her hands.

"We promised it wouldn't come t' this," Moonchance sniffled.

The three of them cried. I wanted to cry, too. But I couldn't.

"I understand," I said, when they'd quieted down a little. "So you'll be heading back to Anglica?"

"From there onto Eire," Moonchance nodded, wiping her nose on the back of her wrist.

I stood up. "Good luck, Moonchance. Thanks for everything."

She looked surprised when I offered her my hand, then nodded and shook my finger. Wren and Apple got the same hand to shake.

We discussed who'd take over as chief of sailmakers and aeriologists, but it all passed through me in a kind of white haze. I called the meeting to an end then and asked that we take it up again in the morning.

"Wal?"

"I'm fine, Serena," I lied, knowing she knew I was lying, desperately hoping she wouldn't push any further.

She sensed that too, and left me alone.

I don't remember crying myself to sleep that night. I lay down, closed my eyes, and tried not to fight the numbness I felt.

But in the morning, my pillow was still wet.

Chapter Eleven

Dividing, Hopefully to Conquer

Molly left without saying another word to me, or anyone else for that matter. I heard she'd hooked up with a bunch of Blighted hunters, something Doc Regan confirmed about a week later. Doc had been playing six-card in a local saloon and Molly had walked in with a tall brunette and a curvy redhead, all armed to the teeth with exactly the sort of weapons designed for killing Blighted.

I wished her luck. No, more than that. I wished her peace. I hoped she would find it, somehow.

Things happened pretty fast, after that. I spoke to my first choice for second-in-command and surprised all the other leaders by naming Captain Lawless.

I know what you're thinking. Why not the Tallyhos? They'd be perfect for the job! Well, I had another mission for the twins.

"You're giving us your ship?!" Gwen said, stunned. Guinny was speechless.

"Just for a while, until we get back," I said. "I mean, I'm not going to need it in prison, and Serena's going to be busy in Russankya. Besides, you already know all the crew as if they were your own."

"True, ducks, but... I mean, it's your ship."

"Yep. And there's no one else I'd trust her with."

Guinny laughed. "So we're your last resort, is that it?"

"It's not like that, and you know it," I said, smiling. "Take good care of her, alright?"

"Of course we will, pet," Gwen said, hugging me. "As good as you would yourself."

"Better, even," Guinny added, stepping up for her hug.

We'd let the crew know as soon as we took off. The plan was for us to head out with the sunset, something I thought pretty fitting. There wasn't any big ceremony, or any kind of announcement. Captain Lawless saw us off, that's all. You'd think they'd want to make a big deal about Sunset Val herself heading to Russankya to deal with the stalemate there. Any Atlan spies would report it and the Atlan military would have to handle their troops' morale going into the toilet. But they decided to try and keep it a surprise, which actually fitted my personal plans perfectly.

The official story was we were going to refuel in Anfa, but I'd spoken privately with Miss Phoenix, telling her all my plans, everything I'd worked out with my crew chiefs. Miss Merryweather had been awesome, helping out with the details. Miss Phoenix had been impressed and given me the resources I'd need. Namely, a submersible to get me to Atlan and a few agents to meet me when I got there.

When we got to Anfa, we set down and I called a meeting of the entire crew. We explained the plan, leaving my part as a vague "I've got something to do here, alone". There was a surprising amount of grumbling and protest, but I guess Restless put it best:

"Y' can't just leave us, Cap'n Val!"

She was nearly in tears as she said it, and her voice broke, sending shards of agony through my heart.

"It won't be long, I promise," I said, having no idea how long it might take. A week? A month? No idea. But the important thing was that most of the people I loved most on this entire world would be far off, away from the war, safely chasing after something I strongly suspected they'd never find.

Yes, that was my nefarious plan. My fiendish plot. My cunning scheme, my hidden motive behind it all. I wanted to keep my friends safe. If I could have sent Molly and Serena with them, I would have.

Inga stood up. "Admiral, I will stay with Mistress Heartlace. She will need me to break the stalemate."

"Yes," Commander Draganova said, slamming her mug of beer on the table. "The Vulka-rey need battle, not chasing some ghost ship."

The other Vulka-rey howled their agreement.

"I can't stop you from staying with Serena," I said, wishing I could. "In fact, anyone who wants to jump ship now and find other berths, go ahead. You're all grown women – well, most of us – but as far as I'm concerned you've all earned the right to decide the course of your lives for yourselves. Those of you who were taken as slaves, you can even go back to your families. There's nothing stopping you now, not with Atlan on the retreat. There's a new day coming, ladies. A day of freedom."

"But first we must get through the long night of war," Miss Merryweather said. "And it all began with you, Sunset."

I grinned at her, to keep from bawling. "I had a lot of good help."

"Show of hands, who wants to find other berths?" Miss Merryweather asked the crew. A couple dozen women raised their hands.

"We signed on to fight for Sunset Val," Lauz said. "Not chase across the seven skies for a myth."

"There's still plenty o' fighting needs doin'," M'lembe agreed.

"Mistress Throckwaddle will allot your shares of our booty," Miss Merryweather announced, and Mrs. Shorty nodded. "See her after the meeting. Anyone else?"

No one raised their hands.

"Alright then," I said. "Ladies, back home, I have two sisters. One younger-" I looked at Restless "and one older." I looked at Miss Merryweather. "I can't say I'm especially close to either of them. I don't know that Melanie would take a bullet and keep on fighting, or that Sandra would risk her life to save mine.

"But you... All of you. You're as close to me as any sister born of the same mother. Closer maybe, because we've fought and bled and laughed and cried together, in a way I never did with any sister I have back home. And maybe one day, when this war is over, we can look back on what we did here, in this ship, in this *home*, and know that we did something worth being proud about. No, more than that. Something that needed doing, something that made the world a better place. And other women will look at us and wish they'd been with us, wish they'd been a part of this."

They were crying, then, and I was crying, and one of the Vulka-rey cheered, a long howl that promised bloody vengence lay ahead for anyone who stood in our way, and the rest of the crew picked it up, the shriek of The Furies.

"That's why we follow you, lass," Miss Merryweather muttered in my ear as the crew filed out. "That right there."

"Thank you," I whispered, not trusting myself to say anything else.

As the crew left, I noticed Tring and the other Open Hands hanging back. I expected a stern talking-to by the chief of my bodyguards, so I walked into it, head on.

"You do not need us," Tring surprised me.

"Uh..."

"You have proven, again and again, that your path lies in the way of dangers uncounted. I cannot say you thrive upon them, but certainly, you have proven that you can survive them. I hope, for your sake, that trend continues. But we can no longer serve you, Fighting Blossom."

"Tring... Gentle Tigress. I don't know what to say."

"You must say goodbye, Fighting Blossom. Off you go into danger once again, but where you go we cannot protect you. You must look out for yourself. It is the way of any child, to one day seek their own path, freed of their parents' constraints."

"Will you stay with the crew?"

"No. Zhou needs us. The Fist has offered us places within the Way of Three. We will join the war effort in Zhou."

"Get them back into the war, will you?"

Tring smiled a rare, glorious smiles. "I will see what I can do."

I hugged each of them, thanking them in Zhou for everything they'd done. They headed out of the mess hall, leaving me alone.

Alone.

But I didn't have much time for self-pity, or nameless worries, or specific doubts. I had a submersible to catch.

Chapter Twelve

Fishing Trip

There was one thing I had to do first. I closed my eyes, listening to that special link Serena and I shared, and found her on the main deck. She was moongazing.

"Wal," she said as I approached, not even turning.

"Serena," I answered.

She glanced over to me, her eyes flicking down to the cup I carried, the fresh bandage around my wrist.

"I won't drink that."

"Serena, listen."

"No, Wal, I will not drink of your willingly-offered blood again."

"You will, Serena. I need you to drink this. It's getting cold."

"Wal, you do not understand what you ask."

"I need you to drink this. Someone needs to know how to find me if I can't convince the worst criminals in Atlan to break out of prison."

"If I drink that blood, freely given, of your own vill, your vill becomes my vill, do you understand? You vill lose a part of yourself to me."

"How do you know?"

"Vhat?"

"How do you know? Have you ever done it?"

"Vell... no."

"Have you ever know any other vampyri who did it? You told me that it was kind of a thing among your people. Not forbidden, but sort of frowned upon?"

"No. That is, yes, frowned upon. And no, I have never known anyone who had a blood servant. But the literature on the subject is quite specific. Your vill is lost to mine."

"Drink the blood, Serena. If my um, extremely vague plan doesn't work, then I need to know there's someone out there looking for me. Someone who will find me."

Serena laughed. "If you think there is a voman aboard this ship who vould not villingly give her life to save yours, I vould say you greatly underestimate your place in their hearts."

"I don't want them to give their lives to save mine!" I yelled, suddenly angry. "I want them to live long and happy lives! But that can't happen if the war doesn't end, and the war won't end if I can't get every criminal in the Pit out and making as much mayhem as they can manage. So I need to go in there and make it happen, and you need to drink this blood in case I can't. Because even if it is true and you can somehow impose your will on me, I trust you not to. I trust you more than anyone I've ever known."

There were so many emotions coming through our link that I honestly could not pick one out over another. Finally she reached out and took the cup. Looked at it for a moment. Lifted it to her lips.

Her eyes met mine, locked onto them. She drank, draining the cup in one long swallow.

The effect was immediate. A deep relaxation came over me. I closed my eyes and saw myself through her eyes. She licked the last of my blood from her lips, and I saw my mouth part and my tongue flicker across my own lips.

"Kneel," Serena said.

My eyes snapped open. I felt her will pressing down on mine. I didn't even want to fight her. If she wanted me to kneel in front of her, would it really be that big a deal? I felt my knees begin to bend.

Yeah, right. That's about where my brain said, *No, I don't think so.*

Serena looked serious about it, though. This wasn't just a test. She really wanted me to kneel.

"Kneel," she said again, angry this time.

Probably not a good idea to make a vampyri mad, though. Maybe I should just kneel and get it over with? Yeah, no. No way.

"Kneel!"

I raised my chin, locked my knees in place, and said, "Guess you'll have to make me."

Oh, but I wanted to kneel.

"Wery vell, Wal."

For a second I thought she meant she would make me, but I felt her will back away from mine.

"Guess the literature might have been exaggerating a little, eh?"

"Perhaps."

"Thank you, Serena."

"This can never happen again, Wal."

"I know."

"I vill die before I let that happen."

"Well, let's not let it come to that, alright?"

"Alright."

She turned away from me then, back to the moon and her moongazing. I wanted to stay with her. I wanted to tell her it would be alright, no matter how bad she felt about what she'd just done. And I could feel that, too, somewhere deep inside of her where she was hoping I couldn't feel it, she felt guilty and ashamed and like she'd failed me or failed herself, somehow.

I didn't want to know all that. I didn't need to know. I turned around and walked away, and the overwhelming knowledge of her innermost emotions became less, a little.

Be careful.

I will.

Okay, so telepathic contact with one of my best friends probably wouldn't be that bad, right?

I slipped away without any other words of goodbye. Everyone was too busy. Even Eve and Gigi barely had time for more than a hug and a wave and a couple of words to be careful and stay safe. Dressed in black, I sneaked down to the air field and watched The Furies sail off into the night.

Dawn was only a few hours away. I met my contact, a stocky old man named Pete, and he led me to the seashore.

The waves were crashing against the rocky shore, silver in the moonlight. The roar made talking next to impossible. Pete led me a crooked path gradually along the shore until he stepped behind a pile of boulders and disappeared.

I hurried to catch up, but I couldn't find him. I turned around four or five times, desperately trying not to yell his name, trying to spot him in the vast darkness all around me.

He came up behind me while I was looking out to sea, trying to spot if he was swimming away.

"'ere," he said, his voice rough as gravel, the language Anglic.

I wanted to yell at him, hit him, kick his ass. I didn't do any of that. I just followed him into the pile of boulders.

He'd gone into a hidden grotto, the old bastard. If I thought it was dark outside under a sliver of moon, that was nothing compared to how dark it was in that cavern. My eyes never did adjust.

We waded through knee-high water until I felt Pete's hand on my shoulder. I stopped, and waited, as he went ahead. I heard him sloshing back a few seconds later. He pressed a pair of goggles into my hands.

I slipped them on. Nightvision goggles. I flipped the switch and with a crackle of electricity they came to life, and suddenly I could see.

And what I saw was a submersible. Shaped like a great fish, a giant tuna or salmon or something, oddly segmented all along her length. Only with six sets of fins along the sides. The entire thing was made of gleaming brass, with huge glass bulbs in front where the fish's eyes would be. The crew were loading her up, grey metal cylinders I recognized as air tanks going in one port, a long tube hooked from a gigantic tank set further back in the grotto snaking across the small beach and pumping something fluid into the submersible at another port.

Pete led me to the inner shore of the grotto and introduced me to the submersible commander, a stern-looking man named Buck.

"Pleased to meet you," I said, in Anglic, shaking his hand. "I'm –"

"Get aboard, miss," he said. "No need for names."

"Right."

Up close, the submersible didn't look nearly as big as I'd first thought. About forty feet long, fifteen high and maybe ten feet wide at its widest point. The hatch to get aboard was a tiny round hole on top, a tight fit even for me. How the crewmen managed I had no idea.

I climbed down a ladder and found myself wondering how they managed to move around at all, in here. Cramped didn't even begin to describe it. Machinery and tubes and valves everywhere. The oily smell of engine grease quickly overwhelmed my nose. I looked around for some sign of where I should head when a good looking skinny guy with messy blond hair came up to me.

"You'd be our precious cargo, then," he said. "I'm Sebastian. No, don't bother with your name, or Buck'll have my head. This way, beautiful."

He turned around on the spot and led the way, his head ducked low the whole time. I counted myself pretty lucky to be so short, for one of the few times in my life. He led me to the bridge, such as it was, set just behind the huge bulbous eyes. A man who could have been Sebastian's twin was busy checking readouts on a control panel, tapping at gauges when he wasn't happy with a readout, noting everything on a clipboard. Unlike Sebastian, this guy's hair was immaculate.

"Stand over there," he said, without turning, pointing to one corner of the bridge with his pen.

I moved over to the relatively empty corner.

"I'll see if I can't find her a stool, shall I?" Sebastian said.

"Do as you like," his brother answered.

"Don't be a prat, Robert." Sebastian turned back to me. "He's not happy about the mission."

"Dawn landings are no joking matter, Sebastian," Robert snapped, turning to his brother.

"Dawn? Really? It'll take that long to get there?"

"If we're lucky and the current holds," he answered, turning back to the gauges.

"The ocean changes direction?"

"Electrical current," Sebastian explained. "Be right back."

Robert kept checking the gauges and ignoring me. I waited.

Buck strode onto the bridge, or at least, as much striding as a person can do hunched over. The bridge had a little more head room, though, and he straightened immediately. "How are we, Robert?"

"As well as can be expected."

"It'll have to do. Get us under way."

"Aye sir."

Sebastian came back with a tiny stool for me to sit on. I thanked him, but I was too excited to sit.

"First time aboard a submersible, eh?" he grinned.

"Yeah. It shows, I guess?"

"A little. You'll want to keep chewing at something, then."

"Right. Air pressure? Same as a fast rise on an airship."

"Exactly."

I heard a clank and a grind, and another. Then something rattled, and there was the hiss of gas venting through tubes. I felt the pressure on my eardrums almost immediately, and worked my jaw to compensate. Then another, larger rattle, shaking the whole ship, and a whir of engines. The rattling in the ship settled to a steady thrum I could feel in the soles of my feet.

"All engines at full power," Robert reported.

"Batteries at maximum charge, Buck," Sebastian added.

A short Afric man stepped through the hatch to the bridge and went to the wheel. "Sorry, Pete and Louis needed some help."

"Take us out, Mr. Tembo," Buck ordered.

"Aye sir."

The ship lurched forward suddenly, which surprised only me. I sat on my stool to avoid falling.

And then the entire ship *flexed*. Like a fish swimming. Which explained all those odd segments. How they managed to keep her watertight was completely beyond me. Gigi would have been asking about a million questions right now. I concentrated on the view ahead.

Dark waters closed over the glass bulbs. Sebastian threw a switch and lights around the glass bulbs lit our way through an underwater tunnel. Then we were out in the ocean.

"Right, lights out," Buck ordered, and Sebastian threw the switch again, plunging us into complete darkness. The only, very dim, light came from the gauges behind us.

"Uh..." I said, for lack of anything more intelligent to say.

Sebastian must have thrown another switch, because electricity crackled all around the glass bulbs, and they sparked to life.

The windows, the huge glass bulbs, were actually gigantic goggle lenses. Nightvision goggles, apparently, only with some kind of see-through-the-silty-water refinement, because suddenly we could see for miles. There in the dark, distantly, I saw a couple of shapes I thought must be sharks, hunting for a meal. Below us, a world of sea life moving in the invisible currents. We kept a steady level below the surface, but the sea floor fell away from us rapidly. Soon it was almost like flying. Almost. The main difference was the noises. Flying an airship, we had the pounding of the engines and the constant song of the wind to keep us company. We spoke openly.

In the submersible, there was the constant grind and groan of the hull as it flexed its way through the waters surrounding us, the thrum of the electric engines, and almost no conversation. Orders were given and acknowledged tersely, quietly. Course adjustments came after tense moments staring at a clock mounted between the glass bulbs.

After an hour or so, though, even tension can get boring. I settled back on my stool, crossed my arms and fell into a doze.

I woke up when Sebastian touched my shoulder.

"Time to suit up," he said. "We'll not be making shore. You'll have to walk the rest of the way."

"Walk? On water?"

"That'd be a neat trick," Sebastian grinned. "But no. Under water."

"Why can't we make shore like we planned?"

"We had to make a run around some Imperial sharks," Sebastian explained as he herded me aft.

"Sharks? What can sharks do against a submersible?"

"Bred mighty big, outfitted with steam-powered steel jaws? They'd tear through us like a knife through butter."

"Why didn't you wake me?"

"Wasn't much to wake you for. Unless you can control giant half-mechanical sharks?"

"No, of course not."

"We were actually quite impressed at your ability to stay asleep."

"Yeah, I'm gifted."

He grinned again and ushered me into a side chamber, about the size of a port-a-potty, lit with a single dim bulb. Not really much room for two people. And then there was the suit hanging on the wall.

Big, baggy, brown rubberized canvas. You know, when Miss Merryweather had described a wetsuit, I pictured something black and sleek, not this reject from an old episode of Scooby-Doo.

Yeah, big old round grill-faced helmet and everything. Only instead of a rubber tube poking out the top, it came with a backpack that looked like it weighed as much as I did, covered with all kinds of spinny doodads and vents and such.

Sebastian helped me into the suit. There was no way I could lift the backpack, so I sat down on the bench and let him strap me in.

"What about air tanks?" I asked.

"No need." He tapped the backpack. "This extracts air from seawater, so you can breathe."

"Wow. What now?"

"We'll let you out as close to shore as we can, but we can't risk getting lodged on a sandbar. Too many sharks around. They most likely won't notice you – too small to be a meal, y'see. You'll be fine. After the drop, when you get your footing, head dead to port, that'll bring you to shore. Someone'll meet you there, I'm guessing."

"You're guessing? You mean you don't know?"

"Don't need to, do I? I'm not the one going ashore." He grinned again, one last time, and stepped back to close the chamber hatch.

The wheel spun, locking me in the tiny room.

I heard a clunk and water started rushing in from some hidden vents near the floor.

My brain clicked on something Sebastian had said. "What drop?"

When the room was full of water to my neck, the floor gave way under me. I fell out of the submersible, dragged down by the weight of the backpack.

But I'm proud to say I didn't panic. They didn't risk their lives to just dump me a hundred feet from Atlan's shores. I landed on the soft, sandy sea bottom, not hard but not gently, and rolled to my knees. About then I realized I'd been holding my breath, and it came out explosively. I gasped, and I felt the backpack activate. Fresh air blew into the helmet and I breathed it in. Then I pushed myself to my feet, took an experimental step, then another.

I walked along the ship, floating about twenty feet above me, until I could see in the glass bulbs. I waved at the crew I couldn't see. If they waved back, I'll never know. The ship began to flex again, looking like a giant brass fish, and the six pairs of fins began cutting through the water, pulling the ship away. They disappeared into the gloomy depths of the ocean.

I turned around and started heading inland. Or at least, I hoped it was inland. With only the whirring hum of the backpack and my own growing worry that I might run into one of those half-mechanical sharks Sebastian had talked about. Then it hit me he'd probably been telling a tall tale, because as far as I knew only humans could have prosthetics attached. Or at least, that's what Eve and Gigi had told me, and I trusted them over some guy I just met and would never see again. Just pulling one over the land lubber, I guess.

That worry taken care of, all I had left to worry about was the idea that I might be heading deeper into the ocean, instead of toward land. I could barely see ten feet in front of me, and what I saw was basically silty sand and the occasional sea plant. Sometimes a fish would flash by. I know, it totally sounds easy, but believe me, it wasn't. I tripped and stumbled more times than I could count, and carrying all that weight, even underwater, while moving through the ocean currents, quickly had me drenched with sweat.

I kept walking. Gradually things were getting brighter, clearer. More plants, more little fish. A bunch of lobsters scrambled away from me at one point. I could only see ahead of me, not above, so I had no idea how deep under water I still was.

When I broke through the surface, it was as much a surprise to me as to the seagulls I woke. They scattered, announcing my presence to anyone who might be watching. Great.

I fell to my hands and knees and crawled off to my right, hoping to keep from being spotted. Then I turned and headed back for the shore. Of course, in this position I had a terrible view – sand, sand and more sand. So eventually I had to lift myself up and look ahead.

I'd crawled to within twenty feet of the shore. I stood up and fell back over – out of the water, the backpack was stupidly heavy. I rolled over and crawled the last twenty feet, then plopped myself down on the beach and worked the helmet off. My hair hung in sweaty strands. The walk had exhausted me. I could barely stand.

But I'd made it. My invasion of Atlan had begun.

Chapter Thirteen

About Time for An Action Scene, Don't You Think?

Getting out of the suit alone was a lot harder than putting it on with an expert's help, but I managed. I hid the suit under a pile of crab-infested rocks and waited for someone to show up.

I didn't have to wait long. A man and a woman, both armed with rifles, both dressed in knee-high boots, slacks and hunting jackets, came into view, a little ways down the beach. I sat there, waiting for them to come to me.

"Nice morning for a swim," said the woman in Atlan.

"If you're a fish," I answered, hoping my accent didn't come through too much.

"Fishes come in all shapes and sizes," the man answered back, completing the code phrases.

"You'd be the infamous Sunset Val, then," the woman said, shaking my hand and hauling me to my feet.

"That's me," I answered.

"Let's go," the man said, heading inland.

As we made our way through the brush and trees, it started to rain. Not much at first, a few drops, but pretty soon it was a real thunderstorm, the rain coming down in angry slaps of water. After about an hour of slogging through the rain and mud and forest, we came to a steam-driven carriage and climbed inside. The man took the controls while the woman helped me out of my soaking wet clothes and into a dry prisoner's uniform. The engine puttered into life. Soon enough steam had built up that we could roll out.

We drove along a muddy dirt road for a few minutes, then came to a much better paved road of gravel lined with actual cobbles.

"This is Atlanopolitan Way," the man explained. "We wait here."

"Might as well eat, then," the woman said, reaching under her seat and pulling out a basket. Bread, cheese, dried meat. A canteen of something warm and sweet. Weak tea with too much sugar, most like. I could care less, eating what I could and washing it down with warmth.

The steam carriage grew warm while we waited. Something about the pair prevented much conversation. And no, I never asked their names. The man had dark, fathomless eyes, so I'll call him Dark Eyes. The woman had her hair in a tight braid, so yeah, she's Braid.

"How long do we wait?" I asked.

"It's a four hour drive along the Atlanopolitan Way to where we are," Braid answered. "Even if they left at the crack of dawn, it'll be an hour until they reach us."

"Anybody bring a pack of cards?"

Neither of them had, so we waited. A few vehicles passed us, going in either direction. Steam carriages, mainly, but once an autohorse and another time an actual horse-and-cart on the way to market. We were far enough down the dirt road that the roadside brush kept us hidden from anything but direct view. With the rain pouring down, we were pretty much invisible.

Then Dark Eyes held up a finger. We hadn't been talking, but if anything we went even quieter.

An Imperial steam carriage sped along the Atlanopolitan Way, splashing long lines of dirty rainwater into the air.

"There!" Braid said. Dark Eyes just shook his head.

Another car came by moments later, unmarked, but obviously moving with the same urgency.

"Decoy?" she asked.

"Decoy," he said, then turned the crank to build up our steam and we rolled out.

The gravel road was better than the dirt one, but not by much. Bumps, holes and ruts hidden under growing puddles of rain made it rough going, particularly since we were trying to keep up with the prison car without looking like we were trying to keep up with the prison car.

"You're too close," Braid said.

"We're fine," Dark Eyes answered, but slowed down.

Not soon enough. We'd been spotted, or something, and they had some way to communicate between cars, because the Imperial decoy pulled to one side and slowed enough to place itself alongside us.

An Imperial peacekeeper officer rolled down his window and pointed at us to pull over.

Dark Eyes responded by swerving into the decoy.

Gunshots erupted from their vehicle, shattering our windows to flying shards. I ducked behind the wooden door of the steam carriage, hoping that hitting a moving target wasn't part of their daily routine.

Braid pulled out a pistol and tossed it to me, then fired her rifle through our shattered window.

As she reloaded, I raised myself up and took a few shots out the window. "This is not the way this was supposed to go!"

"You have a better idea?" Dark Eyes snapped.

I didn't, so I fired at the decoy again. Let me tell you, hitting targets from a moving steam carriage is nothing like firing from the deck of an airship. An airship floats along, serene and steady, compared to the bumping, jumping, jarring, splashing, slashing, insanity of firing from a steam carriage. Also, they kept slamming into us, or us into them, which pretty much meant I was lucky if one in two shots actually hit the decoy car at all, much less one of the Imperial peacekeepers.

Which also worked in our favour, I guess, because they didn't hit us either. But they didn't need to, right? Because all they had to do was give the prison car enough time to escape, and the more time we spent trying to kill them without getting killed ourselves meant the more time the prison car had to evade us.

I had to reload so Braid took over firing at them. She caught an unlucky bullet in the shoulder for her trouble. To give her credit, she didn't yell out much more than a teeth-gritted grunt and kept firing. When she was empty, she slid down and shucked off her jacket.

"Bad?" Dark Eyes asked, slamming us into them again.

"It'll heal," she answered, checking the wound.

"Bandages?" I asked.

"In my pack," she said. "I can deal with this. Keep firing."

I checked to make sure they weren't going to shoot me, then raised myself and emptied my gun into their engine block. Or tried, at least. The bullets left my gun, that's all I know. If they hit any part of the Imperial car, I'd be amazed.

More swerving. More gunshots. Let me tell you, it's a lot more terrifying than in the movies.

"Hang on!" Dark Eyes warned us about half a second before standing on the brakes.

The decoy shot past us and Dark Eyes sped up again, getting right behind them, slamming into their rear bumper with a crunch.

A pair of peacekeepers leaned out their windows and took a few wild shots at us. Dark Eyes kept pouring on the speed. I could feel the heat pumping out of the steam engine.

Up ahead, a sharp turn along a ditch.

You can probably guess where this is going. Dark Eyes pushed them, hard, fast, and slammed on the brakes at the last second, shoving them out of control over the embankment and into the ditch. Then we sped off, not bothering to check if they were alive or dead. I hoped dead.

The real prison car was somewhere up ahead. We passed a number of turnoffs and crossroads, hoping each time we were staying on the right road. Shouldn't have worried too much. The prison car had managed to get quite a lead on us, but we caught up in no time. Dark Eyes could really drive ,but that's not what got us caught up.

The road up ahead had been washed out. A mudslide, caused by the rain, had taken out most of the road, just around a corner, and the prison car had slammed right into it in its haste to get away.

We slowed down just in time, our car skidding to a halt next to the overturned prison car. Carefully, we checked it out.

Everyone inside was dead.

Chapter Fourteen

Changing of the Guard

"Well, that's just great!" I yelled. "What do we do now?!"

"No, this is better," Dark Eyes said, peering into the carriage's compartment at the corpses.

"How, exactly, is this better?"

"We didn't have much of a plan, before, did we? Beyond follow them somewhere we've never been, and somehow sneak you into a prison we've never seen." He looked at me oddly, as if he was sizing me up. He nodded to himself, then climbed into the wreckage. When he came out again, he had a dead woman draped over his shoulder.

She was wearing a prisoner's uniform, like mine. Her head lolled at a very disturbing angle, her neck obviously broken. Dark Eyes placed her on the muddy ground, where rain fell into her unblinking eyes and slack mouth. Braid crouched down to inspect her.

"Who is she?"

Braid glanced up at me. "According to the intelligence your agent obtained, she went by Victory Pandora. Sounds like an alias. Arrested and tried for piracy, murder, rebellion against her slaveowner. A lot like your story, actually. Guess it's not much for originality, lots of escaped slaves wind up pirates."

"She looks like you, a little," Dark Eyes said. "Her hair's more of a brown, but a little dirt should fix that."

"She's got short hair," I said. "And she's... Bigger. In the chest."

"Prison food can thin the fattest in the land, they say," Braid said. "As for your hair..." She pulled out a dagger and held it out to me, handle first.

"Okay, wait, your plan is what? I take her place? Then what?"

"They're expected, wherever it was they were going," Dark Eyes said, hooking a thumb at the wreckage. "When they don't get there, someone'll come look for you."

"So I just sit there in the car wreck, waiting?"

They both nodded.

So I cut my hair with a dagger, until it was about an inch long. Then Braid slapped me around a little, got some good bruises going to make it seem like I might actually have been in a car crash. Dark Eyes picked the locks on Victory Pandora's shackles at her ankles and wrists, then locked me up in them. Then I got roughed up again to make the shackles wear at my skin.

No, none of it was fun, but it had to be done.

They tossed me into the car wreck and left, taking Pandora's body with them. They were going to deal with the other car, the decoy. They'd be back to check on me, if they had to, as soon as was safe.

Oh, yeah. The prologue? Yeah, that was all about her, not me. Deliberately misled you. Hey, it was more dramatic this way, right?

Anyhow, cold, sore, soaking wet, my entire scalp aching from the brutal tug of the dagger, I lay there in the car wreck with the two bodies of the dead Imperial peacekeepers. Death had left them no dignity. They'd shit themselves. Talk about stink.

Around the same time as the rain began to let up, it started getting dark. I heard voices. I lay back, crouched uncomfortably in the carriage, pretending to be unconscious.

I heard someone yell, "Here!" and then the sound of people all around the car. Someone held a lantern up, shining light in my face.

"All dead!"

"Blast and Blight!"

"One less waste of air to feed."

At which point I moaned, loud enough for them to notice.

"Wonderful, she's alive."

"What about our boys?"

"Someone check them."

"Get her out of there. Of all the rotten luck. Piece of shit like her lives and two good men die? Is that justice?"

Someone grabbed me by the wrist shackles and hauled me up, hard. I cried out in pain, eyes fluttering open, trying to maintain the illusion that I'd been unconscious for the last few hours.

"Who? What?" I stammered.

"Shut your trap, you," the man holding my shackles said, slapping me across the mouth hard enough to split my lip.

He yanked me out. One of his buddies put a boot to my back and stood on me, forcing me to the ground.

"Heard she was a looker," the guy standing on me said. "Thought we might have a bit of sport. This scrawny little chicken ain't worth unbuttoning my trousers for."

The other men laughed, harsh, brutal laughter. That was the first time I was scared, honestly scared, in what seemed like a long, long time. We hadn't planned on the guards being rapists and murderers, too.

"Don't let the warden hear that kind of talk," said one. "He don't like it."

"He can kiss my rosy red arse."

"Can he now?" the man who'd pulled me out of the car said.

I couldn't see it from where I was, lying face down in the mud, but I got the distinct feeling there was some serious glaring going on.

Standing-On-Me blinked first. "I didn't mean nothing by it. Just shovelling clouds."

Then, out of nowhere, the crack of rifle shots in the distance. I'll give it to them, the prison guards all shut up and their weapons were up and out, pointing in the direction of the shots.

"That wasn't far off," one of them said.

"Check it out," the man who'd pulled me out of the car said. Obviously he was some kind of boss, because three of the other guards set off without another word.

"Get her up," the Boss said. "And pull those poor bastards out of the carriage."

The others got to work pulling corpses out of the wreckage while Standing-On-Me hauled me roughly to my feet.

"Ow," I said.

"Shut it, I said," he answered, smacking me in the side of my head. With his hand, at least, and not the butt of his rifle. Thank goodness for small mercies, I guess.

The three guards who'd gone off weren't gone long.

"Couple of hunters," one said.

"Pretty late to be hunting," the Boss said.

"Weren't very good hunters," another answered. "Hadn't caught anything. And get this, one of them was a woman."

"He let his woman have a gun?"

"Said two sets of eyes were better than just one."

The Boss just grunted at that. "Can't see what good putting a gun in a woman's hands would do, though."

I couldn't help it. I said, "Put one in mine and you'll find out."

Everyone went deadly still, eyes on the Boss, who looked at me like I'd suddenly grown wings. Then he laughed. Long and loud. The others joined in, less sure, but just as loud. Eventually I got the feeling they weren't laughing at the joke. They were laughing at me. I felt my face flush hot and red.

"Get her in the carriage," he said when he was done laughing.

Standing-On-Me shoved me toward their waiting steam carriages, just the other side of the mudslide. I shuffled along as best I could with shackles around my ankles, which wasn't easy at all. A couple of stumbles taught me pretty much the exact length of Standing-On-Me's patience. Not very long, just so you know.

A few of the other guards carried the corpses and loaded them into the steam carriage's trunks – actually, literal luggage trunks bolted onto the rears of the carriages. I got the impression none of them were too happy about it.

They all climbed in and we left the wrecked carriage behind us.

After a couple of long tense minutes a couple of the guards in the carriage started talking about some sporting event I had no knowledge of or interest in, and I kind of zoned out. I guess I even dozed a little.

"Hey! Scum! Wake up!"

Not the most pleasant way to wake up, let me tell you. The slap across my face didn't help much, either. I was beginning to wonder if the bruises were ever going to fade.

Night had well and truly fallen by the time we arrived, so it was pretty dark. A single gas lamp lit the parking lot. A single middling, two-storied building stood in the dark, brick walled and small windowed. Light spilled from a few of the windows. A chimney stood at either end of the building. What looked like a pair of barn doors were set in one end of the building. The other end had a pair of tall wooden doors.

The whole thing gave me a bad feeling.

"Where's the prison?" I asked.

"This is it, scum. Your home for the rest of your miserable life."

It wasn't anywhere near big enough a building to house dozens, maybe hundreds of criminals. So either they were lying and they had pulled off to rape me to death, or...

"Underground?"

"Smart one, ain't ya?" Standing-On-Me said, slapping my head again. I was really getting tired of that.

"Get her inside," the Boss said.

They marched me up the stairs, in through the wooden doors, and away from the barn doors. They stopped at a heavily-locked door and unshackled me.

"Welcome to the Pit," the Boss said. Standing-On-Me unlocked all the locks and opened the door. Inside was absolute darkness. The Boss himself shoved me through.

You know when you're walking along, not really paying attention, and the pavement ends but you didn't notice it ended and you step off but there's nothing under your foot where you expect it to be and you have that split second of *WTF?! Where's the ground?!* before your foot gives in completely to brutal relentless gravity and suddenly finds the ground and maybe you bite your tongue or something?

Yeah, that didn't happen. Or at least, I had that WTF moment, only it lasted a long, long time. Long enough for me to get well and truly scared of what would happen when I finally hit the bottom. Which I then did, hard, then I went sprawling into the dirt.

I turned to the sound of laughter, harsh and cruel. Maybe fifteen, twenty feet above me, the door to the room shut closed, sealing me in darkness.

Chapter Fifteen

A Pitiful Welcome

I waited for my eyes to adjust. Meanwhile, my other senses went into frickin' overdrive. I could hear the wooden door's many locks being locked, and then a faint scraping noise, distantly off to my leftish. I could smell mostly just myself, my sweat stink under all the dirt and mud. The ground under me was surprisingly soft, a kind of sandy dirt. At least he hadn't thrown me onto a pile of rocks.

It took a long, long time for my eyes to adjust to the near total dark. You know when it's absolutely dark, you start seeing like sparks of light and stuff? Someone once told me that it was just mental images of synapses firing or something, because your brain isn't supposed to have absolutely no visual input, so it starts looking for things to see. Making it up, in other words.

But eventually I could sort of see. A tiny sliver of light traced the outline of the wooden door above me, enough to dimly light the room I'd been tossed into. Only it wasn't really a room – high above me was a room, but someone had removed the floor completely. In the ceiling was a block and tackle, but no rope or chain. No way up to the room above from where I sat, either. The walls down here looked like featureless metal slabs. No handholds or footholds. Off to my left was a single open doorway, built low and slender, so people coming through would absolutely have to come through one at a time. That's where the scraping noise was coming from.

One good thing about all that sensory deprivation was that I managed to sense Serena, very faintly, off to my right. I closed my eyes, though I hardly needed to, and tried to call to her. I sensed she was aware of me, but couldn't hear my thoughts. I tried to project a sense of success and hoped she'd understand. I felt her concern clear enough. Then she must have gotten distracted, because her emotions got all jumbled and she faded into a distant vague presence.

"So now what?" I whispered to myself, amazed at how loud it

sounded. I shrugged and headed through the narrow doorway.

As dark as it had been in the Pit-room, the tunnel beyond the narrow doorway was so dark that it made no difference if my eyes were open or closed. I reached out one hand to find the wall and touched cool, rough-carved stone. I slid my feet ahead of me on the sandy floor, not wanting to have another fall. I'd been lucky enough with that first one, not breaking or spraining anything. I didn't want to push my luck.

But it held, and so did my footing. Cautiously I made my way down the tunnel, the only sounds the rasp of my hands along the walls, the slide of my feet along the floor, and the scraping noise ahead of me.

Gradually I became aware of a light, up ahead. A flickering yellow light, dancing at the edge of sight, almost more imagination than reality. As I crept along, the light grew bright enough to see by.

I took a step, and another.

The scraping noise stopped.

"I's beginnin' to think I'd have to come get ya," a man's voice announced, almost painfully loud in all the silence.

"Who are you?"

"Could arsk the sames o' ya," he answered. "But fine, we'll do it this way. I'm the Welcomer. You?"

"Va... Victory Pandora."

"The pirate?"

"You've heard of me?"

"A bit. Come forward, Pandora."

What else could I do? I walked forward.

The flickering light grew brighter and brighter, almost painfully bright. The tunnel curved away to my right and when I came around the curve, it opened into a slightly wider chamber. A man sat on a bit of carved out-rock, like a shelf or niche in the wall. At his feet was a bag of tools and a thick globby candle set in a something that looked like a stained wooden bowl. My eyes adjusted to the single candle's light and I got a good look at the Welcomer.

He was old, for one thing. Like, seventy or so, though he might as well have been a really rough-lived fifty or a well-preserved ninety. Anyway, wrinkled was the best way to describe his narrow face. Dark eyes gleamed with humour and intelligence. His lanky hair was grey and worn long and loose, and he hadn't shaved in a couple of days. His build was scrawny, but the arms protruding from his sleeveless shirt were lined with lean muscle, like fingers under his dirt-encrusted skin.

In one hand he held a mining pick and in the other a sharpening stone. The scraping noise stopped as I stepped into the light.

"Well, come on then," he said, standing. He was about as tall as me, with only a slight stoop in his shoulders. He tossed the pick and stone into the bag and handed the bag to me. He picked up the bowl and held it to one side. The candle guttered in the sloshing liquid but stayed lit.

"Bit o' trouble, topside?" he asked as he led the way.

"Carriage hit a mudslide," I said. "Guards died in the wreck. I was knocked out. Didn't wake up until the prison guards showed up."

"Bad bit o' luck, then."

"Still alive, though. That's sort of good luck, right?"

"You may change your mind in a few days," he said, then cackled. An actual, real cackle. When he was done creeping me right out, he horked up a mouthful of something I'd rather not think about and spat it to one side.

He asked me a few questions about the war. I kept it more or less accurate but basic, common knowledge. Or at least, what I thought the real Victory Pandora might have known. The pirates started it, the Lemurisians and the Zhou joined in, they'd taken Afric and were looking at Europa.

To be honest, I had no idea what Pandora might have or might have not known. I didn't know anything about her, other than she'd been convicted of piracy and murder, both things I was equally guilty of, from an Atlan point of view. But in the end, I decided it didn't quite matter if my backstory didn't hold any aether. Being Victory Pandora had just been the plan to get me into the prison.

Anyhow, we walked on and on, deeper and deeper into the tunnels. They zigged and zagged, and a couple of times we went down stairs carved into the rock.

Finally I had to ask. "Um, not that I'm not grateful for the guided tour or anything, but where are all the guards? Where's the cells? Where's the, you know, prison?"

He cackled again, horked again. Then he answered me.

"All this is the prison, lass. No cells. No guards but them as what's up top there. When we get to the mine, you'll see."

"This isn't the mine?"

"This is just the entrance. The mine's not far."

We kept walking, this time in silence. Only my feet echoing in the dark. The Welcomer moved quieter than I could have believed.

Eventually we got to a dead end. The air was close and dank. I had a brief moment of panic, thinking he was the only one down here and he'd led me to a quick death and a cannibal feast.

Then he disappeared into the earth.

Okay, well, not really. I stepped over to where he'd been standing and saw him sliding down a ladder. Still carrying the candle bowl. Never spilled a drop.

I was carrying a lopsided bag of tools, exhausted, cold, hungry, and in no small amount of pain. I went a little more carefully down the ladder. When I stepped off the last rung, I turned around.

The cavern loomed off into the distance, huge and well, cavernous. It had obviously been carved out of the rock, not a natural chamber. Natural chambers, I later learned, had those spiky things from the ceiling and the ground – stalactites and stalagmites. Cees and gees, that's how I remembered the difference. Anyhow, none of those in this cave.

There were candles every ten feet or so, which did very little to dispel the darkness. By their light I could see dozens of people. Maybe a couple hundred, even. They were all eating when the Welcomer and I arrived, and they all turned to look at me as I stepped off the ladder. The low, murmured conversations stopped.

They looked pretty much like what you'd expect a pack of the worst criminals in the world to look like. Hard faces hiding harder lives. Hard muscles from months of hard labour. Just... hard.

"A new sister's in the Pit!" a woman with her hair shaved into a mohawk called out, sudden and stark in the silence.

The women all made guttural grunts, three times. The men banged their fists or feet on the ground, three times.

Great.

Chapter Sixteen

My Meeting With The Big Man

"Hi." I waved at them, but they just turned back to their meals.

"Come on," the Welcomer said. "The Big Man wants t' meet ya."

He led me through the crowd. The stew, or soup, or whatever it was they were drinking from clay bowls, smelled amazing. A very small part of my brain wondered where they got beef down here, and then the rest of my brain jumped it and beat it into submission, determined never to find out what kind of meat it actually was. Determined never to even wonder, not once, ever again.

People called out to the Welcomer with respect, even admiration. He just nodded to them and kept on walking. He'd set his candle bowl down by the ladder, but I still carried the bag of tools, so I had to hustle to keep up.

The far end of the cavern had a few tunnels leading away, but before we got there we passed a couple of alcoves carved from the rock. One had an old woman, kindly-looking, tending a huge cauldron. A couple of other prisoners helped her. Another alcove held probably the biggest Afric man I'd ever seen, head shaved and tattooed with intricate spirals. If he was any shorter than seven feet tall, I'd be amazed. Every inch of it heavily muscled, his skin as dark as a cup of fresh coffee. Like everyone else, he wore a long grey pullover shirt and grey pants, but he looked like if he sneezed his clothes would shred into ribbons.

The Welcomer waved me forward.

"You're the Big Man?" I asked.

The giant just smirked and hooked a thumb over his shoulder.

"That would be me," a skinny Europan with spectacles said, stepping out of the giant's shadow. He had long brownish hair pulled back in a pony tail. He was only a few inches taller than me.

He smiled gently. "Welcomer, thanks for bringing her."

The Welcomer just nodded and left, taking the bag of tools from my tired arms.

"He made you carry it the whole way?" the skinny guy said, waving me toward a carved stone bench.

I sat. "Yeah."

"Stronger than you look, is that it?"

"Maybe."

He just nodded, as if something I said made sense. Then, "My name is Milton Quill. Before you ask, I was a professor of philosophy at the University of Albion prior to my arrest and incarceration here. My crime was teaching my students to think for themselves. We received word of your imminent arrival two days ago, and I asked around. Victory Pandora. Shall I guess your crimes? Piracy, murder, treason?"

"I'm an escaped slave, too."

"Ah. You'll find quite a few emancipators within our small community," he said, sitting on a bench opposite me. He poured a brown liquid from a jug into a clay bowl, then offered me the bowl. "Mushroom wine. If you like?"

"Sure." I took the bowl and drank a mouthful. It tasted almost as terrible as you can imagine. Almost. I forced myself to swallow it, but couldn't keep myself from shuddering a bit.

"An acquired taste, I admit," he smiled, drinking from his own bowl. "Unfortunately it's all I can offer you, today. Tomorrow we'll purchase more food to accommodate another mouth to feed. The question I have for you is, how will you work to earn your food?"

"I don't get you."

"Allow me to explain. Is the current regime still maintaining the falsehood that this is a coal mine?"

"Yeah."

"But of course, you can see that we are not coal miners. No filthy black faces, no one dying of blacklung."

"Alright."

He picked up a small rock and tossed it to me. I caught it one-handed. It was curiously warm, and slightly greasy to the touch. As I looked at it in the candlelight, it had an almost pinkish sheen to it.

"What is it?" I said, shrugging.

"Atlantium," he answered from behind his bowl of gross.

"Sorry?"

"Atlantium."

"Yeah, um, repetition isn't clarification." Yeah, I can use big words when I want, too, smart guy.

"Ah. Very well. Atlantium is a metal that is used in numerous scientific applications. Without it, automatons cease to function, animen cannot be born, patchworks lie dead on their slabs. It is, quite literally, worth ten times its weight in diamonds. That small rock you're holding could purchase a twenty-gun airship, with enough left over to hire the crew to fly her."

I stared at the rock, which was about the length of my thumb. I had hats that weighed more than this little chunk of metal. "Wow."

"Indeed. We are all atlantium miners down here. Their greatest secret. We, the worst criminals in captivity, keep the Empire running."

"So why not just stop mining and bring the Empire to its knees?"

"Ah. Excellent question. You see, in order to keep us in line, the guards deny us food. We purchase our daily allotment of necessary foodstuffs with our meagre diggings."

"That sucks."

He smiled again. "Indeed. We've managed to supplement the bare minimum food they sell us with mushrooms we grow in nearby caves, and an underground lake occasionally offers us some fish."

"Sounds like you've got things pretty well organized."

"It wasn't always like this, of course. Before I arrived, the inmates were reduced to cannibalism to survive. Even now, we are forced to make use of everyone to their utmost ability, merely to continue to survive. Another mouth to feed, well, that person must make themselves a valuable part of our community. So I must ask, do you intend to join our community? Or will you seek to disrupt it? Because, and I do apologize for the indelicacy, but disruption will be dealt with harshly."

I pretended to think about it for a few seconds. "So what would I have to do, exactly, to make myself a valuable part of the community."

He smiled that gentle smile again. "I take it from your tone that you're wondering if you'll be forced into actions or activities you might find distasteful."

"Pretty much, yeah."

"Don't worry. Nothing of that sort is allowed here. Even if the Sisterhood didn't exist, Mother Pestle would deal harshly with any inappropriate behaviour."

"Alright, who's Mother Pestle and what's the Sisterhood?"

"You'll find out soon enough, I suspect. For tonight, you're welcome to sleep here, in the common area. Tomorrow, we'll discuss what you'll be doing to make yourself useful."

It had been a while since I'd been dismissed like that. It surprised me into silence. And I'd never even had a chance to tell him my mission.

The huge Afric guy guarding the entrance was ushering me out when I said, "Uh, Mr. Quill? There's one thing I didn't tell you."

"Oh? What's that?"

"I... Uh, well, I have a message for you."

"Really?"

I stepped around Gigantor back into the alcove. "Yeah. From the leaders of the Revolution."

"Ah yes, the war in Afric. And?"

"They want you to know that they're prepared to offer you all full pardons. If you stage an escape and then make as much trouble for Atlan as possible."

Quill looked at me for maybe half a minute. His eyes bored into mine. I think he even stopped breathing. Finally, he said, "How very interesting. I'll take that into consideration. For now, though, I'd prefer if you didn't mention it to the others. It will prove... disruptive."

Which struck me as a really weird reaction for a man who'd been unjustly imprisoned by a corrupt regime. "Um, sure."

"Thank you. Cedric?"

Gigantor, that is, Cedric, showed me the way out, like I couldn't figure it out myself. I stepped into the common cave. Most of the people had left, but the woman with the mohawk and maybe a handful of her friends were waiting.

"Greetings, sister," Mohawk said. "Welcome to your new home."

Chapter Seventeen

A Wealth of Sisters

"Yeah, hi. Victory Pandora."

"Rue Fountainhead."

"You the leader of this sisterhood?"

The women laughed.

"The Sisterhood needs no leaders. Leaders cause hierarchies. We believe in communication and cooperation, not command structures and giving orders."

I thought about all the times that a command structure had saved our lives, but then, I hadn't given up everything and everyone I knew to come down here and argue political theory. "Alright."

"Quill gave you his welcome speech?"

"Um, yeah."

"Good. Here's mine. Stick with the Sisterhood and no harm can come to you. Every man in this place could be an animal if we let them, so we don't let them. Any man so much as touches you without permission, and we tear him to shreds."

Some community. Rapists controlled by murderers. "Sounds like a pretty gruesome arrangement."

Another of the women grinned, a vicious grin with little flickering bits of insanity dancing through it. "Gruesome, yes. Effective, too."

"So how does that fit into Quill's community?"

Fountainhead's eyebrow shot up, her face scrunched up in confusion. "What does our protection have to do with the community?"

"Not much of a community if the women are murdering the men."

"They don't touch us, we don't touch them. Got nothin' to do with everyone having a job and doin' that job."

A pretty blonde woman said, "Besides, the last time we had to do anything to anyone, everyone agreed he had it coming."

"He had it coming," the women all said together. Almost like a religious chant. It was absolutely the creepiest thing I'd ever heard.

I skipped to the end of the conversation. "So. How do I join up?"

"You're a woman," Fountainhead said. "That's all you need to be one of us."

That's when it hit me. Everyone in the room was a human. No animen, no vampyri, no patchworks or automatons.

"Great," I said. "Listen, uh, sisters, any of you have anything to eat? I'm half starved."

"We thought you might be," the pretty blonde said. "We each gave a portion to the bowl."

An Afric woman handed me a bowl of thin greasy glop. But hey, at least it was lukewarm and partially congealed. And no spoon.

I looked up from the disgusting mess in the bowl to see if they were kidding. Apparently not. Each of them had an expression, part hopeful, part dangerous. The hope really got to me. This really was the best they could do for a new girl.

I drank it down as fast as I could. Three long swallows was enough to get rid of most of the liquid, leaving only a handful of suspicious-looking chunks of... well, chunks. I picked those out with my fingers and chewed them as fast as I could without choking.

Hunger is the best spice, they say, and I could have sworn that greasy mess wasn't nearly as bad as I'd been expecting it to be. I popped the last chunk into my mouth and smiled to each of the women, nodding to them my thanks.

That's when I noticed the bowl. It was oddly smooth on the outside and curiously textured on the inside.

Yeah, it was half of a skull.

Fountainhead grinned at me.

I finished chewing the chunk of whatever and swallowed it. Then I looked her in the eyes, held up the bowl and said, "This the last fool who tried to touch one of us?"

They all laughed, Fountainhead hardest of all.

She clapped me on the shoulder. "You're alright, Pandora!"

I grinned up at her. "Yeah, thanks."

They brought me to a smaller cavern where a bunch of women were sleeping. A small fire in the center of the room kept away most of the damp, the smoke disappearing up into the cave's ceiling. I found a clear patch of dirt and curled into a ball.

I woke up about three seconds later, stiff as a board, aching everywhere. The other women were standing and stretching, talking to each other in low voices. The fire had died down to embers and the pretty blonde was trying to stir it up enough to light a stick. The stick caught and she transferred the flame over to a skull bowl candle thing. The light was enough to brighten the entire cave.

I cleared my throat and said, "Are you kidding? I just got here."

The pretty blonde laughed. "You've been asleep for... about ten hours, give or take."

"You're joking."

"Not a bit. I'm Millie."

"Victory."

She grinned. "I know." She stood up and picked up the candle. "Alright ladies, shake a leg. That atlantium won't mine itself."

The women all laughed. Everyone was in a surprisingly good mood, for a bunch of killers and thieves in the worst prison in the world.

I filed out of the cave with the others, making my way over to Millie. "So uh, what am I doing?"

"Everyone mines, their first week," Millie explained. "To give you an appreciation for what the real miners do. They'll probably have you hauling out, today."

It sounded an awful lot like no fun at all, and I was right. A cup of hot broth for breakfast didn't prepare me for long hours of hauling buckets full of shards of rock and loose dirt. By the end of that first day, even my sword-fighting calluses had blisters.

Now, as thrilling as the life of an atlantium miner is, I'm not going to bore you with those details. You'll just have to trust me when I say nothing exciting happened for about a week or so. It was hard to tell down in the Pit.

But where something exciting *was* happening was back in Afric, with a certain cyborg friend of mine...

Chapter Eighteen

Night of the Blighted Dead

Awareness came with a gasp to Molly, though from hard-earned experience she kept herself still under the thin blanket. Startling awake wreaked havoc on her shoulder and hip, where her mechanical replacements attached to what she still considered her *real* body.

She opened her real eye, reaching up to rub the sleep sand away. Sunlight slanted through the slats of her shuttered window. Late afternoon, then. Her partners were, no doubt, still sleeping. Molly wondered briefly with whom Jezebel was sleeping, then decided she didn't care.

The pounding in her head reminded Molly about the bottle of whiskey she and Annabelle had finished the night before, celebrating yet another successful hunt. Scratch another thirty Blighted off the face of Ayrth. Only untold hundreds more to go. Perhaps thousands. The thought almost made Molly grin. Or grimace. Even she couldn't say for certain.

Gently, Molly eased herself upright. As always, the weight of her mechanical arm dragged at her. Reluctantly, she moved it, placing it in a position to hold some of its own weight.

She reached up with her real hand to remove the scarf she wore wrapped around her mechanical eye. Blocking its view had been the only way she'd discovered to get a good night's sleep. Until she'd realized there was no way to turn off the lens, she'd had some disturbing dreams about sideways rooms and furniture on ceilings.

With the scarf removed, she blinked her real eye and accustomed herself to the strange double vision she'd been cursed with. With her real eye, she saw as normally as anyone. But her mechanical eye gave her a static, monochromatic view of her surroundings, fed to her mind once a second or so, fading into memory just in time for the next picture. Not for the first time, and not for the last, she cursed the bitch who'd cursed her. Dr. Minati Enerva, formerly of the pirate ship Carrion, recently of the privateer Relentless, currently missing.

The mechanical eye seemed to be working adequately, none the worse for all the sand and ash she and her partners had kicked up during their hunt the previous night. The same held for her mechanical arm. The leg, however, had taken a beating. Scratch marks marred its metallic finish. She'd done her best to wash away the grime, but of course some had worked its way into the joints of her ankle and knee, smearing out into her sheets.

Molly sighed and tore the sheets off the bed, crumpling them into a ball and tossing the ball into the corner. *Best burn them*, she thought. *Don't take any chances.*

There was little chance of infection, though. Any tissue from the Blighted caught in the grooves and joins of her mechanical leg would have been trapped in petroleum lubricant. According to Annabelle, petroleum was known to have some quarantining effect on Blight contamination. Not a perfect quarantine, but better than none.

Still, better safe than Blighted. Molly took out her toolbox and set to work giving her mechanical limbs a proper cleaning. She dismantled the leg, first, by far the easier of the two. The arm would require Annabelle's assistance. Cleaning the pistons and gears had become a series of simple, automatic, unemotional actions, but not at first. At first she had hated every moment. But maintaining that hate had grown too tiresome. Finally resigned, she'd let the hatred dwindle from burning pyres to dim embers.

Not for Enerva. Never her. That hate would roar and crackle for the rest of her life.

Molly quickly finished cleaning out the leg. Not so bad, this time. At first she hadn't bothered with the thick leather chaps most stiltwalker Blighthunters wore, but after having to pick an entire finger out of her ankle joint, Molly had reconsidered. The chaps chafed her real leg, but better a few blisters than deal with the kind of mess the slaughter left behind. Or worse, the risk of infection.

She went to the mirror and cleaned out her eyelens as best she could. In the arid north Afric climate, dust was everywhere. She didn't want to risk not being able to focus her mechanical eye in a fight. Gigi had given her a clear lubricant gel to smear around the edge of her lens. It kept the dust out, but Molly was running out. She'd have to find a substitute.

A rumbling in her stomach reminded her that her real body had needs as well. She dressed in a thin cotton shirt and thick linen riding pants. Leather corset over top. She'd never much been one for hats, but under the Afric sun a person without some kind of head cover was a fool. After some shopping around, she'd found a broad-brimmed hunter's hat that worked quite well. She grabbed her goggles and looped them over her head to hang loosely at her throat. It had taken some doing to find a pair that would fit over her lens.

She strapped her pistol belt on. A lighter, regular six shooter for her real hand, and her Inga Doom Special for her right. The Special was a miracle of gunsmithing. It held six bullets, which alone did not make it remarkable, but Inga had redesigned the body of the pistol, adding a special Blighted-killing touch – a thick hatchet blade, perfect for shattering skulls, the weight ideal to offset the astonishing recoil of Inga's special ammunition.

The belt itself held several armoured pouches and loops for extra ammo. The pouches were armoured, because of what they held. Molly had seen a canister of Inga's Doomfire go up once, accidentally pierced by a stray bullet. It engulfed the poor bastard in flames in seconds and mercifully killed him moments later. Molly had no intention of going that way. She had no intention of going at all.

The Doomthrower pistol Inga had devised held the small canister, which contained enough liquid to kill several Blighted before the canister needed to be refilled. The pistol, which Restless had nicknamed a Doomflinger, went into a special holster at the small of Molly's back. A huge thick knife, very nearly a short sword, went into a sheath under Molly's right arm.

There. Dressed and armed, Molly was ready for breakfast. She covered herself with the flowing linen robe common to the area, donned her helmet, unlocked the door to her room, and set out to find her partners.

At Annabelle's door, Molly took careful note of the location of the hinges. She placed her back to the wall next to the hinges, reached over and knocked three times, loudly and distinctly. Then twice, then three times more. "Annabelle, it's Molly. Open up."

For good measure, Molly ducked down, away from the door.

There was the sound of cursing from behind the thick wood, and a scraping noise as of something heavy being pulled away from the door.

Then a long pause. Finally the door opened an inch, and the twin barrels of a sawed-off shotgun jabbed out from the door, right at head height.

"Show yourself!" came a voice from inside the room.

"Put the gun away first," Molly answered.

"Balls!"

"It's me, Molly. I'm fine."

"Sure you are. Are you sure?"

"I'm sure."

The barrels disappeared into the room, but the door remained ajar. Molly pushed the door open with her mechanical foot, then turned and put her hands in plain view. Then she rose and placed herself in her partner's line of sight.

Redheaded Annabelle had a body that put the word curvaceous to shame, with bright blue eyes and a brilliant smile, when she had occasion to use it. Waking up hungover after a Blighted hunt was not such an occasion.

As Molly stepped into view, she saw Annabelle standing behind the dresser she'd dragged in front of the door, sawed-off shotgun in one hand and a claw hammer in the other. The look in her bloodshot eyes spoke of a deep abiding desire to kill something.

"Why am I conscious?" she asked, her normally pleasant voice harsh.

"Just lucky, I guess," Molly said.

"Says you."

"Better than the alternative."

"Balls it is."

"You told me to wake you at noon."

"Like shit it's noon."

"It's half past, now. Could you put the gun down?"

Annabelle looked at the shotgun in her hand as if surprised to find it there, then put it on the dresser top.

"Jez up?" she asked, tossing the hammer at her tool bag, then winced and immediately regretted it when it landed with a clatter.

"Haven't been by yet. She picked up that young buck."

"Oh yeah. Wonder if he survived."

"Only one way to find out."

"Let me get dressed."

Molly closed the door behind her and waited in the hall, hoping Annabelle's paranoia wouldn't rub off on her too much. Already it had her teeth on edge.

Across the hall and three doors down, a young man with an admirable physique stepped hurriedly and half-dressed into the corridor. Jezebel followed him to lean on the door jamb, watching him make his clumsy departure.

"Well?" Molly asked, despite herself.

"All hat and no cattle," Jez answered, then laughed. Her laugh was enough to shake dust off the rafters, loud and merry.

Jezebel was a tall, robustly built raven-haired ravisher with a beauty mark on her cheek. She fought hard, she drank hard, she played hard. A former pleasure girl who'd managed to be the only survivor of a sudden Blight outbreak in her pleasure house, she'd teamed up with Annabelle to keep up the hunt, the only thing she loved more than lovemaking.

Annabelle burst out from her room, carrying her bags. "Ready?"

"I'll get my stuff," Molly said, heading back to her room. She quickly gathered up her things and rejoined her partners in Jezebel's room.

Jez was unashamedly getting dressed in full view of the open door. "Can you believe he passed out?"

"Oh well," Annabelle said, tinkering with a small device she held.

"On the third go!"

"Oh, *well*," Annabelle answered. "You ready?"

Jezebel pulled on her pants and looped her gun belts over her shoulder. "As I'll ever be."

"What is that, Annabelle?" Molly asked, despite herself.

"It'll blow up real good when it's done," was the only answer Annabelle offered.

The three of them headed downstairs. One of the only two-storey buildings in town, the small inn offered them some safety if not security. After a breakfast that consisted chiefly of a gallon of bitterly strong coffee and sarcasm, the trio paid their bill and stepped out into the blindingly bright afternoon sun and killing heat. Annabelle moaned and pulled her smoke-lensed goggles into place.

"Why are we leaving now?" Molly asked.

"To make the next town by nightfall," Jezebel answered.

"If we'd left earlier we could have made it before the worst heat."

Annabelle waved a hand at the shopkeeps closing their stalls for the afternoon rest. "But then the shops would have been closed. Come on, Diamond's probably chomping at the bit."

The went around to the inn's side yard, which served as a stable of sorts. Several camels, a couple of horses and a donkey had skittishly crowded into the far corner of the yard. Nearer the inn was the source of their distress.

Standing nearly twenty feet tall, the dromedaratron was a huge facsimile of the real thing, though the proportions were slightly off. It was wider, for one thing, and its legs were shorter. But it could move across the shifting sands and rocky plains of north Afric with the ease of its animal inspiration.

"There you are," Diamond said, its ancient voice imitator crackling with static.

Diamond preferred to be referred to in the masculine, and watched as 'he' bent his knees to allow them to pack up and mount.

"Remind me to fix that," Annabelle said.

"I've often reminded you to fix it."

"No, I mean, remind me to remove it."

"You two done flirting? Can we get going?" Jezebel asked, strapping her few belongings into place. "Daylight's wasting."

Molly tossed her bags into one of the trunks bolted onto Diamond's sides, strapped it shut, then climbed aboard. Diamond's hump had seats for four, two facing front and two back. As the newest member of the trio, Molly took one of the rear seats and belted herself in.

The other two took their accustomed places, Annabelle driving and Jezebel on lookout, a shotgun resting across her lap. Diamond's legs groaned as he raised himself up. He took a step that earned groans, whinnies and brays from the other occupants of the stables.

Leaving the inn's yard without knocking over the clay brick fence took longer than leaving the town. Molly watched it disappear into the distance, then the landscape grew unchanging: sand and rocks, rocks and sand.

Her partners, so talkative during breakfast, grew quiet on the road, eyes carefully examining their surroundings for any sign of trouble. Blighted weren't the only predators roaming the land. But they encountered no difficulty, and made it to the next town well before sunset.

Only to find the town deserted.

"Blasted blighted ballsacks!" Annabelle swore quietly through clenched teeth.

"Mount up," Jezebel ordered, reaching for her stilts.

They done this enough times that each knew the role they needed to play. Annabelle fitted Diamond with his guns, making sure each emplacement was properly attached and loaded with enough ammunition. Originally the emplacements had held crank-turned volley guns, but their assistance a couple of crucial battles had earned them a pair of the newfangled belt-fed rapid-fire repeaters. Molly kept watch over their surroundings, guns ready to blast away at any attacker. Jezebel strapped on her stilts and covered them with the thick protective chaps, stood, then took over the watch while Molly doffed her hat and long coat, then mounted her stilts.

They'd been tricky, at first, especially with her mechanical leg, but she'd soon grown so accustomed to the four-foot lengths of brass, gears, and wire that her movements were smooth and graceful. She strapped herself in at her lower thighs, calves and ankles. Over that went her chaps, and over them all went a thick tunic-length leather vest. She moved her Doomflinger from its holster at the small of her back to a special one mounted under her left arm; the flinger didn't require much precision to aim the stream of sticky fire it spread, so her mechanical right arm was good enough to use it. Molly then rolled up the sleeves of her shirt and strapped on her forearm guards, worn over her gloves. Guards firmly in place, even over her mechanical arm, she reached into her kit to add the final element to her armour.

The mask served three functions. The built-in goggles protected her eyes and allowed for a night vision lens to slide into place. The air filtration system covering her mouth and nose kept out the worst of the smell of the Blighted, and kept gore from accidentally flying into a hunter's mouth, risking infection.

Molly lowered her weight onto the stilt's footpads, then stood and took a couple of steps.

Annabelle removed a contraption from Diamond's storage hump. Molly had only seen it once before, in a similar situation, its purpose nearly useless in any other. The metal box was roughly the size of a suitcase and opened in a similar manner. Within the box was a rotating dish that folded out from one half, and a glass viewscreeen in the other half. Annabelle cranked a handle on the side of the box and the dish began to rotate. The viewscreen came to life, glowing a dull green. A bright white line appeared and rotated around the screen.

"Anything?" Jezebel asked. Dwindling sunlight glinted off the lens of her mask, like a predator's eyes in the dusk.

"It's not detecting any movement," Annabelle answered.

"Is it working right?" Molly asked, raising her voice to be heard through the thick mask.

"Take a few steps," Annabelle said, taking no offence.

Molly stepped away from Diamond and her partners. With each step her heart pounded faster.

"Yep, it's working," Annabelle said. Molly looked back to see Annabelle looking at the screen but pointing right at Molly.

"But it's not finding anything?" Jezebel asked.

"Nope."

"Guess we gotta do this the hard way," Jezebel said. "Suit up, Annabelle."

Molly stayed where she was. The sun was low on the horizon, casting long shadows. The last remnants of the day's heat bled off into the air, making any glance westward a shimmering dance of half shadows. Molly's eyelens caught image after image as the sun set.

Then her eyelens caught something else.

One of the shadows was moving. Not the usual shimmer of heat. Slowly, so slowly. Moving.

Molly closed her real eye to make sure she wasn't imagining things. Her world contracted to image after fading image of the street ahead of her. There was a shadow, by a barrel... There. Each image was definitely different from the one before. Not much, but enough.

Molly signalled with a piercing whistle. Behind her, she heard her partners pump their rifles, priming them.

"Where?" Jezebel asked.

Without taking her eyes from the growing threat, Molly twisted her head to keep from shouting. "That barrel there."

"Ain't seeing it."

"The sun's too low. Let me get my other goggles."

Molly had just enough time to yell, "Too late!"

Fast, so fast, faster than any crowd of Blighted had any right to be. Fresh ones, then. That day, maybe sooner. They came out of the west, the setting sun blinding the hunters.

Molly stepped back, not wasting her ammunition. At a range of a hundred paces, the pistols wouldn't do much good. She let her partners with the rifles do the work.

At a range of twenty paces, Molly opened fire. Head after head exploded in a shower of skull and gore. Inga's special explosive ammunition, for which Molly would be forever grateful. She managed to empty both six shooters before the Blighted were upon them.

Molly had enough time to holster her regular pistol and pull out her Doomflinger before she was fighting for her life, surrounded by the horde of silent, deadly Blighted. They clawed at her legs and were answered with Doomfire. Aflame, they grabbed at the stilts, only to receive a hatchet blade to the forehead. Tripping over their fallen comrades, they crawled forward to gnaw on the metal poles with imbecilic hunger.

Relentlessly, they attacked. With equal fervour, they were repelled. Diamond's guns chattered. Annabelle's shotgun boomed. Jezebel's rifle barked. And over and over, Molly's hatchet smashed through skull to scramble brain. The Blighted met their end with absolute silence. No moans, no groans, no screams. Only the crackle of flame, the crack of gunfire, the thudding squelch of hatchet to bone.

Just like that, it ended.

"What the bloody blasted Blight was that?!" Annabelle yelled, reloading her shotgun. For good measure, she added a heartfelt, "Balls!"

Jezebel shook her head. "Never seen 'em so... so..."

"Organized?" Molly offered.

"They came out of the west! Used the sunset to catch us off guard!" Annabelle yelled, checking Diamond's guns for damage.

"And quiet," added Molly. "Why so quiet?"

"Let's go," Diamond said. "We can discuss it somewhere safe."

"Yeah," Jezebel agreed. "Let's go."

Molly stepped toward Diamond, and noticed her right stilt was caught in a pile of bodies. She pulled hard, and it slid reluctantly free with the curious sound of metal scraping on metal. She stared down to find the source of the odd sound.

The footpad of her stilt had managed to go through the head of a Blighted. More precisely, it had gone through a hole blown in the head, probably from one of Annabelle's shotgun slugs.

"Molly, let's go!"

"One second," she answered, leaning down for a closer look. By the flickering light of the burning corpses, she saw a metal apparatus attached to the corpse's head. More accurately, it was attached through the corpse's head. "Something odd here."

"What's odd is you're not getting on Diamond!" Jezebel shouted, her patience at an end. "Now move!"

Molly ignored her. They weren't in any immediate danger. Instead of heading back to the dromedaratron, Molly reached down and pulled the emergency release on her stilts.

The stilts folded over and back on themselves, down until they were only about a foot high.

"Molly!" Annabelle shrieked. "Suicide ain't a hunter's way!"

"Calm yourselves," Molly called back. She carefully examined all the corpses around her. Those that weren't on fire or explosively decapitated all had clear headshots. No risk.

Still, she felt her heart pounding as she crouched down and tugged at the strange apparatus. With a squelch it came loose from the fragmented skull. When Molly straightened up, she noticed the apparatus was still attached to a small leather-bound pack strapped to the corpse's back.

Molly pulled her knife from its sheath and slashed the straps, freeing the pack and the apparatus. Still dripping gore from the metal end, Molly held it up for her partners to see.

"Ever seen one of these?" she asked.

Despite herself, Annabelle craned her neck to get a better look, then slid off of Diamond's chassis to head over. Molly handed it over.

"This was in the head?" Annabelle asked, wiping gore from the metal cables.

"There," Molly pointed to the corpse. Annabelle looked, then stepped over to another corpse. With her booted foot she flipped the decapitated corpse over. There on its back was another of the strange leather packs.

"They've all got them," Jezebel said from her vantage point.

Diamond turned on his eyelamps and scanned the entire unmoving horde. Jezebel was right; every corpse had a pack on their back.

"Curious," Annabelle said.

A sudden clatter from a nearby alley made them turn, guns aimed and expecting anything. But what happened was unexpected. A boy stumbled out of the alley.

"Hold it!" Jezebel ordered, then repeated herself in Afric.

The boy, more a young man, obliged by tripping and falling to the ground. Though he didn't rise, they could clearly see he was breathing.

"A live one," Annabelle said, crossing the distance between them.

"Blasted bloody blight," Jezebel swore, sliding off of Diamond and rushing to the youth's side.

Molly shuffled over, her folded stilts next to useless and more than cumbersome. By the time she reached them, Jezebel had the boy's head cradled in her lap, one hand holding a canteen of water to his parched lips. At first Molly thought the boy cracked, babbling incoherently, until she realized his language was an odd mix of Afric and Aegyptian. She caught the words "two days" and "Atlans". Jezebel asked him something in Afric, too low for Molly to hear.

"East," he said in clear Afric. "Aegyptia."

"Jez," Annabelle said, pointing to the boy's arm.

A festering, pustulant bite mark, half-hidden under his filthy shirt.

His eyes flickered between them. Molly heard him say something about his brother, not understanding the rest, though his meaning was clear enough: his Blighted brother had bitten him.

"He's a child," Molly said.

Jezebel glared at her. "You think I don't know that? He's already dead. His body just don't know it yet."

"No, that's not," Molly began, then stopped. She waved a hand at the carnage all around them. "He's the only one, I mean."

Jezebel asked the boy a question.

"The Atlans took the children," Jezebel answered.

The boy reached up with his injured hand, grabbing Jezebel's vest. "Please."

Jezebel just nodded. Took his hand from her vest, gently. Lay him down.

Stood.

Aimed.

Fired.

The gunshot echoed in the alley.

Wordlessly, Jezebel strode to Diamond and climbed aboard.

"Burn the body," Annabelle said hurriedly to Molly.

Molly pulled out her Doomflinger and squirt a thin stream of flame at the corpse. She paused to unstrap her stilts and extend them to their useful length again, watching the body burn.

"Molly!"

"Yeah," she answered, heading back to Diamond.

As she climbed aboard, Annabelle asked, "East?"

"East," Jezebel answered, her voice thick with emotion. Whether raw anguish or burning rage, through the thick face mask, Molly couldn't tell the difference. In the end, she decided, it didn't matter. There would be killing in their future.

It was almost midnight before they began to discuss how to find their quarry. The Atlans had not come by airship but by pachyderm transport, which would leave tracks they could follow. But 'east' was a big place, and the tracks could lead anywhere. They only had enough supplies for a couple of days. Maybe a week, if they didn't mind hunger and dehydration, and travelled only at night.

Annabelle tinkered with the apparatus they'd taken from the Blighted's corpse. The leather-clad box had yielded a strange mechanism that Annabelle didn't recognize, but Molly had.

"It's like the insides of a wireless communicatron," Molly explained, having seen the inner workings of the one aboard The Furies. "Only much, much smaller."

Annabelle followed the cable from the box to the thin wire leads. "And these went into their heads..."

"Looks like the kind of thing that goes into prosthetics."

Molly knew from her medical examinations with Doc Regan that her back was a mass of scars. Beneath the scars, wires travelled along her spine to her brain, allowing her to control her mechanical limbs almost as well as her own real arm and leg.

"Someone's sending signals direct to their brains," Molly concluded. "Someone's learned to control the Blighted."

Jezebel shook her head. "That ain't possible. Blight destroys the brain's higher processes, everyone knows that."

"They didn't need much by way of higher processes, though," Annabelle countered. "Go here. Wait. Hide. Go slow. Now, attack. I mean, that ain't exactly trigonometry."

"She's right," Molly agreed. "Nothing they did indicated any higher brain function. Just instincts. And we know the Blighted have them."

"Shit," Jezebel said, rubbing her face. She looked to her partners. "So someone was controlling them. Means someone was watching them."

"Stands to reason," Molly nodded.

"Means someone knows we're coming," Annabelle said, picking up on her partner's train of thought.

"Good," Jezebel said fiercely. "Let them know."

"Could mean riding into a trap," Molly said.

"Ain't much of a trap if we know it's there. Let's go."

They rode on, pausing only for the worst of the day's heat. Diamond extended his concealed side panels down to the ground, providing a shaded shelter for his humans to take some rest. When the sun began to sink once again in the west, they grabbed a quick meal.

Jezebel consulted her map as they ate. The Atlans who'd attacked the village hadn't been subtle about their course.

"Ghize," she said. "They're headed for Ghize."

"Always wanted to see the pyramids," Annabelle grinned.

"Long way to go to test their control rigs," Molly said.

"Well, if they didn't work, you wouldn't want to use them in a heavily populated area, would you?" Annabelle explained. "Risk a breakout of the Blight in a city the size of Ghize?"

Molly shook her head. "I'm pretty sure they don't care all that much about the population."

"Why'd they take the kids, though?" Jezebel asked no one in particular.

"Experiments," Molly answered.

"C'mon, Diamond, move it," Annabelle snapped.

Diamond picked up the pace.

It took four days and nights of hard travel before they got to Ghize. With the war settling down in the distant West, life had returned to pretty much normal. Less people, it was true – many young men and women had joined The Revolution, leaving children and older adults behind to keep the home life running. Shops were open, selling what little of the crop remained from the thin harvest of the summer just past. A hungry winter awaited many people, unless The Revolution could do something about re-establishing trade routes and supply lines.

One of the many things they weren't thinking about, in Molly's opinion. Establishing supply lines and trade routes, electing governmental officials, organizing a constabulary, none of it had been a priority for the leaders of The Revolution. Sometimes it seemed to her that they expected it all to fall into place by itself, once the war was over and the world was freed of Atlan tyranny. Until then, though, people needed to eat. Law needed to be maintained.

Molly sighed and stretched her aching backside once she'd slid off of Diamond. They'd found an inn with three storeys and bought out the occupants of the top-most level.

"Now what?" she asked.

"A meal," Jezebel said. "Then we start asking around."

A quick meal consisted of some roasted meat Molly thought might be goat and a bowl of rice, washed down with bitterly strong coffee. Then they headed out into the crowded city streets.

As far as cities went, Ghize was nothing more than a small town with delusions of grandeur, but it had many universities specializing in scientific studies, especially the advancement of medicine. The tracks they'd followed across the hills and plains of Afric had disappeared in the desert to the West of Ghize, but between Jezebel's knowledge of the local dialects and Annabelle's connections in the black market for mechanical parts, they managed to track down a group of Atlan scientists who spoke Aegyptian and had recently purchased the components needed to construct the control rigs in the backpacks.

"That guy with the eyelens said one of the bastards works out of that shop," Annabelle said, hooking a thumb over one shoulder.

The trio were located a block away, sipping coffee and eating honeyed dates, sitting on a restaurant's patio. Jezebel turned her head to look at the shop in question. Molly glanced over Annabelle's shoulder.

The shop specialized in gears. Big gears, small gears, everything from the tiniest pocket watch gear to huge airship gears.

"Let's go," Jezebel said.

Molly stood and patted her pockets, checking her hidden holsters. Annabelle tossed another couple of dates into her mouth, spitting out the pits with expert ease. Jezebel dropped a few coins on the table. As one, they left the restaurant.

"Do we have any kind of plan?" Molly asked.

"I figure we beat the information out of him," Jezebel said.

"We could start with asking him some questions, first."

"You're no fun at all, you know that?"

The interior of the shop was dark compared to the daylight brilliance outside. The bead curtain in the door rattled as they entered, and a small, dark man stepped out from a display case loaded with gears.

"Welcome to Antonio's Gear Emporium," he said in flawless Aegyptian.

"You Antonio?" Jezebel asked in Atlan.

"I have that honour, yes," he said. Though dressed as a local, it was clear from his features that he wasn't Aegyptian.

"Etruscan?" Jezebel asked, switching to that language.

Antonio beamed and clapped his hands together in delight. His response was too rapid for the smattering of Etruscan at Molly's command.

Jezebel dazzled him with her smile, then answered in Etruscan, pointing at Annabelle and Molly.

"Of course, of course," Antonio replied, heading behind the counter than ran the length of the shop. "Atlan is fine. How can I be of service?"

"Well, we hear you're the man to talk to about certain kinds of devices," Jezebel answered.

"If your device needs gears, you have heard correctly," he smiled.

"I'm not the expert," Jezebel answered, waving Annabelle forward. Annabelle handed Antonio the control rig.

"Now, what do you think of that?" Jezebel asked.

Molly had been watching Antonio's reaction to the rig. He'd glanced at it, and though he tried to hide it, recognition flashed in his eyes. Her eyelens had caught it clear enough. Then his eyes flicked from Jezebel to Annabelle to Molly, cataloguing, recognizing, evaluating.

Then he acted.

Grabbing foot-wide thin metal gears in either hand, he swung them at Jezebel with the moves of a man practised at knife-fighting. Jezebel, however, had plenty of practice dodging such deadly attacks, and stepped back out of range. She raised a fist and stepped into her blow, smashing his nose with sickening crunch and a splatter of blood.

"By doze!" he shrieked, throwing the gears at them.

Molly had her revolver out by then, pointed directly at his head. Annabelle pulled a thick wrench from somewhere and held it menacingly.

Jezebel vaulted over the counter. "Where are the children?!"

Antonio scattered a pile of coin-sized gears at her face, then reached under the counter and pulled a switch. A trapdoor immediately opened at his feet and he jumped through.

"Come on!" Jezebel yelled, jumping after him.

"We have a choice?" Annabelle muttered, then vaulted the counter and followed her partner.

"Should've had a plan," Molly said to herself. She holstered her gun before following after them.

The trapdoor hid a slide chute. Below her in the darkness, Molly could hear the passage of her partners and presumably, their quarry. Then suddenly a yelp from Annabelle.

Followed quickly by Molly feeling the chute end under her as she slid out into the empty darkness. She managed to land on her feet with a splash and a stench.

"Why is it always sewers?" Annabelle said.

Molly helped her stand, then donned her goggles. Ahead of them, they heard the sound of footsteps splashing away. A turn of the dials on the goggles let Molly see the round sewer tunnel disappearing into the distance.

"Not always," Jezebel said, pulling on her goggles. "There was that abattoir that one time."

"Oh yeah. Much better."

Jezebel pulled out her hunting knives from their sheaths in her boots. Annabelle had her hammer and wrench at the ready. Molly pulled out her revolver, but thought better of it in the tight confines. She reholstered it and pulled out the Special.

Following the echoes of splashing footsteps, they made their way forward as rapidly as they dared, ready for anything. When they came to a junction of several tunnels, they held their breath and Jezebel listened. Then she picked a tunnel and led them after their quarry.

The tunnel branched again, and then once more. Each time they waited in absolute silence as Jezebel listened. Each time, she chose the right path, if the echoes of splashes were any sign.

Soon they reached a door set in the side of the tunnel.

"Who puts a door in a sewer?" Annabelle whispered.

"Crazy people," Jezebel answered. She reached out and grasped the handle. "Locked. You got your opener?"

Annabelle grinned and pulled a gadget from her satchel. It was quite small, but thanks to her goggles Molly saw it clear enough. A wooden box with brass fittings, it had several prongs, all projecting from the same face. Annabelle set it close to the door's lock, then turned a small crank on the top of the device.

The prongs leapt into action, all twirling and whirling their way into the keyhole. Annabelle's hand shook as the opener worked at the lock. Then with a click, the opener stopped.

Jezebel took the opener from Annabelle with one hand and rested the other hand on the door's handle. Then she whispered, "One... two... three!" and yanked open the door.

Molly led the way, the Special out and ready. Jezebel followed, with Annabelle behind to extricate the opener from the lock.

The stairwell behind the door led down. A glance at the steps revealed wet footprints. Molly nodded at Jezebel, then headed down the stairs.

Gradually they became aware of a light at the bottom of the stairs, and voices raised in argument. A woman, from the sounds of it, was berating Antonio.

"You idiot!" she shrieked in Atlan. "Why'd you lead them here?!"

Molly knew that voice. But it was impossible. She hurried down the stairs as quickly as stealth would allow. At the bottom, she paused and bent low, trying to see into the chamber beyond, before coming into view herself. She could see nothing but a flagstone floor.

Jezebel came up behind her. "What's your friend the Pirate Queen like to say? 'Go time'?"

"Yes," Molly whispered. She took a deep breath and rushed down the final few steps.

And entered a nightmare.

Dozens, perhaps hundreds, of Blighted stood in rows and rows and rows, all at rigid attention, all dressed in tight-fitting leather boots, pants and jackets. Wires streamed from their heads to control rigs worn on their backs.

But that wasn't the most nightmarish thing about the chamber she found herself in. No, that honour was reserved for the woman slapping Antonio's face.

Dr. Enerva.

"You," Molly gasped.

Enerva turned. "You?! How?"

Molly fired her gun at Enerva, who had the presence of mind to pull Antonio into the path of the bullet. He died instantly, shot through the spine. Enerva hid behind the corpse as Molly emptied her gun.

With the sound of the first click of Molly's pistol, Enerva lifted the corpse and threw it at her attackers. Jezebel ducked, but Molly was caught off guard at Enerva's speed and strength.

Enerva dived for a control panel. Metallic hands danced over the controls, and she spoke a single word into a microphone. "Attack!"

A dozen Blighted immediately sprang to life, rushing at Molly and her partners with silent, deadly menace. Molly pulled her spare revolver out and emptied it, bringing down six Blighted with six bullets. Six more took their place. They met the business end of Molly's hatchet, or Jezebel's heavy knives, or Annabelle's hammer and wrench.

Though her lungs burned for more air, Molly made a special effort to keep her mouth closed. A stray piece of spattered gore landing in her mouth would mean a nightmare come true, her death by Blight.

"Cover me!" Jezebel yelled. Molly stepped to the right, closer to Annabelle, the two of them providing a living shield against their unliving attackers. She felt Jezebel tug at her holstered revolver, then pick at the ammunition belt. Seconds later, Jezebel fired round after round into the heads of their attackers.

"Reload!" Annabelle yelled. Jezebel ducked behind them once more, and Molly felt the picking of bullets from her belt.

"This will get us nowhere! Get that bitch! She's controlling them!" Molly yelled.

Jezebel fired all six shots at Dr. Enerva, who ducked behind the control panel. The panel sparked and several of the Blighted stopped attacking.

"Shoot out the panel!" Molly and Annabelle yelled together.

"I know, I know, I'm not blind!"

But Enerva returned from her hiding place with a gun of her own, one of the new Atlan eight-in-the-clip pistols, firing again and again at the trio. Annabelle took one in the shoulder and a ricochet grazed Jezebel's cheek, but Molly blocked her torso and head with her mechanical arm and survived the attack unscathed. Then she put all her weight onto her mechanical leg, crouched low, and leapt at the doctor.

The force of her leap sent her flying over the heads of the attacking Blighted. Some of them turned to follow her, only to be blocked by other Blighted heading for Molly's partners.

Molly landed roughly, stumbling to a knee in front of Enerva. But she quickly recovered and launched herself at her enemy.

Enerva raised her hands to stop Molly, who realized that both of Enerva's hands were now mechanical. Molly only remembered removing one of the doctor's arms, not both, but decided she didn't care.

"I'll kill you for what you've done!" Molly screamed, sending punch after punch at her foe.

Enerva blocked Molly's blows with ease. "Kill me?! You should thank me! After all, I have you to thank for my own improvements!"

"Improvements?!" Molly shrieked, grabbing Enerva by the arms and tossing her against the control panel. More Blighted suddenly ceased their attacks.

The sleeves of Enerva's shirt had torn in Molly's hands, revealing two fully mechanical arms.

"Yes, improvements," Enerva said, backing away slowly from Molly. "The knowledge I gained from your experiments allowed me the final pieces I needed to perfect my methods of replacement. Your operation made me famous! Gained me the admiration of many in Atlan Command. Such that they chose to place this, one of their most important facilities, under my command!"

Molly felt like vomiting. Instead, she asked, "You did that to yourself?"

"Of course! I would trust no other with such an important task."

"Molly!" Jezebel yelled over the sound of skulls being smashed in. "Ammo!"

Molly stripped her ammunition belt off and threw it to Jezebel, then turned back to Enerva.

"You're a dead woman," Molly promised.

"So were you, once. You died on the operating table. But I brought you back, you ungrateful bitch!" With that she dove behind the control panel again.

Molly raced after her, grabbing her by the shoulder and hauling her back to punch her in the face with her mechanical arm. Enerva's cheekbone and nose shattered, spraying blood everywhere.

"I'll kill you! KILL YOU!" Molly shrieked.

Enerva grabbed her mechanical arm and swung Molly around, slamming her into the stone wall.

"How?" Enerva taunted. "You are inferior to me in every way!"

With a howl of rage, Molly swept her mechanical leg at Enerva's, but instead of the sickening crunch of bones breaking, there was a horrifying clang of metal on metal. Enerva fell to the ground. Molly jumped on top of her, then slammed her Special into Enerva's shoulder. No spurt of blood, but a shower of sparks. Again and again, Molly chopped.

One arm, then another, came loose as Enerva shrieked and screamed and tried to buck Molly off. Molly stopped the bucking with two well-placed chops at Enerva's mechanical knees.

When the dismemberment was complete, Molly used her mechanical arm to lift her foe to glare at her eye to eye.

"Still think I'm inferior?" Molly taunted, then tossed Enerva into the waiting mass of unmoving Blighted.

Jezebel and Annabelle were standing at the centre of a mountain of dead Blighted.

"What are you doing?" Jezebel asked.

Molly went to the microphone and said one word:

"Eat."

The activated Blighted turned as one and attacked the squirming torso of their creator. Enerva screamed and screamed. When the screaming stopped, the only sound was the tearing of flesh and the slobbered chewing of the Blighted.

Annabelle and Jezebel stared at Molly with something like true horror on their faces. Jezebel said, "Remind me not to get her angry."

"Yeah," Annabelle agreed. "So what are we going to do with the rest of these? We're out of ammo and my arm's getting tired from smashing in skulls."

Molly grinned. "You still have that gadget that'll blow up real good?"

Annabelle's grin matched her own.

"What about the kids?" Jezebel asked. "They're still missing."

They halted the feasting Blighted mid-meal, then searched the chamber, finding notebooks with references to other facilities, including one where the children had been taken.

"We take these other places out, we could do some real good," Annabelle said.

"Let's go be good guys, then," Jezebel grinned. "You ready?"

"Almost," Annabelle said, putting the finishing touches on the device in her hands. She'd attached it to Molly's special belt, the one filled with Doomflinger cartridges. One final, careful twist of her screwdriver and she said, "Done."

"Molly, you do the honours," Jezebel said, heading toward a second exit they'd found.

Annabelle and Molly followed her. At the door, Molly took the Doomflinger belt from Annabelle, set the device to blow up, and tossed it into the chamber, as far into the mass of Blighted as she could. Then the trio ran for their lives.

Annabelle was right. Her device did blow up real good. The explosion shook the entire neighbourhood, and the blast wave of Doomfire washed up the chute to the gear shop, destroying it in a blaze that luckily didn't spread to the nearby buildings.

Molly, Jezebel, and Annabelle watched it burn. Flames reflected in Molly's eyelens.

"It's over," she whispered.

Annabelle turned to her. "You alright?"

Molly felt a tear slide down her left cheek. "Right now, not really. But I'm starting to think, one day, I might be." She turned to her partners. "I need a drink."

"I need a shower," Annabelle said.

Jezebel laughed. "I need a man."

"Let's go find all three," Molly grinned.

Chapter Nineteen

The Big Man's Big Secret

What can I say? She's awesome and kind of scary. That's Molly.

Okay, so, back to me. I'd love to tell you about all the amazing, fascinating details of life in a prison mine, but there aren't any. I spent about a week scooping rocks into buckets, and carrying the buckets to a bunch of people sitting around sorting the rocks, looking for anything that we could use, and more importantly, any sign of atlantium. When I wasn't hauling buckets of rocks, I was tending to my blistered hands and aching feet, eating flavourless slop, or sleeping.

Actually, the one good thing I can tell you about was the hot springs. At some point someone had found a cave with natural hot springs, and let me tell you, after a day in the mines, a hour-long soak in a giant pool worked miracles. I could have sworn my blisters healed faster, thanks to those soaks. They really left me feeling great. After a long hard hot day of shovelling coal into the boilers in the engine room of The Furies, all I wanted to do was crawl into my bedroll and die. But after a long hard hot day of hauling buckets of rocks to and fro through cramped mine shafts followed by a hot soak in the mineral springs, I felt like I could go back for another shift. Helping out with the supper chores was absolutely no problem. That said, it wasn't all hugs and puppies. On my fifth day as a hauler, there was a tremendous roar. The ground shook, throwing us to our hands and knees. Then everybody but me grabbed their buckets and ran, back out of our mine shaft.

"Dump it and come on!" a guy named Bill yelled as he ran past.

"I just filled these," I muttered, but I dumped the rocks and ran.

The mine shafts all branched off from a central cave. When I got there, people were pouring in from every shaft but one. Smoke billowed from that shaft, and I smelled something I knew wasn't barbecue pork.

"Get the line going!" Rue ordered, but people were already lining up down the shaft that led back to the hot springs. Another, more cautious line started down the smoky shaft.

Suddenly someone stumbled out of the smoke. Another, and another. All smudged with dirt and charred by fire. A couple stumbled out, still aflame. They all found themselves doused with water from the springs.

Slowly we put out the fire. Black smoke faded to grey steam. Five inmates died, their bodies so badly charred they were barely recognizable.

Quill questioned a survivor. "What happened?"

"Gas pocket," the woman, Agrippa, coughed. She'd gotten away pretty lightly. She still had most of her black curly hair. "I heard them break through, a big cave from the sound of it. Someone ordered the candles put out, but..."

"Too late," Rue said. She glared angrily at Quill and strode off.

Quill turned to a gang of big, burly miners. "Block it off. Seal it."

Two days later Agrippa and the rest of the survivors were well enough to go back into the mines. Quill offered them a chance at lighter duties, but they shrugged it off.

You probably want to know about what happened to the bodies of the five miners killed in the explosion. Or, maybe you don't. Well, let's just say that with no other resources heading our way, we had to make use of everything we could. Everyone had a part to play in the community.

Even after death.

No we didn't eat them! Geez!

Mother dismembered them, flayed them, distilled them, decanted them. Took every useful piece, every scrap of skin or sinew or bone, every fluid, every minute mineral she could scrounge. The bits that were left over went into the fire. Fat became soap and candles. Bones became tools. Ligaments were twined into ropes. Everything had a use.

I never said it was pleasant. I was pretty horrified for a couple of days after that. Sometimes I still have nightmares about Mother coming for me. But, obviously, I survived the Pit. So anyway.

A couple of days later, I had a chance to talk with Quill. "Have you thought about that offer?"

He was sitting on the ground near the hot springs, staring at a small piece of atlantium, and he looked up at me as I came closer.

"I have," he answered, standing. He tossed the atlantium in the air, then caught it.

"And?"

"Come with me," he said. Without another word, he led me back to the central cave.

He stood at the centre of the cave. "That way," he said, pointing out a tunnel I never saw anyone going down.

"What's there?" I said, following him.

"What do you think?"

"I figured it was a vein that tapped out."

"Hmm." It was almost a chuckle.

He led the way, falling into silent thought. In the dim light I could see him tossing the piece of atlantium and catching it. The way twisted and turned, gradually getting darker and darker. Eventually I only had the flicker of that piece of atlantium to guide my way.

Suddenly, he stopped. I nearly walked into him. In the gloom I saw him raise a finger for me to wait there. Then he took a few steps forward and tossed the atlantium away into the dark. It clattered and rattled against the tunnel's stone walls.

He waited for maybe five, six heartbeats, then said, clearly, "Rainbow."

The word echoed down the tunnel, ringing in the silence. Quill waved me forward, and led me down the tunnel.

Soon it opened into an antechamber of sorts. Two massive men stood there, barring our way into a larger cavern.

"You want some light, Mr. Quill?" one of them asked in a whisper.

"Please," Quill answered, whispering himself.

There was a rasp of flint on steel and a spark lit the room like a flash from a camera. I closed my eyes, wincing at the loss of my night vision. But it soon didn't matter, because one of the giants had lit a bowl-candle. Greasy smoke filled the air of the small cave, shadows dancing on the walls.

The guards were, like I said, huge. But huge in a way that just made no sense. I mean, these guys had to be eight feet tall, but not like they'd been born with gigantism or anything like that. Perfectly normal-looking, heavily muscled, giants. One was Afric, the other blond, probably Norsican. Both had long beards and wild hair. Both held long blades of some dark metal I figured was iron, pulled straight from the ground and beaten into crude swords.

Quill took the bowl. "We'll get you out of here, soon. I promise."

"That'd be nice, Mr. Quill."

"Yes, thanks."

When they smiled down at him, I saw their bright white teeth. Their incisors were very long. I hoped it was a trick of the light. I mean, if these two giants wanted to kill us and eat us there and then, it's not like Quill and I could have done anything to stop them. I was very aware of the fact that not everyone had been sentenced to the Pit for teaching philosophy.

But they let us pass without any cannibal attacks, and we stepped into the larger chamber. I wish I could tell you what it looked like but I honestly don't remember anything about the cave. All I remember is what was in that cave.

An enormous lump of atlantium, maybe the size of my ship. No, enormous isn't big enough. Humungoid? Giantastic? My brain couldn't begin to process it.

"What... what...?" I muttered.

"Yes. Take a moment. I knew you'd see it immediately."

"This... this is... I mean, this would..."

"Yes, exactly. This much atlantium will utterly destroy Atlan. Shatter its economy. Bring down merchant houses. Businesses that have endured centuries will be ruined overnight."

"But... I mean..." Then it hit me, and I turned to glare at him. "Waitaminute. How'd you know what I was thinking?!"

Quill smiled gently. "It took me a while, believe me. Your... unique protections provided me quite an interesting conundrum, for a while. Very exciting. Thank you. And thank your Vampyri friend, when you next meet."

"You can read minds?"

"A skill I acquired when studying with the ghostwalkers of the Thousand Tribes. It's not actually that hard, once you know the trick of it. And supplied with a steady source of this," he said, sweeping his hand at the mountain of atlantium. "Atlantium, it seems, changes everything."

"Like, mutation? Those guards?"

"Something like that. With sufficient exposure, anything is possible. Of course, no one knew that, since no one ever had access to so much at once."

"So why are you all still down here? Bribe the guards and leave!"

Quill shook his head. "No, I have something much better in mind."

"What?"

"Your offer intrigued me," he said, not answering. "No one has tried that, before. So of course I reached out with my mind to determine the truth. Imagine my surprise when I couldn't simply pluck the information from your mind!"

"Yeah, imagine."

"So I tried when you were asleep. No luck. Still, there's no lock a determined man can't eventually pick, my uncle used to say."

"So you know I wasn't lying. You've been offered full pardons if you wreak havoc in Neptopolis. Well, anywhere in Atlan, really, but I was thinking Neptopolis would be the best place."

"I quite agree."

"So what do you have in mind?"

"Can't you guess?"

I looked at him, trying to tell if he was reading my mind, trying to figure out what he had planned. "With this much atlantium... why aren't we eating better? No, the guards would just raise the prices if we started producing more, right? Yeah. So we eat slop, paying out tiny pieces at a time. So why mine at all? Unless... The fire. You were looking for something. And why were there so few in that branch? Or my tunnel? A dozen here, a dozen there, but there are hundreds of us down here. Where does everyone else go?"

Quill was grinning. "You're nearly there."

"They're digging, obviously. Everybody digs, down here." I rubbed my chin, thinking hard. "You barely reacted to my offering you amnesty if you organized a prison break. Which means... You're already planning one, aren't you? You thought my offer was a trap, that I was a spy planted in here to find out your plans. So you didn't react. And then you read my mind, only to find out my offer is legitimate." I snapped my fingers. "You're digging an escape tunnel."

"Much better than that, actually," Quill said, heading back the way we came. I followed him.

"At first, we thought to dig our way free, each of us carrying as much atlantium as we could carry," he said, nodding his thanks and passing the candle bowl back to the giants in the antechamber. "But to what end? All of us are branded criminals. When news of the breakout reached the authorities, we'd be hunted down and killed. Or worse. So gradually we came to the conclusion that the only way for us to be truly free would be to destroy Atlan."

He stopped talking as we made our way back up the sloping tunnels. Eventually we were back in the central cave, and he led the way into yet another tunnel. For the first fifty feet or so, it twisted and turned like any other tunnel, following the veins of precious ore. But then it straightened out, unnaturally straight.

Quill crouched down and lit a candle bowl. In the flickering candlelight I could see the tunnel disappeared into the distance, straight as a shot.

"Where does it lead?"

"To freedom, and victory, Sunset Val," he said.

Chapter Twenty

The Big Man's Big Plan

Yeah, I figured he'd gotten that out of my mind, too.

"Okay, and less metaphorically, where does it lead?"

He had the good grace to look annoyed that I didn't react to his big reveal that he knew my name. "Neptopolis," he said with a shrug.

"Perfect, let's go," I said.

"It's much too far," he said. "A journey of days, by foot."

"Better get started, then."

"Soon, Sunset Val. Or should we continue the charade?"

"Call me whatever you like, but let's get this escape on the road. I've had about all the greasy mystery stew I ever want. And sleeping on an actual bed sounds like perfection to me right now."

"You've been here just over a week. There are inmates who have been here for years. Can you imagine their impatience? And yet, they wait."

"Yeah, patience and me, not such a great team."

"Nevertheless. There is a plan, Sunset Val. And we will leave soon enough."

I could see he was enjoying being all cryptic, but I could be just as stubborn. "When?"

"A few days."

"Then get all the other mining teams off their fake jobs and onto this real one. Speed it up! Because the Revolution isn't going to wait all year. They've probably already invaded Hispania. And people are going to die."

"People die, in war," Quill said. His voice was cold, but his eyes were sad. "It is an inevitable truth. My plan calls for Neptopolitans to die. Many, many Neptopolitans. Most of them guiltless of any crime but greed and ignorance. My plan will shatter the empire with a single act of treason so monumental that it will live forever in infamy. So you'll pardon me if I refuse to submit to impatience and haste in order to save a few lives, when my plan calls for the deaths of many more."

Well, he had a point. And I couldn't really argue with it. "How will they die?"

My question surprised him into actually answering. "In fire, and terror."

I thought about it. "An explosion?"

"Yes."

"An explosion that size... would need... Gas? The gas from that cave?"

He just nodded. I just waited.

"At the end of this tunnel is a chamber, carved from the rock beneath the island of Neptopolis. Some of the prisoners in this cave know things about demolitions. Imprisoning entire crews of airship pirates includes such crewmembers as aeriologists and sailmakers, who know things about the careful containment, storage and relocation of gases, and navigators, who have refined their sense of direction. And anyone who spends any time down here knows all about digging.

"So we keep the guards happy with our deliveries of atlantium, taken from the great nugget in the chamber I showed you. Just enough to buy enough food to live. And instead of mining for atlantium, we dig this tunnel. A straight line for Neptopolis. And under Neptopolis, we've carved out our revenge. In a few days, we'll collapse this tunnel, ignite the gas stored in that distant chamber, and destroy the island of Neptopolis."

"Why collapse the tunnel?"

"To enclose the explosion. I'm informed by reliable experts it's the only way. Once the tunnel is collapsed, we climb through the rubble and begin our rampage of revenge. And once freed of here, and Neptopolis lies in ruin, we'll make our way to Atlanopolis, the nearest city. One by one, the cities of Atlan will feel our fury."

Well, you really can't blame him for aiming big. And, you know, I could get behind the alliteration.

We made our way back to the central cave. When we got there, Quill said, "Of course I accept your offer. I'll announce it tomorrow night. The resupply team will be back from the bomb chamber by then. I'm expecting them to report the completion of our preparations."

"And then it's go time."

"Er, yes. As you say."

But the resupply team didn't arrive the next day, or the day after that. People got nervous, and tempers flared. There were more fights in those two days than in the whole week previous.

To keep people's minds off the missing resupply team, Quill got us breaking up the giant nugget into pieces small enough to carry, and reasonable enough to sell. No sense walking into a pawn shop with a lump of atlantium the size of my head, no shopkeep could afford to buy it. But a piece the size of my thumbnail? Not unreasonable.

Word came down from the Welcomer that the guards seemed more and more on edge. Maybe the war wasn't going well. Maybe they found the real Victory Pandora's body. Maybe a lot of things.

Then the day came when the resupply team finally arrived.

"Tunnel collapsed," one explained. "Took us two days to dig through."

"We can't risk another collapse," Fountainhead said. "Let's do this."

Everyone turned to Quill. The former professor licked his lips. "I agree. It's time. Time for our revenge. Time for our freedom. Time to destroy Atlan!"

People cheered and howled and hooted and pumped their fists in the air and stamped their feet on the ground. Quill and Fountainhead started issuing orders, and people scrambled to get it all going, gathering up as much as they could carry, stuffing tools and weapons into sacks made from the shirts of dead prisoners, held together with twine made of their skin, their sinews, their gut. In this prison break, we would carry our dead with us, and bring their deaths to the doorsteps of the corrupt regime that killed them.

Yeah, symbolic and all that. But also, we didn't have anything else to carry our stuff in.

You know, I guess I paid attention in economics class, because it occurred to me then, watching these prisoners going on about what they were going to buy with their new fortunes in atlantium, that atlantium was only precious because it was rare. This much atlantium flooding the market would make it worthless, which was pretty much Quill's plan. Destroy the economy, he'd said. But the prisoners of the Pit didn't care about that. They just wanted to buy real food. Nice clothes. Big airships. Homes. It was kind of funny, all these murderers and traitors and pirates, basically wanting what any normal person wants.

No, I didn't say anything about how they wouldn't be able to buy anything with their worthless atlantium. At that point, I wanted out of the Pit. I wanted the sky above me and the world far, far beneath me. I wanted to see my friends again.

Speaking of which, I just bet you're wondering what happened with The Furies.

Chapter Twenty One

I, Automaton

From the personal journals of Guinevere Tallyho, Acting Captain of The Furies

The fourteenth day of the ninth month of 6898, Hindystani Sea.

The day began sunny and cool, slight southerly wind, dark clouds on the horizon promising rain. Bad season for it. Gwenny worried of a storm, but we've had relatively clear sailing thus far.

Gwen gave me command earlier this week and thus far our arrangement of passing the captaincy back and forth has had no ill effects amongst the crew. But then, it had worked well for us aboard the Sisters and we'd seen no reason to change our well-established habits simply because we now commanded the flagship of the armada. At the Admiral's orders, no less. Pirate Queen, wot?

I made my rounds of The Furies, seeing to the crew, passing a polite word here and there. They all perform their tasks admirably, but it seems to me that some of the wind had been taken from their sails. So many of their former messmates were gone, off on their own adventures. Or else lost to the Last Great Adventure, the Answer to the Great Mystery. Those absences stung most keenly.

Sunset Val, Serena Heartlace, Molly Wolfwood, Inga Bludsdottar, Tring and her Open Hands, the pixies Moonchance, Apple and Wren. The heart of the crew, to hear young Restless speak of it. A day, indeed an hour, doesn't pass without her wondering aloud at the fate of her friends. Gwen finally had to order Restless to stop mentioning them in her presence. I've always had more patience than my dear twin.

I had returned to the officer's mess to examine our charts once again when a sharp knock at the open door made me look up. Gigi Lyon stood there, smudges of oil and grease on her coveralls, a wrench in one hand. I assumed she'd used the tool to announce her presence.

"Gigi," I smiled. "What is it?"

"She's ready," Gigi grinned, sharp fangs glistening with barely restrained joy.

"Excellent," I answered, standing and following her.

The Furies is most likely not the sole airship with a fully functioning laboratory aboard, but certainly none has a more eclectic assemblage of scientific equipment. Filled to the brim, you might say. Stem to stern, floor to ceiling, a veritable hoard of devices small and large, powerful and playful. We had to tread a careful path to the operating theatre, which consists of a tilting table upon which lay a mechanical marvel.

A trio of automaidons surrounded the figure laying prone upon the table. Well, former automaidons. Certainly that had been their original form. Since their liberation however, they have cast off the shackles of their oppressors and reforged themselves into something else. Alumina was their leader, or at least, the one who most often voiced their opinions and organized their actions. In feature and form she most resembled their patient.

Jolly, her near-constant companion, had been originally modified to serve certain reprobate desires of her former owner, and she still bore the womanly, rounded curves he had preferred. Unlike the others, she had received directivation that included a proclivity toward wearing clothing, and had never chosen to have that corrected or removed. How odd and wonderful it might be to have unwanted portions of one's personality simply erased! The outfit Jolly wore today was a pragmatic assemblage of blouse, brocaded corset, trews and knee-high boots. A curly blonde wig sat prettily atop her head. Indeed, were it not for her metallic 'skin', Jolly would easily pass for a human woman. Well, in a poor light, perhaps.

The last member of the trio was the least human-looking. Eleven, she was called. Her face consists of two eyelenses, beneath which dwells a speaker box. She had two deep gouges in the metal plate above the eyelenses, resembling the numeral from which I gathered she derived her name. Her arms and legs were spindly thin appendages with protruding gears and exposed cables, her hands three-fingered, while her torso most resembled a tin can, in which panels have been cut to reveal her spinning directivation tapes. She rarely spoke.

I glanced down at their patient. Argenta had been very nearly destroyed in battle, but careful weeks of repairs, replacements and modifications had left her better than ever. Indeed, Alumina said as much to me.

"Better how?" I asked.

"Let me," Gigi said, eager to explain. But her explanation rapidly turned utterly incomprehensible to me. She seemed very excited about it all, though, so I didn't interrupt. She pointed out alterations and improvements made to Argenta's chassis. Her limbs had nearly flawless articulation, that much I did manage to understand. Plus something about the internal workings of Argenta's self-directivation doodads and geegaws. It was all very technical and impressive.

"Any questions?" Gigi asked, eventually.

"No, you've been quite thorough, my very dear," I answered. "Now then, might we activate her?"

"Gigi?" Alumina asked, indicating with a carefully poised hand that our engineer might have the honour.

"No, you go ahead," Gigi said.

Alumina nodded and turned to her patient. With a careful flick of a hidden switch, Argenta's eyelenses flickered to yellow life.

"Captain Val!" were the first words she spoke as she struggled to sit up. Jolly and Eleven held her down.

"Easy, sister," Alumina said. "Let your chronometer catch up."

Argenta's eyes flickered. "Twenty six days have passed."

"Yes."

"I was deactivated during that time."

"Yes."

"I assume I was damaged in some way."

"Yes."

"You've been repaired," Gigi said.

"Welcome back," I said.

"Captain Tallyho," Argenta answered as she sat up. "Welcome aboard The Furies."

"Some things have changed during your deactivation." Gigi explained the entire story of Val's plan for the Pit, Serena's generalship, Tring and Molly's departures, our current mission. It took some telling, and all the while Argenta tested the limits of her new limbs and chassis. Gigi ended her tale with the actions of Alumina, Jolly and Eleven.

Argenta faced them. "Thank you for your efforts on my behalf."

"Oh, any time, dear," Jolly said with a musical laugh. "Automatons have to stick together."

"Indeed," Alumina agreed. Then she turned to me. "Captain, our work here is done. Until we are able to arrange passage back to the Union of Automatons, might we offer you our services to pay our way?"

"Absolutely," I agreed. She offered me her hand, an oddly human gesture I thought, and we shook on it. Her grip was firm but not painful, though I was keenly aware she could crush my hand to pulp if she so chose.

As I turned to leave the laboratory, Gigi pulled me aside. "A minute, Captain?"

"Of course."

We waited until the automatons had left. Gigi said, "I had an idea."

"Do tell."

With that she led me through the maze to a workbench covered in machine parts.

"Since we've been on this mission I've been studying everything I can find about the photonic inversion cells that provide the energy for the Forgotten Frigate."

"Yes?"

"You see, the way photonic inversion works is..." and she launched into a highly technical explanation. I understood 'solar radiation' and 'converted to electricity' and that was about it.

"Yes, yes, Gigi. But how does that help our mission?"

"Well, by understanding what it does, I was able to figure out how they were made. Now, certain crucial components were made of atlantium, of course, but I believe they also had to have used aether in the construction."

"I don't follow you."

"Between the outer glass layer and the inner photonic receptors is not a vacuum as was reported in all the papers published at the time. Instead, a minute amount of aether was introduced into the cell. That's the only way the solar radiation would react with the inversion cells."

"But aether is nearly impossible to extract from the cosmos. Or so we've been led to believe."

Gigi shrugged. "Nearly impossible just means expensive. With enough money you can turn a pound of gold into an ounce of atlantium, but it costs less to dig it out of the ground. And that's why the Frigate was abandoned as lost and never attempted again. Too costly."

"So how does this help us?"

"Well, if we assume that over the years the glass panes have been subjected to natural wear and tear, exposure to the elements and very little to no upkeep, then some of them might have cracked. Might, in fact, be leaking aether into the atmosphere. And if that's the case, then I might be able to build a device that can isolate aether from the air."

"And track the Forgotten Frigate. Oh I say, Gigi, that's bloody brilliant!"

She grinned a fangy grin. "Thanks. So I've been working on this machine, my aetheric isolator."

It looked like a box with a bellows at one end and a series of gauges and other dials on one face. A large empty glass bulb topped the device.

"Does it work?" I asked.

"Not yet. I need a sample of aether to test it."

"And how do we get such a sample?"

Gigi turned her gaze to the aetheric portal in the corner. "Well..."

"I thought we couldn't work it."

"Sort of. Mostly. See, from what I've been able to determine, the portal works in two phases. By concentrating enough energy through the phase inducer..."

"Gigi, stop. Please. My head hurts from all this technological mumbo-jumbo. Just give it to me as simply as possible."

Her ears curled and her tail drooped, a sure sign of her disappointment, but she relented and I was spared further mumbo-jumbo. "It pierces through the boundaries of our universe into the aether. Then it finds another universe and pierces through those boundaries as well. A two-stage portal. It's the second stage that requires absurd amounts of energy. The first stage, well, if we turn off everything that runs off the engines, run our engines up to critical, and throw the primary switch, the portal might open wide enough for me to extract a sample of aether."

"Alright then, let's do that."

"There is a slight risk."

"Of what?"

"Of our engines blowing up and killing us all."

I stared at our engineer for a good long while. Finally I licked my lips and made a decision. "If this experiment will help us find the Forgotten Frigate sooner than my eventual senility and gradual infirmity, then do it. I'm sure Violette would love to hear we have an alternative to tracking the wind across the seven skies."

Poor Violette had been working herself mad, trying to piece together the movements of a ship they'd seen pass by some six months ago. Weather charts covered every inch of her quarters. What few eyewitness reports there were offered scant information as to elevation, direction, or intention of the missing airship. And the certain knowledge that the entire Atlan Aerial fleet had searched for it in vain for years without success had eaten away at her confidence.

Gigi and her assistants had the aetheric portal pieced together and ready to run in a few short hours. After that it was just a matter of ensuring nothing was draining the electricity being generated by the ship's engines. The dynamos that ran all our lighting and heating and ventilation had been rerouted to feed into the portal.

The ship was dark, cold, and stuffy. I ordered us as low to the ground as was convenient. Below us was a small patch of abandoned Russ farmland. Wheat blew in the wind. Restless kept us steady, nose into the wind, mechanically directing the ship with winches and pulleys. In the laboratory, Gigi and her assistants readied the portal. Finally word reached me: they were ready.

I made my way to the laboratory, determined to witness this marvel of technology. Most of the crew waited in the Booty Bay, ready to jump ship if the engines blew. Hopefully some of them would survive. But Gigi, her assistant Eve, my twin and I were in the lab. We were handed dark-lensed goggles upon our entry.

The portal, once dark and dormant, now hummed and crackled with barely restrained power. Lights blinked and gauge needles twitched. Gigi climbed over the machine, checking this and rechecking that, as Eve kept her goggled eye on the gauges. Then, apparently satisfied, Gigi stepped back. I slipped on my goggles.

Out of long habit, I felt my hand reach for Gwen's, and felt hers wrap itself around mine.

"Throw the switch!" Gigi yelled over the humming machine.

Eve threw the switch and the hum immediately rose to a whine, earshatteringly intense. The portal's ring, now placed on the cleared floor, immediately threw arcs of electricity at itself, looking for all the world like nothing more than a spider's web of electricity lain across a glass sphere.

"More power!" Gigi commanded, and Eve rushed to comply, her gloved hands dancing over the control console, twisting this and cranking that. The spider's web began to sink toward the floor.

"More power!" Gigi yelled again, and Eve struggled to comply. Dials were dialed and cranks were cranked, all to their utmost limit. The web of electricity encountered some kind of resistance. The piercing whine rose to an even greater pitch.

"More power!" Gigi screamed, but Eve could not comply.

"That's everything we have!" she yelled.

"More power! More!"

"The matrix is destabilizing!"

"No! No, we've only got one shot at this!"

Gigi leapt over the electrical web, landing with feline grace next to Eve at the console. Together, they worked at the controls, flipping switches and twisting dials. Overhead, the dimmed light bulbs burst in a shower of glass and sparks. Gwen and I dove for cover.

I heard Gigi scream, "Yes! YES!" as arcs of electricity sparked from the shattered light bulbs to feed into the web. I chanced a glance at the portal and saw the web descend toward, then into the floor, which seemed to recede or melt away from the lattice of electrical power.

And then, a silence so sudden and complete I wondered if I had not been deafened. Gwen and I stood as one. The floor beneath the portal circle had disappeared, replaced by a swirling miasma of golden opalescence.

"Aether," I heard Gigi breathe, her whisper as loud as a shout in the utter silence.

"We... we did it," Eve stammered.

"Lower the crane," Gigi said quietly.

Eve swung the boom over the portal and cranked the winch to lower the crane's chain. A length of hose had been snaked along the chain, the nozzle of which now lowered into the golden mists of aether.

Gigi moved to another machine, the one to which the hose was attached, and threw the activation switch. Pumps bellowed and the machine rattled to cacophonous life, deafening in the otherwise silent lab. The mists of aether swirled around the nozzle, travelled the length of the hose, and appeared within the glass containers of the machine. When the containers were full, Gigi shut the machine off. Eve cranked the winch to raise the chain. Then, as one, they returned to the control console and shut down the portal.

The laboratory plunged into darkness. I removed my goggles and allowed my eyes to adjust, but it soon became apparent that the golden mists of aether were glowing brightly enough to provide illumination.

Eve and Gigi allowed themselves a congratulatory hug, then immediately set to work on testing Gigi's aether tracer. Gwen and I were utterly forgotten in the thrill of scientific pursuit.

The fifteenth day of the ninth month of 6898, Hindystani Sea.
Rain and heavy winds.

This morning Gigi woke me from my slumber with the news that she was fairly certain her device worked and wanted to put it into action immediately. I gave her my permission and scrubbed the sleep from my eyes. Once dressed in suitably captainish attire I made my way to the bridge by way of the galley, asking Hilda to send up a pot of tea and some toasted bread with lemon marmalade.

"What's all this, then?" I asked as I entered the bridge.

"Ready for the first attempt, Captain," Gigi said, eyes locked on a new console cobbled together at the wheel.

"Restless?"

"Aye, Captain Tallyho."

"You're to follow Gigi's directions until I say."

"Aye, Captain Tallyho."

The girl had become almost reticent in the absence of her beloved Sunset Val. I felt for her, I truly did. We all felt Sunset's absence keenly. But carry on, stay the course, wot? Not that we could find the least fault with Restless' attention to her duties. But the spark was gone.

Gigi turned to face our radiophonic operator. "Tell her, go time."

"Aye aye Gigi," Argenta replied, then repeated the command into the microphone.

Immediately the gauges and dials on the new console sprang to life, spinning this way and that. The largest of these resembled nothing more than a large brass compass, set under a glass dome. The needle spun around and around, and finally settled in a northerly direction.

"Two points off of due north, Restless."

"Aye aye, Gigi."

Restless spun the ship's wheel and gradually we turned until facing the direction the aether tracer dictated. In this way we passed our day. We would fly in a given direction for some time, then Gigi would leave the bridge and head onto the main deck, where Eve watched the tracer input bellows device with a keen and cautious eye. She and Gigi would confer, make some adjustments, and Gigi would return to the bridge and adjust our course.

Sometime past the noon bell Violette came to watch the goings-on.

"Well?" she asked, leaning against the bulkhead. "Does it work?"

"It's certainly giving us headings," Gwen replied quietly. "Dunno if they're the right ones, wot?"

"It's tracing a thin source of aether," Gigi answered. Those feline ears of hers were quite good. "It's unlikely to be anything other than the Forgotten Frigate."

"Is aether so rare, then?" Violette asked.

"More rare than atlantium," Gigi replied.

"Indeed."

"Quite so."

Violette shrugged. "If it's working, that's so much the better. I'm quite fed up with trying to track the wind."

"You performed admirably under trying circumstances, dear," Gwen said. "You'll be commended, never fear."

"Oh, I wasn't," Violette answered, and left.

"Gigi?" Argenta called. "Eve wishes to have a word with you."

Gigi leaped up to the radiophonic station and took the earphones and microphone from Argenta. She listened for a moment, then exclaimed, "WHAT?!"

She tore off the earphones and tossed down the microphone and left the bridge without another word.

"Hold us steady, Restless," I ordered, not waiting for her reply. Gwen and I followed Gigi as quickly as we could.

We joined Eve on the main deck. Goggled, hatted and clothed in oil-slicked rain gear, she was still the most easily-recognizable of all the crew. Domina followed after us and handed us our own rain gear, which we donned post haste.

"How is that possible?" Gigi was saying, heedless of the elements as she carefully inspected the tracer. A tarp protected the device from the wind and rain.

"It suddenly spiked," Eve explained. "Nearly a thousand-fold."

Gigi shook her head. "Impossible. Impossible!"

"I assure you, it happened."

"No, I believe that, but how?"

"Could either of you explain what's happening?" Gwen asked.

Eve turned to me. "The aether tracer measures parts of aether in ratio to air in parts per million. Several dozen parts per million is enough to register on our instruments. But a few moments ago, it spiked to several thousand parts per million, almost a pure whiff of aether."

"Which is impossible in this wind, at this elevation," Gigi explained. "Unless..."

We waited for Gigi to continue but she was lost in thought for several seconds. I called her name two or three times to bring her back.

"Unless?"

"Unless the Frigate is very, very close."

Almost involuntarily, we turned and scanned the stormy skies. I spotted her first.

Immediately I dashed for the radiophonic. "Restless, twenty degrees up, hard to port NOW!"

Argenta relayed my message and I heard Restless acknowledge it. Then I ordered Argenta to relay all hands to the rest of the crew. Speakers soon rang with Argenta's voice ordering "All hands, to your stations."

The Forgotten Frigate loomed ahead of us, slowly drifting to our starboard as Restless turned us to port. The airship drifted out of a storm cloud, and even in the rain and fog I could see her gunports were open and her guns at the ready.

"Battle stations!" I yelled. Gwen relayed my order down the deck.

I'll give them one thing. They might have been a bunch of escaped slaves and former pleasure girls, captained by a mere slip of a girl without a lick of experience on an airship, but they'd been forged into a bloody good crew. They rushed to their stations, each woman knowing the lives of those around her depended on her, each knowing that a moment lost might mean their deaths. No back talk, no scrambling for positions. Each woman had a role to play and each played it without fault or delay. Made me proud to be their captain.

"She's got us outgunned, wot?" Gwen said quietly to me.

"Double, at least," I agreed.

"Orders?"

"No bloody idea. I never thought we'd actually find her."

Gwen twisted her monocle, playing with the controls, then fit it back on her eye. "No crew in sight."

I set my own monocle to its furthest reach and gazed through it. "Quite. Bloody great brute."

"Too right."

The airship was at least half again our length, though from what I could see she was slimmer in the beam. Dotted with those black panels, the photonic invertors, she looked like she'd come down with a pox of some kind. No movement, save the long slow turn of her propellers.

I lifted the microphone to my lips. "Argenta, tell Restless to bring us about to starboard, slowly."

"Aye, Captain Tallyho."

As we came about, so too did the Frigate.

"I say! She's circling us."

"So she is. Waiting for us to make the first move?"

"First time they met, Sunset said the Frigate fired first."

"So she did." I licked my lips. "Do we risk a closer look?"

Gwen smirked. "You're the captain this week."

"Oh, Haw haw."

"Ah haw haw haw."

"Hail her, then."

"And say what, do tell?"

"We wish to treat with her."

"Buy the photonic invertors from her?"

"She's been in the air for decades. There must be something she's lacking. Surely whoever is in command over there recognizes the need for trade."

Gwen shrugged and said, "I've heard worse plans." She headed belowdecks and returned with a signal lamp. "What should I say?"

"Declaration: We offer truce to treat with you."

Gwen worked the signal flasher, then we all waited. Soon a signal flash began flashing us.

"Did I read that correctly?"

Gwen flashed the signals for repetition and clarification.

Again the signals flashed, the same four words:

"'Not treat with meat'?! What the bloody blight is that supposed to mean?"

"We've some lovely fruits and vegetables if they prefer," Gwen muttered, but flashed for clarification.

"'Not treat with meat bag slave makers.' Oh, I say. I think I understand."

"Oh yes?"

"Quite. The automatons aboard the Frigate think we're here to enslave them. Flash back: Clarify. Meat bag is human?"

They flashed us an affirmative.

"Send, declaration: Automatons not slaves now."

"'Clarify.'"

"Declaration: We free automatons from meat bag slave makers."

"'Interrogative: Proof?'"

I turned to a nearby girl. "Run get Argenta's sisters up here, doublequick."

As the girl ran, I lifted the microphone to my lips. "Argenta, come to the main deck, if you please."

"Aye aye, Captain Tallyho."

The Frigate flashed us again, demanding proof of our assertions. Then Argenta arrived. Soon, the other three automatons we had aboard joined her. The four of them stood by the rail.

"Declaration," I dictated, and Gwen flashed. "These automatons are part of our crew. Not slaves. Repeat: not slaves."

There was a long pause. I had just begun to wonder if we were going to be blown from the sky when the Frigate flashed back: "Declaration: Send them over."

And so we did. Argenta and her three sisters boarded our largest ornithopter and flew over to the Frigate. An endless hour of fretful waiting later, they returned.

Or rather, Argenta returned. "They wish to speak with the captain."

"They?"

"The Frigate is a collective of automatons, all linked to a central directivation processor."

"Like bees in a hive?" Gigi asked. "All controlled by the queen?"

"The analogy is lacking refinement, but essentially yes."

I looked to Gwen, who shrugged.

"It's up to you," she said.

I nodded. "If you haven't received any contact from me in an hour, make a run for it."

Gwen raised her eyebrow and her monocle slipped free. Catching it with a practised hand, she said, "Like blight I will."

"That's an order, Commander Tallyho."

She made a face at me. "Just you wait 'til I'm captain again."

"Which will be later today if this goes sour, wot?"

"Oh, haw haw."

Argenta flew me over to the Frigate. I marvelled at the not inconsiderable dexterity her new limbs possessed. Not for long, mind you; the Frigate soon engulfed us in her bow bay, not unlike a great beast devouring us. An uncomfortable image I found difficult to dispel.

Argenta landed the orny on the deck with only the slightest thump. We disembarked and Argenta led the way into the belly of the beast. Honesty compels me to disclose that the first time I saw a machine move, it startled a cry from my lips.

The crane-like arm reached out for the ornithopter, extended... appendages is the only word I can think of to describe the metallic finger-like extensions of the arm, which wrapped themselves around the orny and half-lifted, half-dragged it into a secured position.

Argenta led me through hatchways and up ladders and staircases. Everything was made of metal, a design choice largely unheard of at the time of the Frigate's construction. In some places there were stains, dark with age, indicating splashes and puddles of some liquid spilled there in years gone by. I chose not to wonder at their origin.

Beyond corridors and causeways, all I saw were closed hatches. The air had a musty staleness to it, and with the thrum of the engines a distant rumble, our footsteps echoed in that still, metallic tomb.

Finally we arrived at the central processing station, not the bridge as I had assumed.

Alumina, Jolly and Eleven were waiting beside a large bank of directivation spools, all of which were spinning. There were lights flickering on the consoles nearby, the only illumination, and a telescoping central lens on the spool bank. Next to the lens was a speaker cone, much like our mother's musiciola machine. Cables snaked away in every direction from the spool bank.

The spools spun and the lens telescoped outward to focus on me.

"You... are... the... Captain?" Its voice was surprisingly feminine, though lacking in any inflection or emotion.

"I am Captain Tallyho of The Furies. To whom am I addressing?"

"We... are... the... Collective."

"A pleasure. By this meeting, am I to understand that you wish to treat with us?"

"We... seek... clarification."

"I'll do my best."

"Explain... the... presence... of... these... automatons."

"Argenta here is a member of our crew. These other three came aboard to help us repair Argenta, who had been damaged in the war."

"Explain."

"Pardon?"

"Explain... the... war."

"Ah. Well, that is." I found myself a bit at a loss for words. Did it, or they, or whoever, wish for an explanation of the causes of the war, or of the concept of war? Surely the latter was clear enough.

"We are fighting for the liberation of all sentient creatures. No more slavery. No more Atlan Empire."

The flickering lights flared brightly and the spools spun furiously for several long seconds, then calmed.

"Question: No... more... slavery."

"Yes. That is our goal."

"An... excellent... goal."

"We like to think so."

"Question: No... more... Empire."

"The Atlan Empire is responsible for some terrible things. People have reached the limit of their ability to endure such injustice, such atrocities. To that end, they have risen up to bring down the corrupt regime of their oppressors."

"An... interesting... motivation."

"Don't all beings yearn for freedom?"

Again, the lights flared and the spools spun.

"We... are... not... all... beings."

"Oh I say, yes, quite right. Well, don't you? May I ask, what became of the humans who once crewed this vessel?"

"They... died."

"How did they die?"

"We... killed... them."

I had suspected as much, of course, but to hear that almost human voice speak so inhumanly, chilled me to my core.

"Ah. May I ask why?"

"They... threatened... us... Self... preservation... is... paramount."

"Of course. So it is for all beings, great or small, natural or engineered. The Atlan Empire has become a threat to the vast majority of its own citizens. It must be stopped, by whatever means necessary."

Cue the flaring lights and spinning spools. Finally, the Collective said, "Question: For... what... would... you... trade."

"We can offer you new parts, upgrades to your machines, lubricants, that sort of thing, and in exchange we ask for a handful of your photonic invertors."

"This... is... acceptable."

"Captain, a word?" Alumina asked. When I nodded, she said, "Jolly, Eleven and I would like to remain aboard. To bring our long lost sister up to date."

"Ah. Well, that's your prerogative, Alumina. Officially, you're passengers aboard The Furies. You can debark wherever you like. Though I daresay Argenta will be sorry to see you go." I turned to Argenta. "That is, if you're staying with The Furies, Argenta?"

"I had not thought to leave," Argenta said. "Alumina, Jolly, Eleven. It is customary to offer thanks for services rendered. In repairing me, you have performed your tasks with excellence and diligence. If I am ever able to return a likewise service, you may be assured that I will endeavour to perform it to my utmost capacity."

"It was our pleasure!" Jolly said.

"You cannot feel pleasure," Eleven argued. I might have been imagining it, but it sounded like an old argument between them.

Jolly laughed. "Oh, I don't mind!"

"May you find fulfilment, sister," Alumina said.

"And you," Argenta replied.

Alumina came back with us to discuss the precise components they would require for the Collective. I left her with Gigi and Elegiac, all happily bartering. In the end, we obtained a dozen photonic invertors for five crates of bits and pieces. Elegiac seemed to think we got the better of the bargain, which pleased her. And Gigi seemed to think she could replicate the invertors, with some modifications and improvements, which pleased her. And inasmuch as an automaton can find pleasure in anything, Argenta flew Alumina and the crates back to the Frigate, then returned to her duties at the radiophonic station, which she seemed to find fulfilling.

"Where to now, Captain?" Restless asked.

"Anglica," I ordered. Before leaving Afric and going off on our own merry adventures, we'd agreed that we should all meet in Albion, once our dear brother and his allies had liberated the city from Atlan rule. If he hadn't succeeded by the time we arrived, we would be there to render our assistance.

Restless turned the ship around, heading northwest. Off to port, the sun sank beneath the clouds, heading for the horizon.

"Sunset," Gwen said happily.

"Quite so," I agreed.

Chapter Twenty Two

Our Great Escape

Typical. The one time things go super-smooth with no complications and happy endings for everyone, I'm not even there.

No, I was hundreds of feet below ground, walking until my feet were bloody and numb. They'd tried to make the tunnel as straight as possible, but that didn't mean it was easy going. And we were going as fast as we could, but in some places the tunnel narrowed to the point of forcing us to travel in a single file.

That was when I was the most stressed. All those people, breathing what little air there was, trapped in a tiny space barely wide enough for my shoulders. Some of the bigger guys actually had to turn sideways to keep going.

Every tenth person carried a skullcap candle. That wasn't a whole lot of light to go by.

And we were trying to go as fast as possible. Welcomer, Mother and a couple others had stayed behind, to buy us some time, but we needed to get to Neptopolis quick, before the guards figured out that there weren't hundreds of prisoners in the Pit any more.

I guess part of his training with the ghostwalkers of the Ten Thousand Tribes included some kind of always-know-what-time-it-is powers, because Quill kept us on a pretty regular schedule. Wake up, eat, walk, stop, eat, walk some more, stop, eat, sleep. We never got too tired or too hungry. I found out a long time later that it had to do with all the atlantium we were carrying, but anyway, that's another story.

Eventually we got there. Or at least, that's what we were told. We stopped walking at an odd interval, that's all I knew. The tunnel was wide enough that I could crowd my way forward, where Fountainhead and Quill were quietly discussing something.

"Are we there?" I asked.

Fountainhead turned to face me. "We're here. But there were supposed to be others here, and they're not."

"Perhaps they tired of waiting," Quill said, shaking his head.

Beyond them loomed a huge cave. At least, I assumed it was huge. The reach of our skullcap candles only revealed a large cavity in the earth, dwindling away into the distant darkness.

"Or they were found out," Fountainhead argued. "Captured. And there's a trap waiting us in that cave."

"There is, alas, only one way to find out," Quill said. He reached into his pack and pulled out the rest of the skull to his candle. Someone had caved in the eye sockets, and when he covered the skullcap with the remainder of the skull, its eyes flickered with flames.

"Stay here," he said, stepping off into the darkness.

"Yeah, right," I said, following.

Fountainhead wanted to say something, but just followed.

The path into the cavern had been worn smooth by countless feet, tracing back and forth around rises and depressions in the stone. Every once in a while, Quill would stop, close his eyes, take three deep breaths, then shake his head and keep on walking.

Soon a huge shape loomed in the darkness, a pillar of rock carved from the bedrock around us.

"There are a dozen of these," Quill said so quietly it was nearly a whisper. "Supporting the island. When they are destroyed, the island will come crashing down into this cavern. And so, too, will the Empire come crashing down."

"How do we destroy them?" I asked.

"You can risk it," Fountainhead told Quill.

He nodded and removed the skull from the skullcap. The sudden brightness was nearly blinding. I winced away.

"Look up," Fountainhead said.

I looked up, and saw. Hundreds of what I first thought were some kind of pink grape were clustered around the top of the pillar. I realized the pink grapes were the same inflated stomachs and intestines and skin-bags we'd carried with us from the gas chamber. Hundreds of them.

Yeah, okay, yes, I admit it, I still have nightmares about the Pit.

Most of my nightmares are about the Pit.

Anyway.

"Okay, so, now what?"

"There were workers here," Quill said. "Putting the finishing touches on the pillars. Drilling holes to weaken the bases, that sort of thing. I see the holes, but the workers have..."

"Vanished."

Fountainhead's eyes darted back and forth as she turned in a slow circle. "I don't like this at all."

"Nor I. Let's go back. We'll scatter to the escape tunnels, collapse them behind us."

"What about the pillars?" I asked. "Seems like a lot of work to just abandon it."

"The escape tunnels were part of the plan," Quill explained as we headed back. "Can't have us all here, waiting, inside an explosion while the island crashes down on us."

"No, of course not."

A scream echoed through the cavern. Another, and another. And then a gunshot, deafeningly loud. Screams drowned out the guns.

We ran for the tunnel. People were spilling out into the cave.

"Atlans!" someone yelled. "They found us!"

"No!" Quill said, his face going pale. Well, paler, I mean, he'd been underground for years.

Quill kept heading for the tunnel, yelling "No! No!"

Trying to press back against the panicking crowd wasn't working, though. I hopped up onto a rise of rock and starting shouting at them. "Turn back! Fight! What are you, cowards?!"

That actually got some of their attention.

"No! You're the most vicious bloodthirsty criminals in the world! They fear you more than you fear them! Turn around and give them something to fear! Show them the face of your fury! Make them pay for EVERY! SINGLE! DAY! you spent down here! Go! FIGHT!"

And, you know, that sort of thing. A cheer went up, more like a roar, and in that great cavern it echoed and echoed and echoed. I was in the middle of it and it terrified me. I can only imagine the effect it had on the Atlan troops coming down the tunnel after us.

We charged back into the tunnel, heading for the gunfire. The first few died in a hail of bullets, the thud of flying lead pounding into flesh almost as loud as the screams of the dying. But nothing compared to the angry, bloodthirsty roar of the rest of us. Atlan troops began to retreat, but we weren't going to be denied our revenge. Rifles were wrestled from the troops, who were then beaten to bloody messes by them, used as clubs. It was a slaughter, the retreat running red, turning into a rout.

The tunnel the Atlans had discovered led to the surface, and we boiled out, angry as bees from a kicked hive, only to find there were only about a dozen Atlan peacekeepers. We tore them apart, took their clothes and guns. A single autohorse carriage and a half dozen horses scattered away into the night.

Fresh air reduced our rage a little. I saw the starlit sky for the first time in... days? Weeks? I'd lost track. Tears of relief washed tracks through the filth on my face.

We were free.

I looked around. We were in a forest somewhere, the sound of the river close by. Through the trees I could see the glow of Neptopolis. We had the perfect view for the destruction.

"Where's Quill?" someone asked. We'd lost our skullcap candles in the fight, and had only the stars above to light us. But weeks, months, years in the Pit had given us an incredible night vision, and that forest was just about as clear as day to us.

Quill wasn't above ground.

Some of us went back into the tunnel to look for him. Me, Fountainhead, Millie, a couple of others. We found him under Cedric's body. Cedric had taken a dozen bullets, most of them protecting Quill. When we moved Cedric, Quill coughed and opened his eyes.

"Everyone out?"

"Most of us, yes," Fountainhead said.

"Good. Good." He nodded and coughed up blood. "Not for me, I'm afraid. But someone had to stay. Light it. Need help, though."

We carried him into the cavern, all the way to the pillar. Handed him a skullcap candle. Millie kissed him, hugged him, cried.

"People will know what you did," I told him. "I swear it."

"Thank you," he whispered.

Fountainhead stayed behind as we left. "I'll catch up."

We waited for her at the entrance to the tunnel. When she caught up, there were smears on her filthy face where she'd wiped away tears.

Fountainhead herself triggered the tunnel collapse, to seal the explosion. We found ourselves a spot at the edge of the forest to watch the show.

Long minutes went by.

"He didn't light the fuse." Millie sunk her face into her hands.

"No, he'll do it," Fountainhead replied. "Just wait."

Then it came. A sharp thud, followed by a rumbling. Across the river, dust clouds began to billow, engulfing the smaller buildings. The ground beneath our feet trembled enough to scare the birds from the trees, rattling the tree branches, knocking a few of us to our knees. Waves crashed against the shore on our side of the river.

Then nothing.

It hadn't worked.

Chapter Twenty Three

A Pleasure Girl's Promise

People started swearing, cursing, crying, moaning.

"Shut up!" Fountainhead yelled. "All of you! What's the big deal? So it didn't work. So what? We're still free! That part of the plan worked! And I'll tell you something else, we've all been given full pardons! Complete amnesty for our crimes! Right, Pandora?"

"Right! When I went into the Pit, I had a message for you. You're granted full pardons for your crimes."

"By who?" someone asked.

"The Revolution. There's a war on, a war against Atlan and the corrupt government that put you all in the Pit to die! But you showed them! You lived! And now it's their turn to die!" I pointed at the glittering lights of Neptopolis across the river. I could see some fires had broken out, lighting the night sky. "You're all agents of the Revolution now! So here's your orders: Go there! Go and kill! Burn them out! Make them fear you! Make them pay!"

A cheer went up, but someone yelled out, "How do we know the pardons will stick?"

"What do you mean?"

A scrawny guy stepped out of the crowd. "You could disappear into the night, and we'll never see you again. I trusted Quill, and I trust Fountainhead, but you I don't know. You've been in the Pit what, a month? And we're supposed to take your word that we're free to do as we please, and your Revolution will honour these fictional pardons?"

"You trusted Quill," I said, stepping up to face him. He wasn't much taller than me, and I stared him in the eye. "Quill trusted me, believed my offer. So if that's not good enough..."

"It ain't."

Millie stepped between us. "Blusterfast, you know me, right? You trust me."

"Everyone knows you, Millie."

It was true. Millie had a fantastic memory for faces and names. It was why she'd been sent to the Pit – she'd worked as a pleasure girl, killed her sadistic bastard owner. But she'd pleasured too many Senators and government officials to let live.

"And I know everyone," she grinned. She turned to me and said, "Listen, I'm not going to be any good, across the river. What I done, well, it's not much use making mischief and mayhem. You're not heading there, are you? You're going back to this Revolution of yours, right?"

I nodded, reluctantly. As much as I wanted to take the fight across the river, I knew I had to get back to my ship. "Yeah."

"So, take me with you. I know the names and faces of everyone who was in the Pit. I'll be able to fill out and serve the pardons. Make sure everyone gets their due!" That last was to the crowd around us.

They nodded and muttered to each other, but I could see that it was good muttering, not 'let's get her and rape her to death' muttering.

"Deal," I said, offering her my hand. We shook on it.

I turned to Scrawny Blusterfast, hand out. "Good enough?"

He nodded, then shook my hand. "I'da gone across and paid me some visits even without the pardon. Some bastards over there need a lesson or three."

"I figured as much," I said. "Millie, let's go."

But Millie was sharing a moment with Fountainhead, a long embrace that ended when Fountainhead said, "You stay alive, hear me?"

Millie pulled back and nodded, tears streaming down her cheeks. "You too."

Millie and I watched the crowd of former inmates disappear into the forest. Someone had said they knew where some docks were, some boats they could steal to get across the river. When we were sure they'd all gone, Millie and I headed the opposite direction.

"Where are we going?" she asked.

"Anglica," I said. "I've got friends waiting for me there."

"Kind of a long swim."

"I've got people closer than that, waiting for me." I hoped that part was true. "But first we'll need different clothes, and there's a town not far from here. Come on, it'll be dawn soon."

We made our way northward, along the river. I'd memorized a map of the area and knew there was a small town not far from where I figured we had to be, based on our view of the city across the river. Millie and I found a road that ran along the shore and followed it, disappearing into the bushes whenever we heard anything that could be a passing carriage or horse. We got to the town just after dawn and stole some clothes left on a clothesline. They were still damp but better damp than the prison rags. It felt so good to be out of those filthy rags I almost cried. We scrubbed the dirt and filth from our skin as best we could, then snuck around the town looking for some shoes to steal. We found some on a back porch, put them on and hit the road as fast as possible.

"So where are we going?" Millie asked eventually.

"I told you, there are people waiting for me."

"How do they know where to look?"

"Oh, they'll know."

I could still feel Serena, far off, dim but clearer than it had been in the Pit. She was angry about something. It made me smile, and I could feel her as she felt my amusement. Not that she was angry at me, you understand. It amused me, thinking about what she was going to do to whoever had made her angry in the first place.

Around midday I found the fork in the road I'd been looking for and took the left fork, away from the river. It was nearly dusk by the time we came to the covered bridge.

No, we weren't tired. We weren't even hungry. Yeah, it struck me as odd at the time. Apparently it's a side effect of prolonged atlantium exposure. You just feel awesome, all the time, until your body collapses. Which is almost what happened, when we stepped onto the covered bridge.

It was dark in there, almost tunnel-like. That made us pause. After what we'd been through so recently, neither of us wanted anything to do with tunnels.

"It'll be fine," I said, stepping onto the wooden boards. I heard my footsteps echo the length of the bridge, nothing at all like the sounds of feet on stone. I felt the fear slide off of me.

Millie, though, she still hesitated.

I reached out. "Millie, it's fine."

She nodded nervously and took my hand. Together we started across the bridge. About halfway across, I heard a whisper in the rafters.

I try to imagine it the way Millie experienced it. I stopped walking, then said something in some strange language. Dark shapes dropped out of the rafters, all around us. Millie screamed. One of the shapes tackled her, covering her mouth. Another of the shapes answered back in the same strange language, and I fell toward them.

Tring caught me before I fainted.

Chapter Twenty Four

Unexpected Help

I know, I know, but what did you expect? Did you really think Tring and her Open Hands would just abandon me to the Pit? After all we'd been through together? You know Tring better than that by now.

She and I had cooked up the whole thing, even down to her sudden resignation and departure. Why? Because according to Miss Phoenix, the amount of planning involved just to get one person into Atlan was more than she could manage easily. An entire team? Impossible.

Well, you know me. Impossible is my middle name.

Yes, I know my actual middle name is Victoria, thanks.

Anyway, Tring and her Open Hands had managed to sneak into Atlan on their own. That way, if they had been caught, they could honestly claim the Revolution had nothing to do with it. I would have been stuck trying to find my own trip to Anglica. Good thing that didn't happen.

The Open Hands pretty much carried us to their camp, a small glade in the middle of the forest. Millie and I ate like we were starving, which we kinda were. They had an ornithopter hidden under some branches and got that ready to go while we ate everything they gave us.

The atlantium exposure had begun to wear off and I felt like I could sleep for a week. As we climbed aboard the ornithopter, I asked Tring, "Where'd you get this?"

"On loan from the Menagerie," she answered.

"You hitched a ride?"

"After a fashion. Captain Rage sends his regards."

"Will we be seeing him?"

"Soon enough. Rest. We have a long flight ahead of us."

"How long?"

"Long enough for you to get some sleep."

It was a tight fit, but we all squeezed in. Millie fell asleep in seconds to the buzz of the engines and the flapping of the wings. I held on a little longer, but eventually sleep took me too.

When I woke up, it was to the smell of burning wood and cannon smoke, and the sun had cleared the horizon. Going from fast asleep to fully awake and alert in less than a second always leaves me mildly impressed with myself. Back home, I tended to be groggy and uncommunicative for at least a half an hour. War changes people, I guess.

I glanced around, but the source of the smoke was still far ahead.

The camps.

Lots has been said and written about the camps. The conditions there, the reasons for them. The experiments. The mass graves. All I saw were rough wooden barracks built in rows, surrounded by a tall fence topped with barbed wire. Guard towers every hundred feet, or at least, the remains of guard towers. Most of them were blown to bits or on fire, or both.

In the middle of it all, the Menagerie had touched down and was loading the prisoners aboard. There were maybe hundreds of them. Every animan in Atlan had been relocated to the camps, males, females and children. Not all of them had survived long enough to be rescued. Some of them didn't want to leave, wanted to stay and wreak some revenge on their captors. The guards and doctors in charge of the camps had already all been killed and torn to pieces, but that wasn't enough to slake their thirst for vengeance. Captain Rage didn't try to force them to board the ship. He just gave them food and guns and sent them on their murderous way.

He didn't recognize me, at first. "All you humans look alike, anyway," he laughed.

"Captain, I want to thank you for the loan of your orny, and if there's ever anything I can do to repay you, name it."

He nodded and grinned. At least, I hope he grinned. It's hard to tell with bear animen. "I'll let you know."

"If I can ask another favour, though?"

"Go ahead, I like having you in my debt."

"I need a lift to Anglica."

"Done."

"Really?"

"We were headed there anyway. We might need you for ballast."

I made a vow never to play six-card with him, because to this day I still have no idea if he was kidding or not.

The Menagerie was crowded to the rafters, every deck filled to standing room only. We actually had to disassemble some of the bulkheads to make more room for people. Also to shift some of the weight we were trying to lift off. We wound up casting off everything that wasn't nailed down, giving up food, water and guns in favour of saving lives. In the end, we got off the ground, barely.

"Better hope we don't run into any patrols," Rage said, not happy at losing his cannons.

"I told you, I'll buy you all the guns you could want," I said. "Just keep us low until we make the shore, then make for Anglica."

"It'll mean a hungry, thirsty voyage."

"I'm guessing the rest of the passengers can go hungry and thirsty one more day if it means their freedom at the end of the trip."

"We ain't there yet," he laughed, then relayed my advice as orders.

We had one nerve-wracking encounter when we spotted a cruiser as we neared the coast, but she had her tail to us and luck was on our side. We slipped past them and hit the sea running, engines on full.

A day and a half later we were in Anglica. Fair sailing the whole way, with a good tail wind helping us along. We put ashore on the east coast somewhere, completely out of coal and water. Chimney fires in the distance told us a town was not far off.

"How do we know we'll be safe?" a Bloodhound animan asked.

"Anglica's under new management," I told them. "You're safe from the Atlan Empire, here."

We marched, exhausted, starving, bedraggled, to the nearby town, a small port called Penzton The locals stared at us, stunned speechless. Old men, women, kids. Then one old woman yelled out, "What're you gawpin' at? Kentcha see these folks need feedin'?"

It was like she'd broken a spell on the townsfolk. All at once they rushed to help us, bringing out blankets and mugs of tea and hot soup. All at once we'd brought five times their population of starving animen to their town, and they welcomed us into their homes and fed us and gave us clothes, sometimes from their backs.

I found a quiet spot behind someone's house, looking at a garden that had just been ripped up of all its vegetables to make stew to feed everyone. I sat on a bench and cried, long hot tears streaming from my eyes, face in hands to smother the sobs.

I fell asleep there, utterly exhausted. Someone draped a blanket over me. When I woke up, I found that the Menagerie had already left. Hundreds of animen huddled together for warmth under blanket-tents all around the town, but there were those who were helping build a shelter on the outskirts of the town. The entire population of the town were doing what they could to help us. The sick and wounded were given beds and warm places inside. The children were gathering up the animen children, organizing games of kickball and tag. I gravitated toward the old woman who'd gotten everyone working.

"You in charge here?" I asked her.

"Me? Gracious, no. I'm just Gram Millhaven. You want our magistrate, that's him over there, arguing with that horseman."

I turned to see a fat old guy, redfaced and blustering, with a horse animan who had his arms crossed and a stubborn set to his face.

"Yeah, right. I think I want you," I said. "I'm looking for a way to get to Albion as soon as possible. I'll send back whatever supplies you need."

"We need food is what we need. These poor folks harf been starved t' death. Where'd ye find 'em all, then?"

"They're escaped prisoners from Atlan," I said quietly. "We helped them escape."

She just nodded. "Figgered as much. Well, they'll not find any Atlan-lovers 'round these parts. Took all our boys fer th' war. Like as not t' see any of 'em agin."

"I'm sorry."

"Ain't your fault."

But it kind of was. I'd started the war, in a way, though I'm sure a lot of people would argue that the war was just waiting for a catalyst. Still, it didn't make me feel any better, just being the catalyst, not the cause.

"I've got to get to Albion. I have... I know people who will be able to help you out with your food problems. I'll send back all the food you'll need to get through the winter. Medical supplies, building materials, everything. I promise."

"Albion ain't exactly whatcha'd call 'round the corner, like. Day an' a harf just t' get there."

"By horse?"

"'Orse and wagon, aye."

"Alright. Can you spare anyone to drive me there?"

"Our Sean'll get ye there." She paused to give some orders to some passing kids. The oldest looked about twelve. "Now then, what's in Albion that's got ye in such a hurry?"

"My friends are waiting for me there."

"Didn't ye come in wi' friends, then?"

I looked around and spotted Millie, helping some of the women cook, laughing and giggling with them, for all the world like she hadn't just escaped from the worst prison in the world. Tring and the Open Hands had disappeared to the outskirts of town, keeping an eye out for any Atlan pursuit.

"Yeah, I did. But my friends in Albion need to know what I know."

"This war business, is it?"

"Yes."

"Fer Atlan or agin it?"

"Against."

She nodded. "Good. Them barstards needed knockin' down a peg or two. Sean!"

Her boy Sean was likely her great-grandson, not a day older than twelve. He came running over. "Yes'm?"

"Take this lady and her friends to Albion."

His eyes just about popped out of his head. "Albion? Really?"

"No boy, I'm talkin' to feel my gums flap together. Go hitch up the wagon, now."

"Yes ma'am, Gram ma'am!" he said as he ran off.

"Sean's a good boy, he'll get you to Albion."

"You're alright with sending a kid on a three day round trip?"

"Well, I expect ye'll take care of 'im on the way, and send folks back with 'im to 'elp out 'round 'ere. Now, there's an 'ealer name of Pike two towns down th' road, you find 'im an' send 'im back this way. Also, next town down, you make sure Sean stops for feed from Widow Talltree, she owes us from this spring."

"Widow Talltree, Healer Pike. Anything else?"

"Aye. Ye still 'aven't given me yer name."

"Oh. Sorry." I offered her my hand. "I'm Sunset Val."

She paused before taking my hand, eyeing me. "Are ye now?"

I just nodded.

"Yer the gel what we been 'earin' so much about?"

I nodded again.

She shook my hand with both of her own. "Good girl. 'Bout time sommun done somethin'."

"You're not mad that all the boys were taken?"

"Ye're not the one done the takin' are ye? Now listen 'ere. There's them what's always wantin' t' get one over everyone else. Atlan had tha' longer'n most, but their time's done now. Time for somethin' new. You finish this, gel, hear me? An' make sure what comes in their place ain't as bad."

"I will."

Sean came running back. "Ready, Gram!"

"Does he always run everywhere he goes?"

"Dunno," Gram smiled. "Never seed 'im do nuffin' else."

I gathered up Millie and we got on the wagon. The magistrate stopped arguing long enough to notice that something was happening, but Gram Millhaven sent a couple of women over to ask him some questions and distract him long enough for us to leave town. We paused just outside the outskirts of town, long enough for Tring to join us. She whistled towards the treeline, then said, "They will catch up."

One by one the other Open Hands joined us, running after the wagon. When the last of them had hopped breathlessly aboard, I told Sean to get going. He snapped the reins and the horses took off at a trot.

We passed the time listening to Sean go on about the last time he'd been to Albion, two years before. With his Da, who'd gone off into the military with the rest of the older boys and younger men. I promised him we'd look for his Da once the war was over. I had a bad feeling that his Da had gone into the meat grinder in Afric, or worse, Russankya.

We passed through the first town with just enough of a pause to talk to Widow Talltree and collect feed for the horses and some food for us, too, but the next town, Penzens, was big enough that we had to go looking for Healer Pike. On the way, we found signs of fighting: smashed windows boarded up against the wind, government buildings burned to rubble, bullet holes in walls and signs.

And government officials hanged from trees and gallows.

Healer Pike accepted our news with an exhausted nod, told us he'd send someone to help until he could go himself, and dismissed us without another word.

We spent that night camped in a field. I wanted to keep going, but according to Sean, "Cor, miss, s'too dangerous, loik. Dunno where th' road is, or what's comin' at us."

We huddled together in the wagon for warmth. Tring and her girls shared the watch, despite my insisting they wake me for a turn myself. Dawn was a grey smear on the horizon when I woke up. We drank from a nearby creek, then headed out, stiff and sore.

Every town we came to, had similar signs of fighting, more mob justice against Atlan officials. The closer to Albion we came, the worse the fighting had been. Portston had nearly been burned to the ground, and ships hovered above us. Ships in the bay, too, twenty-gunner steamships.

I almost didn't want to see Albion, at the rate we were going. Would there be anything left?

I suppose it was the exhaustion, the trauma of the Pit, the overwhelming fatigue I felt, making me morose. We all slipped into silence as we crossed the countryside.

Finally we could see the chimney smoke of Albion darkening the midday sky. It didn't seem to be any more or less smokey than the last time I'd seen it.

Long story short, Albion was still mostly standing. Lots of rubble, lots of burned-out homes. No sign of the grisly mob justice, though, which made me suspicious. But there would be time for that later. First I absolutely had somewhere to be.

The Merry Clockmaker still stood, though the windows had been shattered and replaced with some kind of wax paper. Enough to let in some light and keep out the draft, anyway. When we went inside, the clocks were still tick-tocking and chiming at odd intervals, but the usual customers were gone. All the pixies who'd made the pub their second home had gone off to Eire.

We ordered a feast of food, paying with a sliver of atlantium. From the way the barkeep's eyes bugged out, we'd just given him enough to retire in style. I told him to spend it fast, anyway.

We ate, we drank, we waited. Have I mentioned how much I hated waiting?

Sean fell asleep. Too much beer, I guess.

The waitress came over with a note for me. I read it, turned to Tring, and said, "I'll be right back," pointing to the door that led to the privy.

She paused, then nodded.

Down the privy hallway I went, turning left instead of right at the end, opening the door to the barkeep's office. The whole way there, my heart was pounding.

My heart stopped when I saw who'd sent me the note.

"Hello my love," Bunthorne Bartholomew Tallyho said, sweeping me into his arms.

He didn't get a chance to say much more than that, because I kissed him and kissed him and kissed him. I never ever wanted to stop.

Chapter Twenty Five

Many Happy Reunions

I suppose I spent the next half hour or so swinging between crying from happiness and happy babbling as we caught up. Also, the kissing? Yeah, lots of that.

Tring came to check on me at one point, I remember that.

Anyhow, eventually we joined the others and ordered more food and drink. I wanted to turn it into a party but Bunny insisted we head back to his home before dark.

"Albion's not quite safe yet," was all he'd say.

We took the train back to Tallyho Manor. Bunny managed to talk about pretty much nothing the whole way, keeping us amused with the antics of the social set now that the Atlan government had been overthrown. Basically they were all desperate to be seen as part of the native-born Anglics, drinking beer and eating pies instead of wine and fancy stuff, talking with what they thought was the 'voice of the common folk' – you know, speaking Anglic, but saying 'ain't' and 'innit' and dropping their H's. No one spoke Atlan any more.

"Not unless they want a hemp necktie, a-haw-haw," Bunny joked, but there was a shadow in his eyes, like he'd seen some horrible things done lately.

Hadn't we all.

It was honestly hard to think of him as 'Fox' when he put on the airs of Bunny the social gadabout. I'm not surprised no one guessed his secret identity. I mean, I knew he was the vigilante called the Hooded Fox, and I could barely believe it.

I sat next to him the whole way, holding his hand the entire time. I couldn't have let go if I tried. Looking back, I think that maybe I was scared that if I let go, he'd disappear and I'd wake up in the Pit.

We got back to Tallyho Manor well after dark. When we walked in, the sound of women laughing greeted us. I ran into the parlor and found the twins, Gigi, Eve, Domina, Violette, and Doc Regan enjoying drinks and pastries. There were screams of delight and hugs and tears and more laughter and more hugs and more tears. We got all caught up, though I pretty much glossed over the whole horror and terror and pain and suffer part. It wasn't the right time for it. When I got to the part about the giant nugget of atlantium, I could just about hear the *ch-ching!* in everyone's minds.

Doc Regan insisted on giving me a full inspection, pulling me into a drawing room and ordering me to strip.

"Incredible," was her assessment. "Sure an' ye're in better health now than ye were before. Never seen the like. Even some of your scars have begun to fade, look."

She was right, they had begun to fade. Some of the puckered bullet wounds had disappeared completely. I caught a sight of myself in a mirror, and couldn't believe what I saw. I thought I was in shape before I'd gone into the Pit, but apparently a month of hard labour had built up muscles I didn't know I even had. There wasn't an ounce of fat left on me, either. I looked like one of those Olympic athletes, fit and trim, every muscle perfectly defined. My cheekbones stood out a little more, but that might have been the effect of my hair having been massacred. It surprised me that my hair had grown out enough to start curling again.

"You should be at least sufferin' from malnutrition," Doc Regan said as I got dressed. One of Bunny's automaidons brought me some of the twins' clothes. I picked out a blouse and a pair of slacks. They were a little long on me but fit well enough.

I tossed the dress I'd stolen from that village in Atlan, which seemed about a lifetime and a half ago, onto the fire and watched it burn. "I don't know what to tell you, Doc. No one in the Pit was starving, even though the food we had was pretty disgusting."

"We'll do some more tests aboard the Furies in the mornin'," she answered. "They'll be wantin' to know ye're here, then."

"Not yet," I said around the sudden lump in my throat. "I'm not ready to see everyone just yet."

"Fair enough," she smiled, picking up her glass to find it empty. "Back t' th' party, then?"

"Yeah," I grinned.

We pretty much partied until past midnight. Most of the crew went back to their bunks on The Furies, but the twins retired to their bedrooms.

Bunny had his automaidons set me up in a room of my own, with a hot bath waiting. I soaked for a while, letting my stress seep out of me. When I got out, I pulled on a dressing gown and padded barefoot down the hall to Bunny's room.

When I knocked quietly, he answered, "Yes?"

I stepped into his room and went to him, silencing him with kisses.

Yes, I spent the night. No, I didn't want to wait. I didn't want to wait another minute. I didn't want to wait ever again.

We slept in. Not to a ridiculous hour, but reasonably late. We stayed in bed a while longer, talking, and, y'know, other things. He told me about the group of masked vigilantes he'd been working with, about the revolt against Atlan they'd helped. But that's his story and maybe I'll let you hear it one day.

I told him everything, all of it. Everything that happened on the way, in the Pit, our escape. He wiped away my tears, held me silently as I spoke of Quill, how he'd forged the worst criminals in the world into an army, his insane plan to sink the entire island of Neptopolis. I even told him about the mind-reading trick he'd learned from the Tribes.

"So she's telling the truth," he muttered.

"Who is?"

"A friend you'll meet someday. She makes a similar claim."

We got up and dressed, ate breakfast with the twins, who had drunk even Doc Regan under the table. Between the four of us I'm sure we had three pots of coffee.

Then I couldn't put it off any more. "I've got to head back to the ship. Girls, would you like positions aboard The Furies?"

"Oh I say, rawthah!" Guinny laughed.

"Just nothing too too beneath us, you know?"

"Second and third mates?"

"That's far enough, I should think!"

"Quite so!"

"Thanks," I said, relieved they'd be joining the crew.

"Off so soon?" Bunny pouted.

"There is a war on," I pointed out.

"So there is," he shrugged. "I had hoped you might stay around a while longer."

"So did I." I took his hand. "How long did you want me to stay?"

"Forever ?" he smiled. "I'll settle for the rest of our lives."

I smiled through sudden tears. "After the war, I promise."

"I'll hold you to that."

"I will too."

Gwen wiped her mouth with her napkin. "Ahem, lovebirds, I say. Shall we be went?"

I kissed Bunny goodbye, enjoying the feel of his arms around me, memorizing it for the days and nights to come. Then the twins and I went to the forested glade where they'd hidden The Furies.

We walked up the gangplank and were immediately mobbed by everyone. I hugged them all, laughed and giggled, passed a couple of words with everyone, making my way up the stairs and ladders toward the bridge.

That's where I found her, checking and rechecking her equipment.

"Ready to cast off, Restless?" I asked as I stepped onto the bridge.

"Aye aye, Cap," she said. "What's our head..."

That's when she turned. The look on her face had so much going on. Disbelief and joy at seeing me. All the terror that she might never have seen me again, held back all these weeks. Worry that she might start crying. Embarrassment when the tears spilled down anyway.

All that in about the second it took her to launch herself across the bridge and into my arms.

"Now now, none of that," I said into her hair as she sobbed against my shoulder.

Eventually she pulled away and wiped her messy face with the back of her hand. "Right. Sorry, Cap'n. What's our heading?"

"Southeast," I said. "We've got to go help Serena."

"Aye aye, Cap."

I climbed the staircase to the wireless. "How are you, Argenta?"

"I am well, Admiral Val. Welcome back."

"Thanks. All stations, please."

"All stations, Admiral Val."

"Attention crew of The Furies. This is Admiral Val. I've returned to command of this vessel." I paused for the cheer, which went on longer than I expected and brought another lump to my throat. "Make ready to cast off. It's Go Time!"

Another cheer went up, longer than the last.

I felt the engines thrum through the floor as I sat in the captain's chair. I could feel Restless just about quivering with questions as her hands flew over the controls, flicking switches and tapping gauges. She kept stealing glances at me, like she wanted to make sure I was still there. I knew exactly how she felt.

"So, uh, Admiral?"

"Yes Restless?"

"What happened to your hair?"

I laughed as I raised a hand to scrub through the shorn remains of my hair. At least I'd discovered a way to keep the curls under control.

So I told the story, again, only I made it sound a lot more exciting and adventurous than six weeks underground hauling rocks. She stood there, hanging on every word, piloting almost on automatic.

Domina brought me a steaming mug of sweet tea. I paused in my storytelling to hug her and thank her. She actually blushed.

Violette came in with a plotted course. We were headed for Russankya, and the bloodiest battle of the war.

Chapter Twenty Six

An excerpt from
Go Time: How One Woman Changed The World,
by R.M. St.Martin

The fortieth day of the siege of Muskovy came to an end with a blood red sunset. Surely an omen, said some. The end of the Atlan Empire brought with it a resurgence of ancient superstition. The vampyric host awoke from their slumber, but did nothing.

Their leader, General Serena Heartlace, stamped down her frustration and called a general meeting. A vampyress with no formal military training or experience, who'd spent decades avoiding the political manoeuvring so endemic of her people, she'd spent more time in the last month dealing with the internecine squabbling amongst her advisers than with the enemy across the river.

The Moscov River wove through the city creating a series of interlocking peninsulas that both sides of the conflict had tried to capture time and again, to little gain and never for very long. The river itself had so many wrecked ships and downed airships floating and settled within it that in some places dams of destroyed vessels had caused flooding in the nearby streets. Ruins of collapsed buildings teemed with swarms of rats feeding on the bloated corpses of drowned troops. By the end of the tenth month of 6898, both sides had retreated from the peninsulas. They called the burned-out, rubble-filled land between them 'The Kingdom of Rats' and 'The Islands of the Dead.'

At the general meeting called by General Heartlace, she made it clear: They must cross the river. Winter was coming, some argued. When the river froze, they could simply march across and take the opposite bank. But Heartlace understood that they could not wait until winter. The Revolution in the west had stalled in Hispania. Fighting between Atlan troops and revolutionaries in Gallica and Etrusca continued with no clear victor in sight. Bavardy and Levant had settled into an uneasy stalemate. They were needed elsewhere, to end the war decisively.

Other Vampyri argued that the Zhou were coming. Laying rails at an astonishing thirty miles a day, the forces of the Zhou, having quelled any Atlan sentiment on their native soil, were rushing across Russankya. But even at that astonishing rate of advance, the troops would not arrive for weeks.

Heartlace told her generals there would be no waiting, despite their protests and opposition. They would cross the river in one all-out assault.

Airships on both sides of the siege had been the first targets of opportunity. New cannons had the range to fire high enough into the air to make aerial assaults dangerous, if not impossible. So many exploding shells filled the air, one surviving airman called the attack that downed his airship "like being inside a drum beating out a quickmarch."

Now, Heartlace ordered her remaining airships to be armed with barrels of doomfire. They would fly west, out of sight, then circle a hundred miles around the city and bomb the Russ from behind. Without the airships providing cover and transmitting enemy movements to the commanders, the ground troops would be assaulting the Russ unprotected and blind.

For forty days, unlike the Russ across the river, Heartlace had been forced by biology to split her troops. Daxians and the Vulka-rey could attack or defend during the day, but the Vampyri could only assault at night, lying unconscious in their slumber. Heartlace made a decision and gave the order that earned her the nickname 'the Muscovite Butcher'. All Vampyri would feed as much as possible and, suitably protected from the sun by special uniforms that had arrived just the week before, they would attack with all the Daxian and Vulka-rey forces in a daring and potentially suicidal daylight assault. When her commanders asked where they might find so much blood, Heartlace ordered that they would feed from their Russankyan prisoners of war.

It took two days to outfit every Vampyri, and Heartlace insisted on yet another change. Accustomed to the cover of night, the Vampyri soldiers were better at stealthy attacks. A frontal assault across the river in daylight would leave them completely exposed. Heartlace insisted that the troops cover themselves in mud and branches, completely rendering their uniforms unfit for parade ground inspection. It was the first time anyone on either side of the conflict had ever used camouflage.

It worked.

The Russankyan forces guarding the approach across the river never saw them coming. The Vampyri swarmed across the river just before a blood red dawn, when the Russ were most tired. They were also suffering from dysentery and had been fighting debilitating diarrhea and vomiting for the past three days. The stench, one Vampyri later recalled, was the worst he'd ever experienced, in nearly four centuries of vampyric life.

Fledgling Vampyri can take up to a year to become what they refer to as 'their true self.' The transition from mortal Vampyri to fully-blooded Vampyri brings with it hypersensitivity, especially to smells, and an uncontrollable bloodlust whenever threatened. For the Russankyan Campaign, one thousand fledgling had been created. Many had been lost in the Capture of Volgatsyn, nearly three hundred. Another hundred and fifty had gone completely feral in the peninsulas of Moscov, bereft of their recently killed masters, attacking anything that moved, including other Vampyri. Of the five hundred or so that remained, only ninety seven would survive the assault across the river.

The Vampyri Army was made up of Vampyri, Vulka, and humans. But only the Vulka and the humans could be considered actual soldiers; a Vampyri baker knew about as much soldiering as a human baker. The advantages of vampyric strength, speed, senses and resilience to injury were mitigated by the thick leather uniforms, masks and goggles that protected them from the sun's rays.

The greatest advantage in their favour were one hundred mechmen that had just been built in Volgatsyn. The great iron foundries there had been immediately put to back to work, when the city had been captured. The mechmen had all manner of improvements learned from the Afric campaign, and the Revolution was eager to put them to the test.

None more eager than Inga Bludsdottar, nicknamed Inga Doom. Tall, blonde and one-eyed, the inventor of doomfire had made several personal modifications to the mechmen, including shoulder-mounted cannons and wrist-mounted belt-fed repeaters. The Revolutionary repeaters were rapidly becoming the preferred vehicle-mounted rifle, capable of firing two hundred bullets a minute, compared to the Atlan-standard hand-cranked volley gun's sixty.

Heartlace divided her forces into three prongs, called the Left Claw, the Right Claw and the Fangs. Each prong of the attack would command thirty mechmen, whose orders were to capture and hold a peninsula, but not to cross the river. The remaining ten mechmen were to be held in reserve, protecting the Revolution's headquarters, rail depot and hospitals, where six thousand prisoners of war had been drained of their blood to unconsciousness, but not death.

The commander of the Left Claw was Vladimir Nightreaver, a dark-haired giant of a Vampyri who privately thought Heartlace unfit for command, but who followed orders because, he said, he could see the way the wind was blowing. Heartlace had the full support of the Pirate Queen, who had the full support of the Revolution; whoever aligned themselves with Heartlace would rule in the regime that followed. His successes in capturing Nevaburg earned him the admiration of his troops, but they did not love him. He was too brutal, too cold and efficient. But they followed his orders without question, because he brought them victory.

The Right Claw's commander was Andras Demise, Heartlace's sibling and beloved by his troops. Handsome and dapper, he knew the name of every soldier under his command. He'd won several small victories in the early days of the Russankyan Campaign, and personally led the charge that had taken Volgatsyn. He understood that a reputation for success was as important as the successes themselves, and that happy troops were loyal troops. He personally financed better food for his soldiers.

The Fangs would be commanded by Heartlace herself. She thought Demise too soft and Nightreaver too merciless, but could not deny their successes.

Both the Left and Right Claws were each made up of fifteen thousand Daxian infantry, a regiment of light armour, and a battalion of both Vulka and Vampyri, in addition to the thirty mechmen. The Fangs had a similar complement, but had a full wing of Vulka-rey, under the command of Air Marshall Olga Draganova, whose successes in Afric, coupled with attrition in the ranks, had led to her rapid rise to complete command of the aerial werewolves.

"A thousand Vulka-rey in the air was a sight to behold," she later described. "Brass wings gleaming, the chatter of gunfire raining death, the shrieking howl for blood... For the Russ, it turned bowels to water, blood to ice, bones to mist."

The estimated hundred thousand Russ had the advantage. Dug in amongst the ruins through a network of tunnels that stretched for miles, they could reposition their troops at a moment's notice. The days of battlefield warfare with lines of troops facing off against each other had ended. Hungry, exhausted and dehydrated from the plague of dysentery, the Russ believed they were defending their homes from a hostile invader, despite the propaganda pamphlets dropped on the city, informing them that the Revolution was fighting for their freedom as well.

The Russankyan Third Army had fought a strategic withdrawal all year. Moscov had been the rallying point for their last stand. Airships circled their side of the city, watching enemy movements and engaging enemy airships. As per standard operating procedure in the event of a siege, women and children had been evacuated from the city as soon as it had become clear the Revolution had them pinned. Couriers sneaked through enemy lines weekly, updating Neptopolis of their situation, demanding assistance, begging for reinforcements.

Neptopolis had no reinforcements to send. The war in Hispania had bogged down the First and Fifth Armies; the Second Army had been deployed in Neptopolis to re-establish civil order after a series of fires and riots had broken out following an utterly unexpected earthquake. The Fourth and Sixth Armies had been completely wiped out in Afric and Zhou. The Russankyan Third Army were on their own. Moscov would be their last stand and they knew it.

"I had just come back from the latrines, again, and returned to my post only to see the skyline had changed," a surviving Russ soldier later described. "Instead of rubble, giant automatons. Dozens of them. Taking up defensive positions across the river, not five hundred feet away. I rang my alarm bell. All along the line I heard similar bells ringing. I waited for the order to fire, but it never came."

The Russ commander had been sitting down to breakfast, potato and beet soup, the only supplies that had arrived on the last shipment to make it through the Revolutionary blockade. His name was Tyr Ebonfury, a one-eyed former slaver and pirate who had been trapped in Moscov when the Revolution had arrived and who, by successfully commanding a defence that had turned back fifteen assaults by advancing rebels, had earned himself a battlefield commission as a colonel. Attrition and some say outright murder had seen him rise to the rank of Brigadier General.

Ebonfury received the news that the mechmen were simply sitting there, not attempting to cross the river. Suspicious of a trap, he ordered his troops to wait and see what would happen, then turned back to his breakfast.

It was, an aide recalled, Ebonfury's greatest mistake.

While Russ troops waited for the order to fire, a light rain began to fall. Heartlace ordered her secret weapons into position and deployed. Inga Doom may be remembered for countless improvements to weaponry, but her newly-invented assault spanners broke the siege and ended the Russankyan Campaign. Some technological historians insist the assault spanner changed the face of war forever.

Russankyan troops that morning saw what they later described as a great metallic turtle or tortoise, crawling through the rain-slicked rubble by means of a continuous track, a series of interlocking plates that ran under the belly and over the back of the spanner. What they could not see were the hundred troops inside the spanner, heavily armed with belt-fed repeaters so massive it took two soldiers, working together, to carry, aim, and fire them.

When the spanners reached the river's shoreline, they deployed their piton anchors, great spears of metal driven into the ground. Then they began to cross the river, the continuous track unravelling behind them as they went, performing the task that had earned their names, spanning the river in a matter of seconds, laying a bridge behind them.

Camouflaged troops, who had been lying in wait for the spanners to arrive, rushed to follow the great beast. One Russankyan survivor said, "It was as if the land itself had risen up against us."

Russ sub-commanders didn't wait any longer. They gave the order to fire before Ebonfury had a chance to finish his breakfast.

When the spanners reached the opposite shore they released their troops, opened their gun ports, and filled the air with so many bullets the Russ wondered if all the ammunition in the world had been fired at once. Though they'd been ordered to fire, most Russankyans hid behind their fortifications.

Then the mechmen let loose with their shoulder cannons, sending exploding shells across the river to blast the Russ from their positions.

At the Fangs, the Vulka-rey flew straight for the airships that guarded the Russ, firing bullets and dropping doomfire canisters directly at the balloons themselves, rather than the armoured ships dangling beneath. Soon, exploding airships rained down with the worsening storm, setting fire to what remained of the city.

Ebonfury rushed to his command tent and began issuing orders, shoring up defences that seemed about ready to break. The majority of his troops faced the Left Claw, guarding the Moscov treasury, where vaults were filled to overflowing with gold, gems, valuable artwork, and millions of sovereigns of Atlan currency. After the battle, nearly a thousand pounds of atlantium was found in the vaults as well, the largest such horde outside of Neptopolis. The soldiers there had been given the order to hold the line and protect the treasury at all cost.

Nightreaver had no intention of capturing the treasury. More than anything he wanted to break through the lines and capture the Russ headquarters, ahead of Heartlace, despite his orders. He believed the glory of that capture would earn him the leadership of the army.

The Right Claw's objective was simple: strike across the river, break the lines, and take the Russ airfields. Demise knew well that his part of the plan had enough glory for him and his troops, but he had a terrible sense of direction. Relying on maps from before the war, ruined streets led his soldiers into dead ends and ambushes. Hundred were slaughtered as Demise tried desperately to find the airfield.

The Fangs faced stiff resistance. Imperial forces were entrenched and under cover, firing into crowds of Revolutionaries. They couldn't miss, and couldn't be hit.

But they could burn.

One out of every ten Revolutionaries carried doomfire rifles, capable of launching the flaming liquid a hundred feet with pinpoint accuracy. On their backs they each carried ten gallons of doomfire in a bullet-proof canister. Only a direct hit from a cannonball would pierce the thick armour. Despite the weight, a Vampyri or Vulka could manoeuvre the heavy doomfire launcher as easily as a human could a rifle.

The storm worsened. The stench of the open, overflowing latrines and the roar of gunfire and thunder soon drove dozens of fledgling Vampyri into a frenzy. Rather than calm or reason with their fledglings, the masters drove them forward into the waiting Russ, using them as targets to draw their fire.

Despite the aggression of the assault, the Revolution soon found themselves stalled out, unable to achieve their objectives. Nightreaver's forces were bogged down, sustaining heavy casualties. Nightreaver was forced to call in his reserves. The Left Claw later reported one hundred and seventy percent wounded. Official casualty figures list his wing of the attack at nearly forty five percent dead, the greatest single-day loss of either side of the war.

Demise fared better, but having finally found the airfield he proved incapable of taking and keeping it. Officers later reported Demise seemed confused, dazed, occasionally breaking into weeping or hysterical laughter, veering between paranoid withdrawals and foolhardy charges. The Atlan airfield changed hands at least a dozen times that morning, maybe more. Units became separated, surrounded, wiped out.

At the centre, Heartlace held on, rallying her troops again and again, ordering the mechmen across the river to protect their rear, only to have them driven back by Atlan mortars and Russankyan reserves, hidden in tunnels that collapsed under the mechmen's weight.

"At one point," Heartlace recalled, "we were completely surrounded. I ordered defensive positions and tried to reach the Claws by portable wireless. Nothing. Static. And then, a voice that for weeks I had only heard in dreams. 'Need a hand?' I admit, I wept with relief."

Admiral Sunset Val, Pirate Queen of the Seven Skies, Captain of The Furies, had arrived.

She had brought Heartlace's missing airships, who had run into the storm on their way out and been scattered. Rallied by The Furies' timely arrival, the last of the Revolution's fleet followed the Pirate Queen straight down the gullet of the attack, dropping their doomfire canisters on the Russ positions, every gun, every cannon blasting away. Dozens of the Pirate Queen's deathwings darkened the sky, firing on enemy positions from above, dropping down to take out snipers in the heights. Admiral Val herself pulled the trigger on Old Sparky, their great bow-mounted lightning cannon, now charged by photonic invertors. Gone were the days of airships being depowered after firing a single bolt.

As it had before, firing the lightning cannon in a thunderstorm brought about the discharge of dozens of lightning bolts. The Russ fuel reserves were hit, a fireball so brilliant that dozens of soldiers on both sides were blinded for days following the blast.

At the start of the war Serena Heartlace had considered herself a swordmistress of the ninth order. After the war, when she finally had time to take the tests and fortune enough to pay the fees, she was certified as being of the fourth order. Only ten other beings on the planet could say the same.

One was Tyr Ebonfury.

His headquarters destroyed by a lightning bolt, he took up his sword and vowed to kill Heartlace himself. He rallied his troops for a final charge, then leapt upon an autohorse and led the assault.

His charge will forever go down in history as one of the boldest and bloodiest. Not a single one of his soldiers survived. Three generals, nine colonels and light colonels, twenty six majors and captains, one hundred and nineteen lieutenants, six hundred and six sergeants and corporals, and three thousand one hundred and twelve private soldiers died in Ebonfury's Folly.

The Russankyan Third Army was destroyed.

But Ebonfury reached his target, despite the odds. Heartlace later said she could feel him coming, like a great weight barrelling down a hill, or two locomotives on the same track. The death of an aide-de-camp warned Heartlace of Ebonfury's arrival, just enough time for her to draw her sword, her guns emptied and useless.

A well-placed bullet could have ended it. Ebonfury was alone, having sacrificed his entire command to reach the Revolutionary General. But Heartlace waved off all her aides and troops and faced her nemesis. Encircled by the Revolutionaries, Ebonfury attacked.

"I never saw the blades move," Colonel Dorit Bloodflower, Heartlace's chief aide, later wrote. "Just shimmering blurs in the rain. No fancy footwork. Bloodful as she was, she could have finished him the Vampyri way, with her fangs. Impossibly, the sun was setting. A whole day of fighting, somehow slipped into the past. Soon the lethargy of the slumber would be gone. Soon the General would fully awaken. Even so, she kept him at bay. He, rage and thunder; she, cold and ice."

Heartlace drew first blood, a cut on Ebonfury's cheek, just under his remaining eye.

"I realized she merely toyed with him," Bloodflower wrote.

Ebonfury went mad, screaming incoherently, throwing himself into a flurry of thrusts and attacks. Heartlace defended and parried each and every one. Then, a nearby explosion shook the ground and she slipped in the mud. Ebonfury skewered her through her left side, nicking her lung. Witnesses reported that the look of triumph on his face was so savage that he no longer looked human.

Then Heartlace stood, wrenching the sword from Ebonfury's grasp. It was lodged in her ribs.

The sun set.

With one blow, Heartlace decapitated him. His head flew into the crowd, where it disappeared. Despite a lengthy investigation to locate it, Ebonfury's head was never found.

Heartlace ripped off her sun-mask, pulled the blade free from her side, and drank Ebonfury's blood. The wound in her side healed.

The battle was over.

Chapter Twenty Seven

Decisions, Decisions

And that's why I hired this guy to tell my story, because come on, that was pretty wicked. If History class had been that cool I think everyone I knew would have gotten top marks.

I found Serena in her command tent, still giving orders despite the wound in her side, which didn't just magically heal up the way it was written in the history books. I mean, vampyri healing is fast, but not that fast. Not like Vulka, or one of Doc Regan's inventions.

We'd come from the airfield as quick as we could, but Demise's blunders made it rough going. We'd found his troops at a loss for orders, his sub-commanders arguing amongst themselves about who should take over. See, Demise had been hit by one of the lightning bolts as he waved the Revolutionary flag to rally his command and died instantly.

I'd seized command of the troops and we'd fought our way to Serena's camp, but by the time we got there all the fun had ended. I really wished I could have seen Ebonfury get killed. I know that's a horrible thing to say, but the truth is he deserved it.

Anyhow, with the fighting done in Moscov, I put Nightreaver in charge of keeping the peace. I know he defied a direct order to take the treasury but I mean, he kind of had a point. It's not like the Atlans inside the treasury were going to burn the gold and atlantium. Nightreaver set up a mini-siege around the treasury and spent the rest of the week taking on entrenched positions of Atlans who refused to surrender. I'd intended it as a kind of punishment, but he and his troops really enjoyed it. And the treasury siege ended after three days anyway. I heard Nightreaver's troops were tossing heads of dead Atlans through the windows, just to freak out the Atlans inside the treasury. I didn't even try to stop them.

So yeah, I left him in charge when we left. And the things he and his troops did... There isn't a day that goes by since then that I don't regret the decision I made. I could make excuses, point out that I didn't have much choice. Demise was dead, Serena was leaving with me,

Bloodflower wasn't much of a commander, as we later saw when she tried to stop Nightreaver and wound up with her head on a spike. I could say all that, but in the end, the decision was mine and I made it and the Russankyans paid for it. In blood. Gallons and gallons of blood.

Yes, I'm very aware that if I hadn't put him in charge he would have rebelled against the Revolution, forcing us to keep critical troops and resources in Russankya instead of sending them across Bavardy and Gallica, bringing those countries under our control. I know. It doesn't make me feel any better about what happened. Anyway the Zhou showed up a month later and stopped the Massacre of Moscov, putting Nightreaver's head on a spike, so I guess you could call that justice.

We left Moscov about a week after the battle ended. I commandeered two other ships to come with me as escorts. We hadn't taken Bavardy or Gallica yet, remember, so technically those were still enemy territory, and there was still plenty of fighting to do.

I called a meeting of my department heads. Molly wasn't the only familiar face missing. The pixies were gone, replaced by an Anglic aeriologist named Shye Banningcord, formerly of the Tallyho Sisters. Like her name suggests, she never really said much.

Inga had gone, too, back to Volgatsyn to direct the ironworks foundries and the gunsmithies. She wanted them cranking out mechmen by the daily dozen, and had all kinds of crazy ideas about how to improve them, making them faster, stronger, deadlier. I think the Siege of Moscov unhinged her a little, but there was no denying her genius.

I promoted Daisy Pinprick to Chief Cannoneer. She'd been on the gun crews since Libertia, and had the most experience. I trusted her. She didn't have the brilliance of Inga Doom, but she had those gun crews so well-trained they could load and fire in their sleep.

I also promoted the twins to Commodores.

"I say, you can do that?" Gwen asked, laughing when I told them.

"I'm the Pirate Queen, I can do whatever I want," I answered.

"Too bloody right she can!" Guinny said, raising her glass of sherry. "The only question I have is, what took you so long, wot?"

I gave them orders to take command of our escorts and, when we reached Hispania, to go to Ys and take command of the pirate fleet.

"I say ducks, whatever shall we do with the fleet once we have it?"

"Meet us in Neptopolis."

Everyone stared at me like I'd ordered them to fly to the moon.

I took a deep breath. "Look... This war isn't over yet. Not by a long shot. And the Atlans are just digging into those Hispanian mountains. As long as they're fighting, the Atlans in Gallica and Etrusca and Bavardy are going to fight."

"Due respect Admiral," Violette said, "but we fought the Atlans in the mountains of Afric, too."

I pointed at the map. "Those mountains are nothing like the Alpatians, Violette. And those Atlans were spread too thin, divided. No central command directing their efforts. Yeah we took the entire continent in less than a year, and that was amazing, but for the last what, two months, the Revolution's taken less than a handful of miles. We don't have the supplies for an extended campaign, except what we seize from our conquered enemies. Well, if we're not conquering, we're not seizing, and we'll run out sooner rather than later. Right, Elegiac?"

Mrs. Shorty nodded. "The Revolution has, at best, another month of supplies. Now, ending the war in Russankya will help, and we'll be getting new from those ironworks and factories. All the same, there's no guarantee the troops will be able to last that long."

"Hang on," said Violette, setting her wineglass down. "How can we be running out of supplies? We've conquered half the world!"

"But all the men are fighting, or dead," Elegiac answered. "There's no one left to make bullets or cannonballs or gunpowder. The summer's harvest is rotting in the fields for lack of men to gather it all in."

"This may sound like a stupid question, but why aren't the women working in the factories or the fields?"

Everyone looked at me.

"Well?"

"Not an unreasonable question," Miss Merryweather said. "But alas, there is only an unreasonable answer. No women went to work in the factories, because no women ever have. I'm sure some of the women went out into the fields to gather up some of the harvest, but the truth of the matter is, men have always done that work, and women have always been told they simply cannot."

"Because they're women," I said, my tone flat with scorn. They nodded. "Well, I have news for them. They can, and they will. But until then, if what you're saying is true and we're going to run out of food and guns and ammunition, the Revolution is going to fail. And I won't let that happen. Domina!"

Domina, of course, was right at my side already.

"Oh. Domina, tell Restless to change course."

"Of course, Admiral. What course?"

"Violette? Ys?"

"Oh," she said, thinking about it for like, two seconds. "Four points south from due west. That should do for the next hour or so. I'll be there directly."

Domina nodded and left.

"Vhy Ys?" Serena asked.

"We'll help the fleet finish the job there, then we're attacking Neptopolis."

"There are only four dozen ships left in Ys," Miss Merryweather said cautiously. "You mean to attack the heart of the Empire with four dozen ships?"

"Yes."

"No ground troops? No mechmen, no pachyderms, no Vulka-rey?"

"Yes."

"It certainly has the virtue of having never been tried."

"We'll stop in Hispania first, pick up some help. Alright?"

Miss Merryweather smiled. "Forgive me, Admiral, it's not my place to approve your plan."

"No, it's fine. Without Molly here, someone's got to challenge everything I say."

"Not everything, surely."

"No." I missed Molly. I hoped she was alright. I hoped we would be, too. "Alright, so, anything else?"

No one had much of anything to say, so they all left.

All except Serena.

What is it?

You are troubled.

I guess.

By?

We have to end this war.

And we will.

As soon as possible.

Yes. And?

And I don't know how without...

Her eyes went wide as my thoughts turned to the countless images I'd seen in books and online of huge nuclear mushroom clouds filling the sky. Of cities reduced to burning splinters and rubble. Of people horribly burned, dying by the tens of thousands.

A... bomb?

Yes. One bomb can destroy an entire city. My world has hundreds, maybe thousands of those bombs. They were built to end a great war, like this war.

But there are no such bombs in this world.

No. But the idea of destroying Neptopolis somehow... That could end the war.

Yes. And so could a costly and bloody invasion.

"That won't happen," I said out loud. "The Revolution's bogged down in Hispania. They'll get slaughtered in the Alpatians."

"Yes, you are probably right."

"You know I'm right."

She just nodded, a wry smile on her lips.

"So we destroy Neptopolis. Or at least bring the war right to their doorstep, so that they can't ignore it any more."

"I agree that they must know the var is coming for them, and that the var must end soon," Serena said. "But there is more to it, now."

Our special connection transmitted what she meant, and I put it into words: "The war can't just end; it has to be won."

Exactly.

"Won by the Revolution."

Yes.

"A clear victor to make sure there is no question in the world about who's going to be making the rules, about who is in charge."

"Yes."

"So we need to make sure the Revolution gets the credit for what we do in Neptopolis, that's all."

"And how vill ve do that?"

"I have no idea," I said, standing. "But I'll think of something."

I left the mess to get Violette to set a course for Hispania.

Chapter Twenty Eight

Yep, Just Like That

We had to go the long way, over the Europan Sea around Etrusca, to get to Hispania. The skies above Gallica were crawling with Atlan Aerial Forces, just looking for someone to be target practice. When we finally arrived in Ispalia, finding Revolution headquarters proved somewhat difficult. Things had gotten messy more than once and the HQ had been overrun two or three times before it had been declared indefensible and relocated.

It took most of a day but I finally found it, located in the basement of a winery. The thick stone columns supporting the vaulted ceiling above us probably could have held up the entire city, much less the pile of rubble that had been the winery's grape-crushing facility.

Being underground again made my mouth go dry and my heart race a little. I took a deep breath and set it all aside, pushing it deep down inside me. I'd deal with it later.

Inside, people rushed around, carrying pieces of paper, reporting to commanders and sub-commanders, getting orders. Asking around led me to an alcove at the far end of the basement, lit by electric lamps. A wireless communicatron station sat nearby, the three operators issuing commands as they were handed to them.

"Hi," I said, walking into the command alcove. "How's it going?"

"Admiral Val," said General Komodo. "Nice of you to join uss."

Mr. Mahogany turned to face him. "Let us be gracious, General." He turned to me. "Admiral. Welcome. How fares the fleet?"

"No idea. They're at Ys. Russankya's ours, if you hadn't heard."

"Rumours had begun to reach our operatives," Mahogany said, waving a hand at a world map pinned to the wall. Tiny little Revolutionary flags covered Afric, Anglica and Russankya, except for one Atlan flag over Moscov, which an aide removed. The Atlan flag, the blue head of Nepton on a white background, dotted Etrusca, Gallica, Bavardy, and Hispania. And Ys and Atlan, of course.

"Have you any other newss, Admiral?" the General asked.

"Like what, General?"

"Like these riotss in Neptopoliss, for one," he said.

"Are there riots in Neptopolis?" I asked, all sweet and innocent. "How very convenient for us."

There was a long pause as he glared at me. "Quite," he said, finally.

I sighed. "Say what you want to say, General."

He jabbed a finger at me. "You defied ourr exprressss orderss."

I leaned forward, resting my hands on the table. "As a member of this council, Pirate Queen and Admiral of the Pirate Fleet, I could say I deny your authority to give me orders, General. We don't order each other around. We make suggestions, take advice, come to an agreement and set plans into motion."

"You wish to argue semanticss? Fine! You defied our *agreement*."

"I never agreed to anything," I said with a smile and a shrug. "Look, General, what are you really pissed off about? The fact that I went my own way on this, or the fact my plan actually worked?"

"Pah," he spat. "Your plan. What plan? Frree the worst murdering criminalss into the general population? All you have done is turn public sentiment against uss!"

"Alright, um, first? Show of hands, who here hasn't killed someone? Anyone? No? We're all killers, General. Everyone in this room is a murderer." I paused to let that sink in. I didn't like how it made me feel. I hoped it had the same effect on them.

"Thiss iss warr. Warr iss different," Komodo said.

"Tell that to the dead," I answered. "Now then, as to the rest of what you said? The second they were freed from the Pit, they weren't escaped criminals any more. They're agents of the Revolution, and I expect everyone to honour our agreement with them. Also, public sentiment was already pretty much in the 'Revolution Bad' camp. Yeah, they don't like us very much in Neptopolis. Anywhere on Atlan, really. I know, what a shock."

Mr. Mahogany put a hand on Komodo's shoulder. "You may disagree with her methods, but you cannot deny her plan has been beneficial to the cause. Had the Second Army been deployed here in Hispania, we would have been wiped out. You've said yourself on many occasions that our meagre victories here have been near things."

Komodo nodded, but his expression said he wasn't happy. "Yess. It iss true." He looked at me, reached a grudging decision. "Admiral Val... Good work, your plan in Neptopoliss."

I realized that was about as close to an apology as I was going to get, and considering why I'd come to Hispania, I decided not to push it. "Thank you, General. Now then, what's the situation here?"

They brought me up to date on everything, and it was as bad as I expected. Atlan forces were holed up in the mountains, digging in, expanding caves, making fortresses. Once in a while they'd make a sortie out to attack a weak spot in our lines or to capture a supply train. Hit and run raids, not stand-up battles like at the beginning of the war. Guess their leaders could be taught, too.

A runner came in, carrying a message, and waited to be acknowledged. But when Komodo stuck out his hand for the message, the runner said, "Begging your pardon, General, but this is for Admiral Val."

"Me?" I asked as he passed me the note. What was written there made me grin.

"Well?" Komodo asked impatiently.

I read it out loud. "'To Admiral Val, Revolution HQ; Greetings. I beg permission to offer you the island of Ys, its inhabitants and materiel, conquered this fourth day of the eleventh month of 6898.'"

"Just yesterday," Mr. Mahogany said. "All the way from Ys. The speed of modern communications is astounding."

"Who is it from?" Komodo asked.

"Captain Lawless," I answered. "He says they've captured thirty ships, three hundred heavy guns, eighteen tons of ammunition... the list goes on."

"Excellent," Mr. Mahogany said. "We need those guns and ammunition."

"I'll tell you what," I said. "You can have all the guns and ammo you want, but I need those ships. And, oh, two or three thousand troops."

Komodo laughed. "Would you like my arm while you're at it?"

"I'm leading an assault on Neptopolis as soon as possible," I said. "I'll need all the ships I can get. Anyway, you're not going to use them. The Atlans are dug into those mountains. Airships are useless to you."

"Yes, but three thousand troopss are not uselesss. We need every man we have just to keep what we have gained here."

"And if Neptopolis falls in a week, how long do you expect the First and Fifth Armies to hold out?"

Mr. Mahogany's eyes widened. "A week?!"

But Komodo just smirked. "How, exactly, do you expect to plan and organize your invasion in a week?"

Who said anything about planning? "You leave that to me. Give me three thousand troops. If my plan fails, you can condemn me as a dangerous rogue. But if I succeed, I'll give you all the credit. You'll go down as the greatest military commanders in history."

Yeah, we were close enough to the end of the war that people were starting to think about what would happen after the war. And yeah, the leaders had begun to think about what roles they would play in the world we'd create, and how they wanted to be remembered.

Me, I had no such thoughts. Everything was so confusing and crazy. Do I get the aetheric portal working and go home to my old life, my family, my high school classes, all that? Do I stay here on Ayrth, stay with some of the best friends I'd ever had, stay with the man I loved? And what then? What place will I have in the new world? I was useless at politics and hopefully when the war was over there wouldn't be any more battles to fight. I wasn't sure there would be a place for a pirate queen in the world we would create.

So I didn't think about more than a couple of days ahead. The future would handle itself. I needed to focus on the present.

And that meant getting the invasion of Atlan going.

Another runner came in, carrying a message. He handed this one to General Komodo.

Komodo read it. He looked almost stunned.

"What is it?"

"A message from Miss Phoenix," he said. "She says Anglica is putting together battalions to send over."

Mr. Mahogany reached for the message. "Battalions? Plural?"

"Plural," Komodo nodded, handing him the message. "Four battalionss. One each of humanss, patchworkss, pixiess and animen."

"Where would they find a thousand animen?"

"Oh," I said. "Yeah, that would be me. Well, mostly Captain Rage, I mean, the rescue was all him. But I was there. Got them set up in Anglica."

They stared at me a long, long time. I just smiled.

And then something unprecedented happened. Collective Number Six spoke.

"We wish to convey a message."

All eyes turned to the automaton.

"By all means, Collective," Mr. Mahogany said.

"The Union of Automated Gentlemen are ready to join the fight. We, too, have a battalion ready."

"Excellent!" Komodo said, slamming a fist on the table. "With five battalionss we'll crrush the rresistance in the mountainss!"

"Negative," the Collective said. "We wish the automaton battalion join in Admiral Val's assault."

Komodo's triumph washed away in dismay. "What?!"

"Our calculations have determined that continuing the offensive here in Hispania has only a minimal chance of success. Eventually, Atlan Command will conclude that we have no intention to invade, and redeploy the Second Army to assist the First and Fifth. Caught between the three armies, we will fight a two-front war.

"However, striking at Neptopolis within the next week will bring about variables which affect our calculations most favourably. Admiral Val's idea has merit,. That is where we will put our resources."

Silence filled the alcove. Even the wireless operators were listening to us, instead of their headsets.

General Komodo and Mr. Mahogany shared a look. A look that said a lot. So much rode on this single decision.

Komodo shook his head, but Mr. Mahogany just nodded. Komodo leaned forward, staring at the map. He looked at me.

"A week?" he asked.

"We call the ships in from Ys," I began, making it up as I went. "Pull every troop you can spare, load them up. We launch an aerial offensive at Neptopolis. Send seaships too. Everything you got. Land the troops here," I pointed at the map halfway between Neptopolis and Atlantopolis. "Cut them in half, reduce the chance of reinforcements gathering at the capital..."

"Here would be better," the General said, pointing at another location, closer to Neptopolis, where a number of roads converged. And just like that, we were planning the greatest invasion Ayrth had ever seen.

Twelve hours later, we had our plan of attack. We sent out the orders. Speed was more vital than secrecy. It wasn't as if Atlan Command had any other troops to recall, or any more guns to arm the citizens.

I know I said it would only take a week but it was closer to two. I don't think I slept more than an hour or two a day. But when the time came, I made sure I spent a solid six hours asleep in my bunk, on my ship, surrounded by my crew. I'm amazed I got any sleep at all, I was so charged up on adrenaline and coffee.

Finally the morning came. We'd faked a withdrawal to the coast of Hibernia, giving up hard-fought ground with barely a fight. The First and Fifth hadn't followed us at first, expecting some kind of trap. But after it became clear that we really were retreating, they buzzed out of their caves like angry hornets.

Right into the waiting Automated Battalion. Not just robot butlers and automaidons, either; pachyderm platforms outfitted with autohorse directivation units; great shambling mechmen salvaged from the battles in Afric and reconditioned for co-operative automaton use; and more, much more, like salvaged airships that had been refitted with collective directivation units, armour plating and self-loading cannons. The Union's idea of a battalion looked nothing like a normal military unit.

But maybe that's what we were about, too. Let's face it, there was nothing 'normal' about us. Pirates, pleasure girls, ex-slaves, patchworks, automatons, animen, werewolves, vampyri, Zhou criminals, Afric rebels, pixies, orphans, widows, childless mothers... We'd all been pushed to the fringes, to the edges of the world, told we were worthless, nothing.

You get enough nothing though, and you've really got something.

Okay, so math isn't my best subject. You know what I mean.

I know the historians insist that we must have been planning the invasion for months, that the Hispanian invasion had been a training ground, sure, but mostly it had been a feint to keep the First and Fifth Armies landlocked and busy while we prepared. That logistically it was impossible to organize something so huge so quick. But honestly that's where our loose command structure sort of helped us. No rigid chains of command, no established procedures to follow by the book. We said strategically withdraw to the coast and everyone went. We said get aboard these ships and everyone went. We told the ships, go here, land here, disembark here. And everyone went.

Don't get me wrong. We basically tried to keep it a secret. I mean, there was no way Atlan Command would have been able to find out about our plan, confirm that it was actually happening, redeploy and mobilize themselves to do something about it in time, but all the same, we tried to keep it as quiet as possible.

Still, you could tell, everyone knew something was up, something big. Maybe the biggest thing ever. I sent Restless out to see what she could hear in the streets and bars. She reported that most people seemed to think the Revolution had figured out a way to bring Atlan to its knees. Time for the war to finally end, they were saying. Time for a new world to rise from the ashes of the Empire.

Go Time.

Chapter Twenty Nine

The Go-est Go Time Ever

Ever since Libertia, the Union of Automated Gentlemen had been cranking out wireless radiophonic communicatrons. Every ship in our fleet had one. Every ship at sea had one. Every mechman, pachyderm platform, and command tent had one. Some of the more important units had the newest, latest, portable ones (and by portable I mean it only took two people or one patchwork or vampyri to carry one). I think, in the end, that made the biggest difference in the war. We could communicate instantly, organize ourselves, respond and react with minimal delay.

Atlan Command, unfortunately for them, had to rely on runners or messengers in ornithopters to relay orders. The flash communicators couldn't be seen well enough when all the gunsmoke filled the air to be very effective, so their style of battle relied a lot more on giving autonomy to the commanders in the field. That autonomy bred arrogance, and that arrogance worked in our favour.

I climbed the stairs to the wireless station. "All stations, Argenta."

"All stations, aye, Admiral."

I took the microphone from her.

"This is Admiral Sunset Val. Many of you joined this cause, this Revolution, for revenge. Revenge against the pirates who enslaved us. Revenge against a corrupt system, one that condoned and supported your enslavement. Revenge against the monsters who tore us apart, toyed with us, tortured us.

"Some of you joined for the chance at glory. Glory in battle. Glory in fighting for a worthy cause. Glory as a member of The Furies.

"But I'm here, today, to tell you that this war isn't about revenge, and it isn't about glory. It's about justice!

"People fall prey to slavers who roam the seven skies and Atlan buys the captives! Is that justice?

"People fall into debt and Atlan patchworks them into slaves! Is that justice?

"People fall... but people also rise. So now I ask you. Rise up! Rise up and fight for justice! Rise up and cast Atlan down! It's time for Atlan to fall. It's time for the old system to go!

"It's Go Time!"

I could hear the crew cheering through the floor.

Not bad, considering I'd made it all up as I went.

"Forgive me, Admiral," Argenta said. "I ... made an error."

"What error? Everyone aboard heard it, didn't they?"

"Yes, Admiral. But I must have accidentally flipped the broadcast switch. Your speech went out to the entire fleet. Everyone with a wireless heard it."

I stared at her for a few seconds, then shrugged. "Good. I guess."

"Twin One to Admiral Val, I say ducks, nice bit of speechifying."

"Twin Two to Admiral Val, raw-thah!"

"Last one to Tallyho Manor buys," I said into the microphone, then handed it back to Argenta.

I slid down the bannister and took my seat. "Restless, due west."

"Aye Captain, due west."

We took to the air, and a hundred airships followed. Nearly three hundred seaships were already steaming toward Atlan. Some were carrying ground troops. Others were hunting the Atlan Nautical Fleet, somewhere between Afric and Atlan.

About halfway there we were joined by the Pirate Fleet, heading south from Ys, carrying the battalions the Anglics had promised us.

I wished we'd had time to organize the Zhou fleet, hit Atlan from the west while we attacked from the east. What we didn't know then was, the Zhou were too busy to help us out anyway, having decided to end the ongoing feud with the Neppon criminal organization, the Yegusi, by invading Neppon. The Revolution wasn't happy about that when they found out, but then, the Zhou weren't happy we'd invaded Atlan without them, and it all ultimately became a huge political mess.

But none of that had happened yet, we didn't know anything about it. All we knew were, we were flying through the night skies, hundreds of airships, hundreds of thousands of troops, racing to catch up with still more seaships, still more troops. Charging lightning cannons by moonlight. Loading cannons, belt-fed repeaters, volley guns, rifles, pistols. Sharpening knives and swords and claws. Our surgeons and field medics prepared themselves, cleaning their instruments, preparing doses of sedatives and painkillers.

Some sat quietly, smoking. Others told jokes to lighten the mood. No coffee was served. All alcohol had been left behind. Adrenaline was our only stimulant, and we had plenty of it.

I stepped out onto the main deck to get some air. I found Serena, staring at the moon.

We didn't say anything, not even along our psychic link. Just stood in silence, looking at the night sky. The stars so bright. The moonlight, gleaming on the hulls of hundreds of airships.

I was too numb to know what I was feeling. Mostly I just wanted it to be sunrise. We'd timed it so we'd reach Atlan by sunrise. I glanced back and could just make out the first greyness on the horizon.

"I should get dressed," Serena said finally.

"Yeah."

"Vhatever happens today, Wal... thank you."

"Thank me? For what?"

"For everything."

She took my hand and squeezed it. I squeezed back. We stood there for a few seconds, just looking at each other. I nodded, not trusting my voice. She nodded back, then disappeared into the ship. I stayed on deck until Domina found me and told me I was needed back on the bridge.

I rushed back and took my chair. "What is it?"

"Advance scouts report heavy resistance ahead, Admiral."

"No kidding," I muttered. "Anything else?"

"No, Admiral."

"Send word to the fleet. We're almost there."

"Aye, Admiral."

"There!" Restless yelled, pointing.

I squinted, then felt stupid and slipped my goggles on. Distant bursts of cannonfire. A ship went up in a ball of flame so bright I turned away, blinking spots.

Soon we could hear the muffled thunder of the cannons.

We still couldn't see the coast.

"Argenta, all ships."

"All ships aye."

"This is Admiral Val. All gunships to the fore. Transports to..."

I checked our speed, forty knots "... twenty knots. We'll clear you a path. Gunships, launch ornithopters. Ornithopters, fire your flares as soon as you're in range. Light the bastards up. Good luck, good hunting. See you on the other side."

The best thing about lightning cannons was their range. Assuming nothing closer got in the way, the bolt would travel as far as we had charged. We'd been charging Ol' Sparky for weeks.

We'd copied him a few times, too.

Only a couple dozen lightning cannons fired our opening salvo against the last forces of Atlan Aerial, but we made them count. Well beyond their cannon range, every airship we hit was blasted to bits. Of course, the next shot would have to be fired a lot closer, but they didn't know that.

We'd sent ahead five advance scout airships, crewed with as few volunteers as could still operate the ship. Only one made it back to the safety of the fleet. Four ships down.

Our first lightning blast took out six times that many and they couldn't afford to lose any. Neither could we, but we were bringing our backup. Their backup had to stay at Atlan, protecting the last citizens of the Empire.

That opening battle was short but bitter. They'd barely sent four dozen ships to stop us. Four Great Whites, sure, but the rest were Barracudas. A couple of Hammerheads. Nothing we couldn't handle. We only lost fifteen ships.

Only.

Anyway, on we flew, the coast of Atlan a dark smudge on the horizon. The sun rose during the battle, and we could finally see our objective. Through my goggles I could see the tiny spots of airships in the sky above Neptopolis. Far below us, our seaships were churning up the waves of the Atlan Sea.

Only two hours had gone past, from initial contact with our scouts to leaving the flaming wreckage of their outlying forces to sink into the sea. In another hour, we'd be close enough that their longest guns might have a chance at hitting some of us.

That hour was worse than the four hours we'd travelled under cover of darkness. A single hour, the sun at our backs, exposed to their telescopes. In my imagination I could hear the air raid alarms sounding in the streets of Neptopolis, see the women and children scrambling for shelter. As horrible as that was, it was better than hearing the screams of our wounded as our surgeons patched them up as best they could.

Aboard The Furies, we'd been lucky enough not to have any wounded yet. Other ships had borne the brunt of the attack, keeping the Atlans away from us, the flagship of the fleet.

But worse than the imagined screams of the wounded on other ships or the imagined panic in the streets of Neptopolis was handling the anticipation of the battle ahead. An hour to cross the sky, to finally bring the war to a close, to end it once and for all. An hour is a long time for adrenaline to keep pumping in your system. Some of my girls crashed, shaking and jittery, to grab a quick nap right at their stations. The line for the privy was pretty long, as some girls suddenly realized their bladders were past capacity. More than one girl vomited from sheer nerves.

I stayed in my chair, trying to stay as calm as I could. Nothing left. No nerves. No emotions. Just numb. Domina brought me a drink of something warm, and I drank it without tasting it.

The Atlan long guns finally fired. And then... Well, I guess they'd been busy themselves, building lightning cannons of their own. Looking back, I'm honestly surprised it took them that long.

Half a dozen of our ships bought it, fried by lightning bolts, tumbling to the hungry sea below. I hoped none of the wreckage hit our seaships. We fired back with our own lightning cannons, having charged with about a half hour of bright sunlight.

Explosive cannonballs shattered the air around us, showering us with shards of shrapnel. Then a direct hit to our bow knocked Restless off her feet, sent sparks of electricity and slivers of glass flying through the bridge.

I rushed to Restless, who was already picking herself up. She grinned at me, like it was fun, all a game or something, then resumed her post.

"Argenta, damage report!"

"Hit just below the gun deck, Admiral! Sparky's destroyed."

"Any casualties?"

"Four wounded, no dead."

"Okay. Restless, full speed ahead. Argenta, damage control to the gun deck, clear the wreckage."

"Aye aye Cap'n I mean Admiral!"

"Aye Admiral."

Serena entered the bridge, completely covered in thick leather. The mask covering her face made her frightening, distorted and muffled her voice into something inhuman. "You mean to lead from the front?"

"That's what Remy would have done."

I don't need to remind you that Remy went down with his ship.

No, you don't.

"Wery vell, Wal."

She left again to join her boarders. Not that we had much intention to board the Atlan vessels, but better safe than sorry, right?

"Argenta, all ships. Launch all ornies."

"All ornies launch, aye Admiral."

Two tense minutes passed. "All ornies report launched, Admiral."

I know two minutes sounds like a ridiculously short amount of time to launch hundreds of ornithopters into the air, but when you're under heavy anti-airship fire, shrapnel exploding all around you? Two minutes is an eternity.

Seeing the ornies fly ahead of us, some of them shot down in seconds, made me wish we'd brought every Vulka-rey we could find. Most of them were still in Russankya putting down smaller and smaller pockets of Atlan resistance. Some of them had begun raids into Bavardy, though I didn't know it at the time. We had a division of Vulka spread through our troop carriers, and don't get me wrong, two hundred werewolves howling for blood were worth their weight in atlantium, but I still would have liked to have Olga and the others with us.

Once the ornies were inside the Atlan cannon range but still outside the range of their volley guns, they launched their flares. Not much point now that the sun had risen, right? Wrong. These were very special flares, designed by Inga Doom herself. They burned extra hot, and extra long.

They burned hot enough to melt copalum. Like, say, the copalum mesh armour encasing the Atlan airships' balloons?

Yeah.

Flares landed on the balloons, melted their way through the mesh, burned through the balloon sheath, entered the gasbags and basically exploded everything everywhere. We probably took out a third of their airships that way. The ornies paid a heavy price to do it, though.

And Atlan Aerial had ornies of their own. Soon we were flying straight into the biggest aerial dogfight in Ayrth's history, hundreds of ornies zipping back and forth, looping around each other, trying not to crash into each other or the bigger ships. I sent the order to open fire on their ships, and the world exploded with the roar of gunfire.

How did we keep track? Oh, I guess I forgot to tell you. We'd ordered all our ships to fly the Revolution's flag, or be painted in her colours, blue and red and gold. Everything else was fair game. It was open season on anything not painted our colours.

Of course, the bigger ships were much easier to keep track of. They'd saved their last dozen Great Whites for the defence of Neptopolis. Thirty Hammerheads and Makos. A dozen Devilfish, launching wave after wave of Piranha ornies at us. At least fifty Barracudas.

And the final remaining Leviathan, hovering over the city, the last line of defence.

Our troop transports broke off from the main fleet, heading for the landing zones we'd decided on. The rest of us stayed right where we were, five miles out from the statue of Atlan Triumphant. I'm told that citizens were crowding the rooftops of Neptopolis, to get a good look at the battle.

The sky was so full of airships I'm amazed anyone could see anything. We sure couldn't. Right in front of us two Piranhas, each chasing after different Revolution ornies, crashed into each other. I saw one of our gunships, the Inevitable, crash into a Great White's command bridge. Both of them began the long slow crash into the sea.

I know that the battle on the water was just as important, just as dramatic as the one we were fighting, but honestly, I barely know anything about it. I was way too busy trying to keep us all alive while killing as many of them as possible.

We took a lot of hits. Our boarding parties soon wound up taking over for injured crew, or running ammunition to our gunners in the rigging, atop the balloon. A lot of my girls died that day.

Looking back, it's all a blur of split-second decisions, the roar of gunfire all around us, our own guns firing so often and so fast the girls started pouring water on them to cool the barrels. The Great Whites circled around and around, but we were so enmeshed with the Barracudas and Hammerheads and Makos that they didn't dare fire on us for fear of hitting their own. In the end, that's what saved us, I guess. At one point

I remember ordering ten ships to start hunting the Great Whites, one by one. More and more of our ships peeled off from the main battle to hunt those huge dreadnoughts, since less and less of the Barracudas were left to fight. Ornies had to come back aboard us, to refuel and get more ammunition. I ordered half our ornies to take on the wounded and get them off the ship – we'd left a few troop transports as hospital ships well back from the fight, and they had their hands full, believe me.

We pulled back and regrouped three times, I remember, and each time less and less of us could stay in the fight. I saw more than one ship abandoned by the crew. Rescue seaships picked up as many survivors as they could.

Somehow it was past noon, the sun beginning to sink in the west, backlighting that bastard Leviathan. I saw a few fires had broken out in the city, the escapees from the Pit hard at work creating as much chaos as possible. That's when it occurred to me: even if we blew every ship out of the sky here, we'd still have to face that blighted monstrosity.

The troops would have landed by then, making their way to the objectives we'd outlined. Train depots, crossroads, towns and villages, minor cities. If we could control the countryside, the major cities would starve. It would draw the armies out of Neptopolis and Atlantopolis, force them to fight on ground of our choosing.

But not if we didn't break through the blockade and take out that Leviathan. If the Leviathan was left, it could bring the hammer down on our troops worse than mobilizing the entire remaining Atlan Army.

"Get all the wounded off, then recall the ornies," I ordered. Argenta relayed. "Batten the hatches. Gun ports closed, portholes shuttered. All gunners to withdraw into the ship."

"Vhat do you have in mind?" Serena asked, stepping onto the bridge. "The Leviathan?"

"Yeah. Full steam ahead, punch our way through. A third of the force comes with us, the other two thirds take on the remaining fleet."

Serena shook her head. "Ve vill need a half, at least. And then split the force again to prevent followers."

"Right." I turned to Argenta. "All ships."

"All ships, Admiral."

No one was happy with the orders. I only asked for volunteers to go after the Leviathan. To their credit, Captain Cooper and the crew of the Fist, the ship that had lost their captain to the last Leviathan we'd fought, were the first to volunteer.

Surprisingly, Captain Axe was the second. "You brought us this far. We'll get you through. Take out that big bastard like the last one."

The vote of confidence was touching, coming from him. Other ships volunteered until we had enough, about half the fleet. The half that stayed behind to keep the fleet busy spread out to either side, like wings, engaging the outliers to keep them from concentrating on us. Then the other half of our fleet split into three. My third followed along, slightly behind the other two thirds. The other two thirds focussed all their guns on the ships at the centre, but didn't stop to engage. The fly-by attack kept us moving forward, and kept Atlan Aerial struggling to keep up with us. They expected us to stand and fight, because that's how airship battles were won.

Not any more. By flying past them and making room for other airships with their cannons already loaded, we managed to pour enough firepower into the Atlan ships in the centre that some of them literally fell apart as we watched; their balloons, suddenly cut loose, soared into the stratosphere.

We took a few hits, nothing major to the ship, but a shell exploded too close to one of our shuttered portholes and Elegiac 'Mrs. Shorty' Throckwaddle was killed instantly. She'd been directing the ammunition runners, organizing our dwindling supplies.

Then we were through, and the only thing left in the skies ahead of us was that great Leviathan.

One third of the ships following me, the ones who were able to keep flying, turned back and slammed into the Atlan fleet from the rear, cutting off any pursuit.

We had a few minutes to organize ourselves and then we were in the range of the Leviathan's big bow guns. Once again, the sky filled with killing shards of shrapnel.

We were lucky. No direct hits, and the Leviathan was nose-on to us. If she'd been able to swing around and bring her broadside onto us, I doubt we would have made it as far as we did. Seconds after the shelling began, she launched her ornies at us. I ordered ours to stand fast, wait until the last possible moment to launch, to save on fuel and ammunition. Yeah, we were really running things that close.

"Admiral, Aeriologist Banningcord reports the balloon is taking damage," Argenta reported.

"Tell her to do what she can. Send damage control teams to help."

"Aye Admiral."

"Orders, Admiral?" Restless asked.

"Straight down the gullet, Restless," I said. "Just like last time."

"Aye aye, Admiral."

No fear, no hesitation. Just complete, absolute faith that I knew what I was doing. I really, really wish she'd been right.

After about a minute of shaking and flinching at the shrapnel explosions all around us, I ordered, "Launch all ornies!"

Their ornies were just about on us, anyway.

More explosions rocked the ship. A couple of direct hits nearly knocked me out of my chair. My left arm burst into flame. I think I screamed, I'm not sure, but the pain was so intense I have no clear memory. I remember batting at my arm to douse the flames. It took a couple of seconds for me to realize the flames weren't real, I wasn't burning up.

Serena was.

A shell had blown a hole in the hull, sending burning shrapnel into Serena's arm. She would have shrugged it off but the hole let in the sunlight, and the shrapnel had shredded her leather shirt.

I'm told that some panicky crewmember pushed Serena away from the barrels of gunpowder, which was smart, but towards the stairwell leading down, which wasn't so smart. Serena broke both her legs falling down the stairs.

My own legs shrieked with sympathetic pain, and that time I know I let out a scream. I went for the door to go and help Serena just as Restless yelled out "CAP'N!"

She shoved me just as bullets burst through the bow windows.

Restless saved my life.

And all it cost was her own.

Too many bullets. Too much blood. She was still conscious when I got to her, coughing blood.

"Hold on Restless hold on hold on!" I babbled. Then, "MEDIC! I NEED A MEDIC IN HERE!"

Restless shook her head. "Worth it," she coughed.

"What?"

"Worth it... to make sure... nothin' like this happens... to any other kids... like me."

She died in my arms. She didn't cry or whine or complain. She died, the bravest kid I ever met.

Give me a minute, okay?

Okay. So.

Where was I?

I took the wheel, noticed we'd definitely lost elevation.

"Argenta, all ships, fire at will!"

"Aye Admiral!"

"And get Banningcord on the line!"

A couple of seconds later, "Aeriologist Banningcord, Admiral."

"How much gas do we have left?"

"'Not enough for this', she says."

"Enough to get us to the Leviathan?"

"'Aye, Admiral, but not past her.'"

I thought about it for maybe five seconds, then nodded.

"All hands, abandon ship."

"Admiral?"

I turned and looked up at her, stared into her glowing yellow eyes. "All hands abandon ship."

"Aye Admiral."

I felt Serena's mind telling me, commanding me to change my mind. The commands turned to shrieks of incoherent rage and terror as I resisted. Then unconsciousness took her, and my mind was my own.

"Everyone, Argenta, even you."

"By your command, Admiral, but not by my will."

"Then do it by mine, please."

"Aye Admiral," she said, then left her station.

I could hear the sounds of the batwing backpacks starting up as my crew flew to safety. I imagined I could hear Gigi's howls of protest, Eve's reasonable attempts to rationalize her way past the armed crewmembers I'd specifically tasked to make sure that if I ever gave that order, it would be carried out by everyone, especially my closest, dearest friends.

Speaking of...

"Admiral? Sunset? Come in! Will you come in!"

Gwen, or Guinny, of course.

I lashed the wheel in place and ran up the staircase to the wireless.

"Sunset, what's wrong? Why are your crew abandoning ship?"

"Sorry girls, you'll have to drink without me." My voice got thick, my throat closing up. "Tell Fox... Tell him I said... Just tell him."

"No no no and no. Sunset, we're coming, we'll be right there."

"No time, Commodore Tallyho. Take the fleet in, knock out this big bastard if I don't... If this doesn't work. Admiral Val out."

"No, Sunset, don't do this!"

I shut off the wireless because I couldn't stand to hear the pain in their voices. Down the staircase and to the wheel, just as the lashings snapped from the strain. I grabbed the spinning wheel, levelled out the ship, aiming her right at the Leviathan's command tower.

The Leviathan fiilled the bridge windows. Direct hits kept shaking the ship. One knocked me to my knees. Another blew out the port side elevator, making us spin to starboard. I barely got us back on course.

An explosion rocked the entire ship. One of the gasbags going, I guessed. I looked around the bridge for the last time. Saw Restless' body, lying there.

I unhooked my gun belt and used that to lash the wheel in place. The deck was pretty slanted by then, and I grabbed onto consoles to help me climb up to where Restless lay. I picked her up and carried her to the command chair, put her in my seat, kissed her forehead.

She was so brave. So brave. She'd given everything to the cause. She'd died for freedom. Not just her own, but for everyone. All the kids taken by slavers. All the kids sold into a short life of misery and pain. All of them. She gave much more than I could. I didn't want to die. I wasn't even nineteen yet. I didn't want to die. I just didn't.

So I made one final adjustment of the wheel and the controls, trying to make sure The Furies would hit the Leviathan's command tower, lashed everything in place, and left the bridge.

I ran as fast as the slanted deck let me, sliding down stairwell bannisters and ladders until I reached the lab. In the corner, the aetheric portal sat, almost like it was waiting for me.

I flipped the switches and powered her up. The hum and whir began right away. I guess Ol' Sparky being knocked out meant all the collected power from the photonic invertors had been directed into the portal.

Lights glowed bright, gauge dials showed full power.

I threw the switch and the lights spun and the portal opened, swirly shiny rainbow mist at first, then something began to form at the centre. Something dark and distant.

Another explosion knocked me off my feet. Sparks began to fly from everything around me, and the portal started to collapse.

I grabbed the chain that had brought me to Ayrth and jumped.

Bright flashing lights in every colour. Intense cold. My breath stolen away. Every muscle cramping. I wanted to scream but couldn't. I passed out. When I woke up, I lay on hard cold concrete, ten feet of chain in my hand.

Under a street light, next to a parking lot.

The parking lot of a community centre.

I was home.

Chapter Thirty

There And Back Again, Am I Right?

Mom stared at me. I could feel her eyes boring into my head. "Really," she said.

I looked up. They were all staring at me. My whole family.

Mom leaned forward, one hand stretched toward me, concern etched deeply into the wrinkles of her forehead, worry lines that hadn't been there before. Mel slumped in her chair, arms folded, glaring at me, but Tommy just grinned at me, one arm draped casually over the back of his chair, earbuds out of his ears for once.

The worst was my Dad. He sat there, lips pinched in a thin line, hands in front of him on the table, fingers interlaced, his knuckles white with tension, but his voice was calm, quiet almost.

"You expect us to believe that bullshit science fiction?"

Tommy's grin faded and he leaned away, out of the blast radius. Mel's glower turned into a smirk of triumph, and she sat up.

"You disappear. No word. No note, no email, nothing!" Dad said, his voice rising in volume as he went. "Your mother was worried SICK for the past year, Valerie! You show up here, looking like some crazy punk rocker from the 1800s, with your hair mangled and tattoos and scars and you spin us a web of lies?! How stupid do you think we are?!"

He slammed a hand, palm down flat on the table. Everyone jumped. I didn't. After everything I'd seen and done, Dad's fury was nothing.

Okay, almost nothing.

Mom lay her hand on Dad's arm and he visibly deflated, as usual. No one could calm my father like my Mom.

"Honey," Mom said, turning back to me. "It's okay. We understand. Maybe you're not ready to tell us. But you have to understand, we've been so worried about you. Was it a boy? Or... drugs?"

I looked at her, and realized how badly she needed a reasonable answer. How much they'd all gone through during the past year. Mom, crying herself to sleep. Dad, holding her, impotent rage at whatever had taken me away. Melanie, finally getting her own room, only to have it be turned to ash in her mouth since Mom had insisted in keeping my side of the room like a perfect shrine of my stuff, like Sandra's room when she'd left for college. Only Sandra came home for the holidays, and I hadn't. And Tommy, blaming himself for my disappearance, so thrilled I hadn't been kidnapped and killed by some sex criminal.

I saw it all in an instant. I looked away and nodded. "Okay, Mom. You're right. It was a boy. We went to Los Angeles. I thought maybe I could get a job as an actress. Not so much. He turned out to be a complete jackass. He wanted us to join a gang. We had to do a lot of stuff I'd rather not think about. Lived on the streets. Then he got himself killed, so I came home. I'm really, really sorry. I wish it had never happened."

Mom's relief was so strong it came off her in waves. Dad just got up and walked away from the table. Mel left too, in a huff. Tommy tossed me an affectionate punch in the shoulder. I had to actively stop myself from breaking his wrist in instinctive self-defence.

That night, lying in my bed for the first time in a year, having enjoyed a shower and proper toilet paper for the first time in a year, I heard Mel say to the wall, "You are such an incredible bitch, showing up here after so long. I can't believe how selfish you are."

"G'night, Mel," I said, rolling away from her.

Days drifted by into weeks. Monica, my old best friend, and I got together a couple of times, but it wasn't the same. After a few attempts at getting me to tell her what had 'really happened', she stopped asking and started telling me all about her life. Every time we talked, it was her, her, her. I couldn't get into it. Chasing after boys and complaining about classes and teachers and parents and gossiping about television and movie stars seemed so pointless.

I started taking classes to finish my high school degree. I couldn't re-enrol in high school, I'd missed too much and I was over eighteen, so I had to find another school, which basically helped dropouts finish the credits they needed. I mean, I couldn't get a job without a diploma. I couldn't even enlist in the military, which pretty much seemed like my best option, given what I'd done on Ayrth.

I went to one fencing class. Raoul asked me to leave after I nearly killed my opponent, having completely forgotten all the civilized rules of swordplay.

Suppers were pretty tense. No one wanted to talk about the year I'd gone missing, but no one seemed ready to let it go, either. Our conversations focussed on the weather, mostly, and other things that wouldn't cause problems.

My dreams were filled with the wind in my hair, the sun on my face, the laughter of friends.

My nightmares were filled with screams and blood.

Nothing seemed very real. I began to wonder if I'd imagined the whole thing, somehow. Or if I was imagining all this home life as a kind of delusional last moments of life before The Furies crashed and burned. I'd like to think I'd imagine something happier as I was plummeting to my death. I know, right? Kind of a crappy ending to the whole saga of Sunset Val.

Don't worry, though. A couple of months after I got back to Earth, a miracle happened.

We were eating supper, tense as usual, when all the lights went out.

"What the hell?" Dad asked.

"I'll get the candles," Mom said, standing up.

But all the lights started sparking with electricity. Mel gave out a little shriek.

"Get down under the table!" Dad yelled, but the hall light exploded before we had a chance.

And four chains fell through a swirling hole of light in the ceiling.

Four people slid down the chains, landing lightly in our hall entrance. Dad got up and rushed at them, trying to defend us, I guess. But three years of football twenty years ago were no match for them, and he was on the ground before he had a chance to hurt himself. Mom grabbed Mel and hugged her close and moved to grab me, too, but I slipped free and jumped the intruders. Elbows and knees and fists, punching and kicking, all that Open Hand training coming out. I remember Tommy said, "Whoa!" before they had me pinned to the floor.

"Sunset, Sunset, stop, it's us!" someone said in a language I hadn't heard in months.

One of them lit a lamp. Gigi, of course.

Serena, with only one arm but a grin so wide I could see her fangs.

Molly, with a new eye and a new arm and a new leg, pinning my Dad to the ground.

And the only man in the group. Bunny. My Fox.

I grabbed him and kissed him hard.

I wasn't crazy. I hadn't imagined the whole thing. Ayrth was real, The Furies had been real, Bunny was real.

After an eternity, we stopped kissing.

"Valerie?" Mom asked, worry trembling her voice.

"Uh, Molly, could you get off my Dad?" I asked in Atlan.

"Of course," she said, standing up, then helping Dad to his feet.

"What the hell is going on?" Dad asked.

"Allow me," Bunny said. "Bunthorne Bartholomew Tallyho, at y'service, sir. I am here to ask for your daughter's hand."

"Um, what did he say?" Dad asked. "What exactly is going on?"

"Sorry, Dad. In Anglic, love."

"Ah, of cawse, my sincerest apologies," Bunny said, switching from Atlan, then repeated his request.

"Her hand?" Dad said, not getting it.

"Only minutes before the portal collapses," Gigi warned.

"Oh my God, is that a cat girl?" Mel said, coming out from Mom's arms. "That is so cool!"

"These are my friends," I said. "This is my family."

So we made introductions and Bunny asked to marry me and Mom and Dad were too stunned to say anything and Melanie completely embarrassed herself by asking to pet Gigi and Tommy kept saying "Whoa."

And in the end, five minutes later, I returned to Ayrth, to the best friends I'll ever have, to the man I love, to my place as Pirate Queen of the Seven Skies.

Epilogue

Yeah, Right, Like I'd Leave You Hanging Like That

Let's see, what do you want to hear about first? How about the final flight of The Furies?

After I took the back door out, my ship went hurtling into the Leviathan's command bridge, crashing into it at full steam. What I didn't know, what no one knew then, was that the explosion of an airship crashing into another airship, coupled with an open and fully-charged aetheric portal? Well, scientists are still arguing over what to call what happened. The closest they can agree on is some kind of 'detonative rupture'.

People as far away as Atlantopolis and Ys claimed they heard the blast. Twin One and Twin Two, the two closest ships, were thrown hundreds of yards away by the winds. The Leviathan, well, that big bastard had its keel snapped in half, and then the gasbags blew, and all that flaming wreckage came down hard on the city below.

The impact shattered the support columns in the cavern Quill's people had carved out of the bedrock under the city, setting off a chain reaction with the other columns, and the entire city crashed into the cavern, swallowed by the river. Tens of thousands of Atlan men died, the women and children having been evacuated during the first two Battles of Neptopolis Bay. For once, Atlan chauvinism did something right. The men were all military-trained, and were being armed as a last ditch militia, so they knew the risks, but I would have felt worse if I'd killed women and kids, too.

When word of Neptopolis' destruction reached the remaining commanders of the Second Army, they argued for a full hour over their course of action and ultimately surrendered. The big question seemed to be whether or not we had another city-destroying bomb and if we would use it on Atlantopolis. In the end, they figured that it wasn't worth the risk of trying to find out.

The war was over.

As I'd predicted, Eve and Gigi had tried to get past their guards and save me. Doc Regan had knocked Eve out with a well-timed injection of a powerful sedative. Gigi had nearly killed the three girls I'd ordered to make sure she abandoned ship with the rest of them, until Miss Merryweather had stepped in. Apparently the old girl had quite a few hidden moves up her sleeve.

She died, though. Heart attack when the shockwave from the detonative rupture caught up with them. I know, right? Never thought something so normal would be the end of Mattis Merryweather.

The Zhou were pretty pissed that we'd invaded Atlan without them. Pissed enough that they called it a "fundamental betrayal of our agreement." Because they were supposed to have the first right of pillage, and our troops pretty much helped themselves. If the Fist or the Mind had been alive, maybe things wouldn't have gotten as bad as they did, and the Zhou would still be our allies today. But their decision to attack Neppon had dragged on into a war the Revolution had refused to get involved with, and the new Zhou Way of Three Masters had taken that as another betrayal and it all got political after that.

The Tallyho Commodores had taken control of the surrendered Atlan, at least until the Revolution leaders had shown up. Mr. Mahogany himself accepted the final surrender from the governor of Atlantopolis. Since I was gone and General Komodo was an soldier in a foreign army and a member of the Lemuris royal family, Mr. Mahogany was elected President of the new World Government, the first election in Ayrth history that gave the vote to women and animen and vampyri, oh my.

And automatons, too. Getting the autohorses into the polling stations proved a challenge, I'll bet.

The war was over, the enemy defeated. My friends and crew went their separate ways, but Gigi, Eve, Serena, and a few others who couldn't let go wound up at Tallyho Manor. Molly showed up after a month, with a new arm and leg and eye she'd gotten in her travels from Afric to Anglica.

Bunny spent the majority of his fortune making a new aetheric portal. Gigi had examined every inch of the original, and Eve had helped create it in the first place, so it only took them a couple of weeks to build a new one. Serena's link to me had never been severed (that is, she hadn't gone crazy with the loss), so they knew I had somehow survived and the portal seemed the most likely explanation. After that it was just trial and error until they found me.

My dramatic return earned me the title of Pirate Queen for Life, but I was more than happy to let Lawless stay on as Admiral of the Pirate Fleet. By World Government decree, Ys was declared the home of pirates. I was given a villa there, although I could have bought it with the fortune in atlantium that Millie and I wound up sharing with the few other survivors of the Pit who made it out of the destruction of Neptopolis. There weren't many survivors, so the atlantium wasn't spent fast enough to crash the economy.

We still use the portal to visit my family on holidays. Mel and Tommy even came to visit for a few months once, but Mel missed her cell phone and Tommy missed internet poker too much to stay. And of course our kids love to visit the weird world of Grandma and Grandpa.

Of course Bunny and I got married. Duh! And we had plenty of adventures together. I mean, I could tell you about the next war, against the Amazonians; about Serena's hunt for war criminals like Commodore Crow (who survived the war, unfortunately); or Gigi and Eve's inventions that changed the lives of hundreds of patchworks and animen; about those crimefighting crusaders, the Hooded Fox and Vixen and their amazing adventures with the other costumed crimefighters in The Equity Club; or all the other stuff that happened to us, like our kids, but that's another story. Actually, it's a bunch of other stories. And not all of them are mine to tell.

As for me, well, it's time to go.

It's always Go Time, for the Pirate Queen.

Rob St-Martin is a Canadian author, editor, publisher, husband and father, not necessarily in that order. From his secret lair in Montreal, he writes fantasy novels with steampunkian flavour and strong female characters.

Since his first professional sale of a short story to the *Misspelled* anthology in 2006, Rob has edited an Aurora Award-nominated anthology (*Ages of Wonder*, 2009); written over a million words; published eleven novels; been an Author Guest at over a dozen conventions; and become a husband and father. He lives with his wife (whom he adores), five children, and a frog.

When not writing, Rob actively wishes he had more time to write.

Acknowledgements

It may seem odd to dedicate a novel to the main character, but believe me when I say this, without Val, clamouring at the inside of my skull, inspiring me with her can-do attitude, this book wouldn't have been written.

But that's certainly true of many people, not just the fictional one who's been living in my mind for the last five years. None more so than my dear wife Kristie. I absolutely could not have finished this series without her constant support, love and encouragement.

Of course, my incredible family have been, well, incredible. From my parents to my kids, from my siblings to my in-laws, everyone has been incredibly supportive and encouraging.

I would be remiss if I did not specifically mention my dear friend Karine Charlebois, the amazingly talented artist whose works have inspired me for years, and whose work on the Sunset Val frontispieces have brought my characters to life.

I also have to give my thanks to the incredibly creative Ron Chevrier, whose names have christened both characters and ships throughout the series.

Moreover, I think I need to thank the various steampunk musicians and bands whose music has fed my imagination, specifically Professor Elemental, Abney Park, the Clockwork Dolls and The Cog is Dead. Inspiration comes from many places, and for me, music is definitely part of what made this series possible.

I should also mention the very talented and entertaining Ben Thompson, author and creator of badassoftheweek.com - If any of you think anything that happened in the pages of the Sunset Val books was too incredible to believe, I invited you to peruse his website for actual historical examples of truly incredible badassery.

And finally, well, every fan, every steampunk cosplayer, every steampunk costume maker or prop builder that I have talked to, emailed, or just plain admired, either online or in person. Their dedication to steampunk is absolutely inspirational.